ELLENVILLE PUBLIC LIBRARY & MUSEUM
40 Center Street
Ellenville, NY 12428
Phone: 845-647-5530 www.rcls.org/epl/

APPLEMERE SUMMER

Further Titles by Harriet Hudson from Severn House

THE WINDY HILL
CATCHING THE SUNLIGHT
TOMORROW'S GARDEN
QUINN
TO MY OWN DESIRE
SONGS OF SPRING
THE STATIONMASTER'S DAUGHTER
WINTER ROSES

Writing as Amy Myers

MURDER IN THE QUEEN'S BOUDOIR
MURDER WITH MAJESTY
THE WICKENHAM MURDERS
MURDER IN FRIDAY STREET

APPLEMERE SUMMER

Harriet Hudson

This first world edition published in Great Britain 2005 by
SEVERN HOUSE PUBLISHERS LTD of
9–15 High Street, Sutton, Surrey SM1 1DF.
This first world edition published in the USA 2006 by
SEVERN HOUSE PUBLISHERS INC of
595 Madison Avenue, New York, N.Y. 10022.

British Library Cataloguing in Publication Data

Hudson, Harriet, 1938-
    Applemere summer
    1.   Booksellers and bookselling - Fiction
    2.   Bankruptcy - Fiction
    3.   Family - Fiction
    4.   Kent (England) - Fiction
    I.   Title
    823.9'14 [F]

    ISBN-10 : 0-7278-6299-5

Typeset by Palimpsest Book Production Ltd.,
Polmont, Stirlingshire, Scotland.
Printed and bound in Great Britain by
MPG Books Ltd., Bodmin, Cornwall.

Author's Note

Applemere is a hamlet near the village of Fairsted which lies on a fictitious branch line of the now lost Elham Valley railway line in Kent. In this novel's predecessor, *The Stationmaster's Daughter*, set before and during the First World War, the age of steam was in its heyday, but now, in the 1920s and 1930s when this novel is set, it is slowly chuffing out of use. Applemere Halt, constructed solely for the use of Applemere House, lies a short way from Fairsted at the end of a winding lane from the House itself. In the late nineteenth and early twentieth century, royalty and other world leaders had frequently used the Halt, but by the time of this novel Applemere House itself is changing, waiting for a new role in its life. Fortunately Jennie Pencarek is living in the cottage next door to it . . .

My thanks are due to Severn House whose splendid team have once again been of so much help in the publication of this book, to Tony Benfield, David Bosomworth and to my agent, Dorothy Lumley, of the Dorian Literary Agency, who first had faith in these Applemere sagas.

Prologue

*T*om, Freddie, Jack and herself. Jennie saw them as clearly as though that golden day of long ago were yesterday. Under a blazing hot sun they half ran, half walked along the footpath by the railway to Applemere Halt. Tom, the leader, the eldest of the three Trent children, unpredictable, tall even at fourteen, fair-haired, and the one they all looked up to; Freddie, the youngest, the good-natured dark horse, forever following in the shadow of his admired older brother; dear Jack Colby, her childhood sweetheart, now long dead, and herself, Jennie Trent.

In the distance she could glimpse the enchanted roofs of Applemere House, where royalty was said to dwell and kings and emperors visited. It was her twelfth birthday and she was so happy she wanted to rule the world. They were laughing, carelessly swiping at the growing corn, startling birds from their nests, and sending rabbits scurrying for shelter. They had no idea that their lives were to change that day.

The day they had met Anna.

One

A Kentish garden in summer. Was there anything more lovely – even though the twins were creating havoc in the orchard? Jennie luxuriated in a brief moment of tranquillity, as she saw them turn their attention to daisy-chains and searching for fairy-rings in the grass. She and Richard had been lucky that Applemere Cottage had fallen vacant at the time they married five years ago in the summer of 1919. The war that had raged for over four years before that was long over now, even if the promised land fit for heroes to live in had not yet materialized.

'We have a Labour Government at last,' Richard had rejoiced earlier in the year. 'Things will begin to change.'

Not to this garden, Jennie thought confidently. She wanted nothing here to change at all. Not the dragonflies darting to and fro from the stream that trickled past in the field beyond their hedge. Not the grasshoppers clicking and chirping in the grass, not the apples forming on the trees, nor the roses that rambled over the fences, nor her precious vegetables. And nothing would change between herself and Richard. They loved each other just as much – more – than on the day they married, and there were at least fifty years ahead to enjoy together.

Her brothers too were happy, despite the coolness between them. Freddie, the younger of them, had married her friend Anna Fokingham, and Tom, the elder, was firmly established with his family. So all (or nearly all) was right with the world.

'Jennie, where are you?'

She jumped up joyfully from the deck-chair, thus ripping the fabric over the frame even further. 'Lord Bookseller's here,' she called out to the twins. 'Come and kiss daddy.'

Richard was early, it suddenly struck her, as the twins rushed up to be swept first one, then the other, into his arms. Normally

2

he wouldn't be home from Canterbury until seven or even eight o'clock, and this wasn't early closing day. Perhaps he'd left the shop in Mr Hodge's hands. His reliable if somewhat dour assistant was more than capable of this honour, but it was still unusual for Richard to tear himself away from his precious books so early. He must have something important to tell her. Yesterday he'd been agog about the forthcoming Mary Webb novel, *Precious Bane*. The publishers' traveller from Jonathan Cape had left a sample copy with him overnight. Although this only contained the usual thirty-two pages, Richard was enchanted by it, and though her previous novels had not sold particularly well he was convinced that this one would.

'It's poetic and passionate at the same time,' he had told her eagerly. 'Passion for love *and* passion for the country-side.'

'Sounds like another *Green Hat*,' she'd commented. Michael Arlen's recently published novel of society life – both public and private – had set cash tills and tongues buzzing. Its chief character, Iris Storm, had definitely been from London society, a society which this new Armenian author had adopted as his own. *The Green Hat* heaved with suppressed passion and dark hints, for Iris Storm had a 'pagan body and a Chislehurst mind'. It was a dramatic phrase that she and Richard, in the small change of marriage, intoned mock-heavily at relevant moments. If *Precious Bane* could match *The Green Hat* in appealing to readers by deliciously shocking them, it might be the making of Pencarek Books.

Jennie had taken a peek at the *Precious Bane* sample, however, and was dismayed. This was no *Green Hat*. As Richard had been, she too was overwhelmed by the poetic beauty and passionate strength of the writing, but that in itself might not seize the wider public's imagination. It couldn't be counted on to be a commercial success.

Something else seemed to be troubling Richard today, however. Her heart sank as she watched him playing with the children. He seemed almost to be avoiding her eye, except when she spoke to him. Then he answered her quietly and briefly. None of his usual glow, his blaze of enthusiasm even when he came home tired at the end of a day's work. None of yesterday's hope.

3

'Never ask a man a difficult question before he's eaten,' Aunt Win always decreed, and Jennie tried to obey, though usually her impulsiveness made her blurt a question out at just the wrong moment. She forced herself not to today, and it wasn't until the twins were in bed, and their evening supper concluded, that she felt the time was right.

'I'll cut some of those sweet peas to take indoors,' Richard offered – was that another reason purposely to delay his coming to sit beside her in the setting sunlight? Jennie watched his long sensitive fingers carefully selecting blooms from the tangled mass, and thought how much she loved him – and how much even the slightest cloud on his face troubled her.

Dr Good-Good had been the Serbians' nickname for him when she and Richard had first met during the war, and his blue Cornish eyes held that dream that had so impressed them – and her. The dream had been a practical one, and he still had it; he'd wanted to help people, at first through his medical role in the war, and now by opening new horizons through literature to those who could or would not see beyond their own front doors.

'What's wrong, darling?' She could leave it no longer. She knew he wouldn't put her off with a 'I don't know what you mean' once the question had been put into words. He was too straightforward for that, thank goodness.

'Pencarek Books is in trouble – not a minor problem, like before. Serious trouble.' He made a face, as if to make light of it, but she wasn't fooled. 'And this time I really don't see a way out.'

A cold hand reached out towards her heart. Why did these things always come when least expected? Just when the sunset was spreading peace and tranquillity over their lovely garden, and she'd wanted so much to enjoy it with Richard. She wasn't being fair, she knew that. He wanted to share its peace too, and she must help him find a path through this latest crisis so that he could.

'Tell me,' she said.

He shrugged. 'Money, as usual. Two travellers today said their publishers want – very politely – cash with order. Including the publishers of *Precious Bane*. I've kept them waiting too long too often, and then the shop rent's due and—'

He broke off, but Jennie knew with sickening clarity what

he was going to say: 'Mr Hodge needs to be paid,' she finished for him. His assistant, Albert Hodge, always insisted on what he called 'biding a while' over when to take his meagre wages, so this must be a serious situation indeed.

Richard nodded. 'I gave his wages to him on the spot, but we both knew that means the rent will have to wait.'

More than that, Jennie thought despondently. Their own rent on the cottage, the shopping bills – the list stretched terrifyingly on. This had happened once before. In the slump of 1921 the recently opened Pencarek Books had faced disaster. But rescue soon arrived in the form of the major bestseller, *If Winter Comes*.

Hutchinson's novel had sold so quickly that autumn that there was room for all the booksellers in Canterbury to sell it at a fast pace. It was a novel of the war, but one with a difference. Mark Sabre was not a hero, he was Everyman, who had gone into the war with such moral fervour. His ideals, although not abandoned, were tarnished with the catastrophic reality of what war had meant, and yet he managed to see hope ahead.

'But if you're right about *Precious Bane*, we should be all right this autumn just as happened with *If Winter Comes*,' she reasoned, 'even if we pay cash with order. After all, *The Green Hat* and *The Sheikh* are still selling well, and the Jeffery Farnol and Hugh Walpole novels do well at Christmas, and the classics sell steadily. And—' she added hopefully, since this was her own pet love, 'the detective stories.'

'It's not enough – and we set out to provide everything to everyone, remember? Brave ideals, but the political books only sell a handful; archaeology and travel books do reasonably well; the second-hand book stock is a drag; the few libraries we supply to naturally need a decent discount, and the publishers refuse to increase our small pittance of a discount or even to supply books on a see-safe basis. We need at least twenty-five per cent, but do we get it? No.'

Jennie laughed – she couldn't help it, despite Richard's desperate face. 'Darling, you're sounding like Albert yourself.'

Albert Hodge's lugubrious complaint was always that 'It'll come full circle, you mark my words.' Albert had begun as a bookseller in the late 1880s and seen the struggles of the

5

publishers and booksellers as they both tried to extract a profit from new book sales. Albert hoped that the second-hand market would revive again.

Richard spread his hands in despair. 'What's to be done, Jennie? I can't force people to read books. We could give up the second-hand market completely, but that stock's already paid for. Why does everything come down to money!' He banged his hand on the side of the deckchair in frustration. 'All I want to do is to sell books, talk about them to people, interest them, and yet I have to spend most days worrying about how to make the accounts add up. If I didn't have you to come home to and the twins and this garden, I don't—'

Jennie froze. She feared Richard's phases of depression. They didn't come very often but they were hard to shift. Even making love failed at the worst times, and it frightened her when he turned from her wrapped in his own impenetrable world.

'Buried in the Book of Doom again?' she asked quietly, appalled that she hadn't seen this crisis coming. In her pleasure in Applemere Cottage and looking after the twins, had she assumed too easily that Richard was faring well enough at the bookshop, simply because he had not indicated anything was wrong?

'How long do we have?' she continued, trying to sound practical.

'I can't run a bookshop without the new books. I can put off the rent a few more weeks but time's running out fast.'

'Shall I—' Jennie hesitated, knowing Richard's pride '—take a look at the accounts? A fresh eye might help. At least it would put me in the picture, and might give me an idea as to how we could tackle the problem.'

For a moment she thought he'd refuse, but he agreed, so the situation must be really bad. Tomorrow she would leave the twins with Aunt Win at the Station House, and go to Canterbury with Richard. It surprised her to realize that she was already beginning to look forward to it. *Any* problem must have a solution, mustn't it?

Once Canterbury had seemed the ends of the earth for her, instead of less than ten miles away. She had grown up at Fairsted Station, and her father, George Trent, was still its stationmaster. It was on a loop of the Elham Valley Line from

Canterbury to Folkestone, and from there she could look through the railway tunnel to the blue hills in the distance one way, and in the other direction towards Canterbury, which then seemed as far off to her as it must have done to pilgrims setting off from London or Winchester to travel to the great cathedral. Now, Canterbury was only a short train journey away for her, yet sometimes she longed to recapture the childhood magic of the unattainable.

Jennie loved Canterbury, especially the cathedral. Every time she walked past its majestic gates into Sun Street, she imagined the pilgrims approaching the end of their journey on their knees. The cathedral had been a battlefield for murder, passion and politics, and yet in its timelessness it inspired only peace and hope.

Pencarek Books was tucked under the shadow of the cathedral walls. The old Sun hostelry opposite and the ancient houses made medieval times seem very close, and watching people pass in and out of the great gate provided endless interest. Before going in, she stopped to admire Richard's window displays – after all, it might encourage others to stop too. Here together were religious and political books, adventure novels, fine bindings and cheap editions all cheek by jowl, yet not clashing with each other. They had a splendid order of Richard's own, calculated to catch the eye of the viewer and to lead it on to fresh fields. She could see an ornately bound *As You Like It* and Barrie's *The Admirable Crichton*, both illustrated with colour plates by Hugh Thomson, and one of his equally splendidly illustrated *Tales of the Canterbury Pilgrims*, which Richard had pounced on joyfully when it was offered to him; there were the new Macmillan Jane Austen editions, and Mrs Gaskell's *Cranford*, illustrated by C. E. Brock. Yet by their side the Jeffery Farnol novels didn't look out of place, nor even *The Sheikh*. H. G. Wells looked proud to be present, and so did Sherlock Holmes. Richard had even put political tracts of today together with Defoe and Swift World Classics editions. Everything seemed to harmonize – it made Jennie want to rush in and buy everything.

'Good morning, Mrs Pencarek. A pleasure to see you.'

Mr Hodge bowed, and she looked affectionately at the small bald spot on the top of his head. Albert Hodge was definitely of the old school, including stiff wing collar and old frock coat, and, if she hadn't known that he possessed the kindest heart of anyone she knew (except perhaps Aunt Win), she would have been terrified of him. She knew he disapproved of her bobbed hair, turban hat and shorter skirts but he tolerated her nevertheless as part of the price he paid for the privilege of working in a bookshop. Even more disapproval wafted over when she began to study the account books, and Richard must have noticed, for he joked with him about how many copies of *The Green Hat* and *The Sheikh* he'd sold that day.

'I regret to say, sir, I have already sold three of the former, and two of the latter.'

Jennie stifled a giggle. Albert disapproved even more strongly of *The Sheikh* than the Michael Arlen novel. She suspected this was because he didn't actually understand what *The Green Hat* was all about. To write that Iris's husband 'died for purity' was merely bewildering to Albert, since sexual diseases – the actual cause of the husband's death – were unlikely to play much part in his life.

The Sheikh had been given an extra long selling life because of the Rudolph Valentino film of the book. Jennie joked that half the women of Canterbury saw themselves as Lady Diana Mayo, ravished time and time again by the masterful Sheikh of the Desert. Albert Hodge manfully considered it his duty to sell it, even though she had seen him urge a copy of the Bible to accompany it. She suspected that buying the novel from Albert Hodge who rigidly stood for everything *The Sheikh* didn't (even though the masterful Sheikh turned out to be a respectable Englishman after all) added an extra frisson for those who bought it. Improving classics weren't nearly so much fun.

The accounts presented a bleak picture. 'You're right, Richard,' she admitted at last. They had no secrets from Albert Hodge. 'We can't go on like this for longer than a few weeks. And it's not your fault, Mr Hodge,' she added hastily, 'you're a marvellous bookseller. But we haven't the capital to ride out bad times even if we can survive until the Christmas sales.'

'So what can we do?' Richard asked.

For the first time, Jennie felt irritated. Was he expecting her to produce a miracle? If so, he would be disappointed. For once she was stumped. 'We'll have to live on stock and pay for whatever little we can buy with cash. You want *Precious Bane*—'

Albert coughed. 'An attractive book, but perhaps if I might make a suggestion, not so instantly appealing as some other novels.'

'No,' Richard said obstinately. '*Precious Bane* will work. It has to. If I can't run the bookshop the way I want to, then what's the point?'

Jennie could see a lot of point. Their livelihood was at stake, not to mention Mr Hodge's. She knew when Richard was really digging in his heels, however.

'If I can delay the rent,' he suggested, 'we can buy a reasonable quantity of *Precious Bane*, which will help tide us over until Christmas, provided we keep our stocks of current fiction up too.'

Christmas! Never had Jennie felt so helpless. It meant virtually depending on one book and old stock. It was hopeless, surely, but she couldn't say so. Could she go back to work in a railway booking office? No, Richard had to earn money or his pride would be hurt. Perhaps Freddie could help get him a job on the railways, or Tom one in the brewery since he was its manager. No, again. That might raise all sorts of problems given the strained relationship between Freddie and Tom. That was the only fly in the ointment in the Trent family. Why did families have to be so *difficult*? Richard had had enough such troubles of his own, and was adamant about not being drawn into any more. Especially any involving Anna Fokingham, now Anna Trent.

Normally Jennie loved visiting Applemere House, but not today. It stood only a mile or so from Fairsted village, half a mile from Applemere Halt station, and a hundred yards or so from Applemere Cottage. It was Jennie's favourite place after the cottage and the Station House where her father lived with Aunt Win, who had moved in after the death of their mother to look after the three children.

Today, following Mr Stevens, the stern-faced butler, through the house, Jennie felt as awkward as when she first came here aged twelve, fully expecting to be turned away. Now Applemere was as familiar and dear to her as her own home, despite all that had happened in the meantime.

'Where are the twins?' Lady Fokingham asked immediately.

She was taking tea in the garden, and Jennie felt a rush of pleasure both at seeing her and at being in the Applemere gardens again. She explained that Lynette and Jamie were at the Station House, because there was something she needed to talk about. She felt somewhat guilty because the twins adored Applemere and she knew Lady Fokingham liked seeing them running about. Whether the gardeners were so keen was a moot point. Almost identical to look at, with their dark brown hair and blue eyes – the latter inherited from Richard – their personalities were very different. Lynette was the more adventurous of the two, always heading for trouble; Jamie was the sturdier one, the rock to whom Lynette returned howling her eyes out when things went wrong. Jennie and Richard longed for another baby, but so far it hadn't happened.

Lady Fokingham looked as slender and elegant in her silky blue slim-fitting dress as she had in her long trained skirts before the war, despite the fact that she must be in her midfifties now. She looked tired though. The war and her experiences in it seemed to have drained the casual confidence she had had when Jennie first met her.

Lady Fokingham must have noticed something was wrong because she quickly replied, 'Oh, that's splendid. I'd been coming to see you anyway. I'm afraid we have to cancel the tennis party on Saturday, our whole house party in fact.'

Despite her worry, Jennie was instantly disappointed. She loved these tennis weekends at Applemere, when she and Richard joined the guests. Jennie had learned to play, and Richard always said he didn't mind. He was happy to watch, for his artificial leg meant he couldn't take much active part himself, though he seemed to enjoy umpiring. Those afternoons were wonderful; the pit pat of the tennis balls, the lovely teas, and the pleasant conversation in the sunshine remained in her memory, perhaps because they were so very different to the war years.

'We all have to go to Montevanya unexpectedly,' Lady Fokingham continued. 'My brother has requested it, which is unusual, and we're somewhat worried as to why he should do so.'

It was all too easy to forget in Jennie's affection for Lady

Fokingham that she was formally the Princess Marie, as well as Lady Fokingham, and her brother Stephen was king of Montevanya. Montevanya was a small independent country situated on the River Danube wedged between what were now Roumania and Yugoslavia, and, like them, an independent monarchy.

'I'm sorry.' Jennie had visited Montevanya once, and still felt a sense of kinship with it.

'Bring the twins here any time you like while we're away,' Lady Fokingham said. 'I know they love the gardens. And would you look after our conservatory – the new gardener might not know which are the tender plants?'

Jennie realized Lady Fokingham was deliberately giving her time to explain what she was here for, but it grew more and more difficult to speak about it. At last she just blurted it out. 'We have a problem at the bookshop. We can't pay the rent at the cottage.' Richard would be appalled to hear her admitting this, but she had no choice.

Lady Fokingham's face wrinkled in concern. 'It doesn't matter at all about the rent. *Ever.*'

It mattered to Jennie and even more to Richard, however. The rent was little enough in any case. 'We'll be able to pay soon,' she assured her brightly.

'I'm sure you will.' Lady Fokingham still looked troubled. 'But if it takes longer, if you need more help – then come to us, Jennie.'

Jennie thanked her, even though she knew there was no way Richard would ever approach the Fokinghams for assistance. He got on with them well enough, and often accompanied her and the twins when they visited Applemere House, but he hated being their tenants.

As usual, this stemmed back to Lady Fokingham's daughter Anna, and the rift between Freddie, now her husband, and Tom. Anna meant trouble, so Richard said, and Jennie was forced to agree that he was right. Nevertheless her friendship with Anna had endured, despite its severe testing. Anna was a rebel. Even when Jennie first met her, she had kicked against the constraints of her upbringing, and later she had become pregnant by Tom. Unknown to him at the time she had given birth to twins whom her parents had promptly had adopted. Anna had tried to trace them in vain, and now that Jennie had twins of her own, she could understand more fully the torment she had gone through. Anna had cut herself off completely from her parents; she never visited Applemere and seldom came to Fairsted. Even though she was now happily married, as was Tom, that didn't mean there wasn't still rancour between the two brothers, which Jennie found hard to bear. Her great fear was that one day it might explode into open warfare.

It did, and at the worst of times: on Jennie's birthday in early August.

Jennie watched proudly as Lynette (naturally the first through the door) rushed up to Aunt Win, whose stern exterior hid a warm and loving heart. 'My dolly's got a new dress,' she crowed, thrusting her beloved rag doll into Aunt Win's face as she bent down to kiss her. It was almost like being a child again herself, Jennie thought, seeing her daughter scooped up into Aunt Win's arms. Dad promptly scooped up Jamie so that the twins should receive the same treatment. In fact, Jennie was never quite sure whether Jamie did want the same treatment, but whenever she saw his large wondering eyes fixed on her she could never resist hugging him tightly too, just in case.

He was confiding to Dad that his bicycle was outside. In fact it was a battered child's tricycle that Richard had bought cheaply for his birthday in May from a family in Elham, but its condition had not registered with Jamie. He had been thrilled to bits, and promptly started to try to get its wheels off to see how it worked.

The twins rushed out into the garden to join Uncle Tom and their cousins Alfred and Arabella. Jennie remembered playing there herself with young Freddie, until elder brother Tom would stroll up and take over the proceedings, which then sometimes ended in tears. They'd both looked up to him then, the debonair, fair-haired god, two years older than herself. Why did families have to change, she thought crossly. At least nothing would happen this afternoon, since it was understood that Freddie and Tom should if at all possible never meet. It was Aunt Win's role to sort out who would and would not be present. Today it was Tom's turn. His wife Mary rarely came to the Station House for such events; she always had a good reason, but Jennie suspected it was because she felt

Tom's family was of less social importance than her own. Today Freddie was working, Dad explained – he was an engine-driver – and Anna was in London.

The birthday tea had barely begun, however, before Jennie to her horror saw Freddie and Anna strolling up the garden path from the rear gate. There was Anna, her slim boyish figure and fair bobbed hair showing off her stylish clothes with perfect poise and elegance. How on earth had this clash happened? Jennie wondered frantically whether she should she cry out 'Look who's here' to alert everyone else, but it was too late.

'What the devil are you doing here?' Freddie asked quietly, as he took in his brother's presence.

Jennie jumped in quickly. 'It's my birthday, Freddie. I'm so glad you could get here too.' She jumped up to greet Anna, who of course just stood there looking faintly amused at the situation.

Freddie, white-faced with anger, turned to his wife. 'You said it would just be us, Anna.'

'I thought so. That's what Aunt Win said,' Anna replied coolly, then turned to the company, full of her usual charm. 'Father George—' That was her name for Dad. Anna never used that particular word, preferring to blot out the whole of her childhood. 'And Tom, it's wonderful to see you all. Richard, darling.' There were kisses for Alfred, for Arabella, for Lynette and Jamie, and even for Jennie. Jennie fumed as Anna's amused eyes looked into hers.

'Did you say that?' Jennie whispered horrified to Aunt Win, at the first opportunity.

'I did not,' came the snapped reply. 'And that young lady knows it very well.'

Somehow tea was survived, with Freddie devoting himself solely to the children, and Anna at her best happily talking to everyone else. Nevertheless Jennie was relieved when they could leave the house and go into the garden for the children's treasure hunt. Seven-year-old Alfred was determined to show his superiority over his younger sister and cousins, and secretly Jennie was delighted when Jamie found the first little parcel. She grew so engrossed in supervising the hunt that she didn't see trouble coming until it was too late.

Richard and the other adults had been playing ninepins, and

Tom was obviously claiming victory, picking up the bag of sweets allotted for the winner. Jennie was jerked to attention by hearing Freddie demand the bag of sweets. 'That's mine,' he said, not loudly but purposefully. That was always Freddie's way when he believed himself in the right. He didn't permit injustice even over a bag of sweets, and more than that was at stake here.

Tom shrugged and handed it over. 'You always want what I have, don't you? You always did. Never played with your own toys, you had to have mine. Pathetic really. You've never changed.'

Jennie froze. Was this a casual reference to their childhood rivalry or was it much more serious? Freddie took it as the latter. His dark eyes were glittering, and his face took on the pugnacious look that she remembered from the war. Then it had won him a medal, but it was rarely seen at home.

'I succeeded,' he retorted. 'She married *me*.'

Dear heavens. For the first time they were directly clashing over Anna – or was Anna just the innocent battleground of a more ancient rivalry? Impossible to tell. Anna looked from one to the other as if she were nothing to do with this argument, and perhaps she would be right.

For one awful moment Jennie thought Tom was going to attack Freddie, and Aunt Win looked as if she was ready to fly between them. The moment passed, as Tom restrained himself, hurling only at Freddie:

'Just keep out of my way, brother mine.'

'Willingly.' Freddie seized Anna by the arm, and without so much as a farewell to anyone frogmarched her through the garden gate to where their car was parked.

There was a menace beneath Tom's words that belied the mild response, and Jennie was in no doubt that the rift between them was far wider than she had imagined.

It was obvious to Jennie how the disaster had come about and at the first opportunity she left the twins with Aunt Win and took the bus to Ashford to have it out with Anna. Despite Anna's wealth, she and Freddie lived in a small terraced house, which Jennie suspected was another bid to enrage her parents. 'How could you, Anna?' Jennie stormed. 'You *knew* Tom would be there. You wanted them to meet.'

Anna looked taken aback, and tears welled up in her eyes.

'You're right,' she admitted, 'but, Jennie, I so much wanted everything to be all right between them again. I hate feeling I've come between your brothers. It's so ridiculous. I was a kid when I knew Tom, and now I'm happy with Freddie, so I thought if I got them together on a happy occasion such as your birthday it would all come right. I did it for you, and for darling Father George and Aunt Win. But it didn't work.'

It most certainly hadn't. And that, Jennie thought glumly, was what usually happened where Anna was concerned. Her plans turned unexpected corners and, hey presto, trouble again.

'We'll have to leave the shop by the Christmas quarterday.' Richard's face was white and strained, and even the twins could not cheer him up. 'I don't know where we'll put the stock. I'll have to sell it on to another trader.'

Christmas was only six weeks away now, and *Precious Bane* had not fulfilled expectations so far as sales were concerned. The reviews had mostly been ecstatic. Edwin Pugh in *The Bookman* had spoken of 'genius'; it had been T. P. O'Connor's Book of the Week with Mary Webb's picture on the cover; L. P. Hartley had written glowingly of it. Only *New Statesman* regretfully saw it as a 'respectable failure'. It seemed *New Statesman* was right, because although everyone agreed it was beautifully written, no one seemed to want to buy it.

'I'm sure the—' Jennie began.

'Don't say the Fokinghams,' Richard broke in mildly. 'It's bad enough that the rent on the cottage is overdue.'

'I dealt with that before they left for Montevanya,' Jennie told him. 'We can leave it for a while.'

He was aghast. 'You discussed it with them without asking me?'

'I knew you wouldn't like it.'

'You were right.' He stood up trembling. 'I will not be indebted to the Fokinghams any more than we have to be. We don't pay much rent, now we can't even pay that – and you took it on yourself to *tell* them so.'

'We'll pay them soon.' Jennie was bewildered. They couldn't just ignore the fact that the rent was due. Of course she had had to tell them.

His anger passed to quiet despair. 'How could you do that, Jennie?'

'How could you *mind*, Richard?' she shot back. 'They're our friends as well as landlords.'

'People like us can never be friends with the likes of the Fokinghams. There's no common ground.'

'Only if we fail to put it there. Can't you see they're lonely with Michael away in London most of the time?' Anna's brother Michael worked for the Foreign Office in London and only came to Applemere for the occasional weekend.

She was never sure if Richard knew about Michael's liking for men rather than women. They never discussed it. 'If Michael doesn't marry,' she continued calmly, 'there'll be no grandchildren.'

Instantly she knew she'd put a foot wrong.

'They have two children, Jennie. Not one.'

The wound inside her opened up again. How could she be loyal to Anna and still be friendly with the Fokinghams? Sometimes she felt she was betraying both. Anna had completely ceased contact with them, and yet she was perfectly well aware that Jennie was on good terms with her parents. It almost amused her, Jennie thought. She justified it to herself that there was blame on both sides. The Fokinghams had behaved badly in expecting to force Anna to renounce her babies for adoption. Anna had behaved equally badly in using Tom to get her pregnant as a means to outwit her parents.

'Let's forget Applemere,' she said to Richard wearily.

'But you never do, Jennie. That's the problem. You *never* do.'

'How could I? It's part of my life.'

Applemere had magically haunted her since she was a child. She thought of her twelfth birthday, when she, Freddie, Tom and Jack had hurried to Applemere Halt. There they had met Michael and Anna, and the door to Applemere was open for good and for bad. Even during the war Applemere had been with her, for she had been a VAD nurse aboard the ambulance train that Freddie had driven and named the Applemere Flyer. A sudden thought – almost a dream – flashed through her mind at such a speed she could not catch it.

Richard sighed. 'Our life's what's important. The days of the Applemere Flyer are over.'

The dream came again, as he mentioned that name and this time Jennie seized it. Certainly those days – thank goodness

– were over in one way. The Flyer had been decommissioned at the end of the war although the engine was still in service in Britain. It wasn't called the Flyer any longer, though. The idea, the dream, moved forward, but frustratingly it still wasn't shaped. Near, oh so near, though. She struggled to keep calm, despite her racing mind.

'Nothing's over unless you want it to be, Richard. Not the Flyer, not the bookshop. After all, we could run it from here, this cottage, in a small way.' No, that wasn't where the dream had been heading. It was a false step. She clung desperately to that fast vanishing dream.

Richard laughed bitterly. 'You think we can live on selling Bibles for christenings every so often? Books aren't like potatoes, they're not necessities except to the few. How are you going to bring the people to the books?'

'Suppose,' she almost choked in her eagerness, 'we don't. Suppose we take the books to the people?' It was coming. The dream. So outrageous, so new, so *obvious*. 'We'll take the books to their doorstep.'

'By horse and cart, I suppose,' Richard snorted. He wasn't taking her seriously. But he would. He had to.

'No! By Applemere Flyer,' she cried triumphantly.

'The train?' Richard looked as if she'd taken leave of her senses. And she had, but in delirious happiness at seeing the solution.

'By charabanc, by bus. Somehow, Richard. We can take all sorts of books, detective stories, classics, encyclopaedias, Bibles, take orders . . . We'll *make* the common ground between people. Don't you see?'

She thought he did. She saw the dawning of hope in his eyes. She saw the new Applemere Flyer. She saw a dream complete at last, and one that they could make come true.

Two

'Jennie, no!' Richard was looking at her in horror.

'But it's *steam*-powered,' she gloated. Oh, the wonder of it. The obvious solution.

'So was the Ark,' Richard said grimly. 'If we have to have a wreck, for heaven's sake let's find a motor-powered wreck.' All the old motor buses they'd looked at in the past ten days were beyond their means, though.

'This one,' Jennie replied with dignity, 'is free.'

'I'm not surprised.' He looked despairingly at what appeared to be a heap of rusting metal.

Even Jennie had been daunted at her first sight of this monster. When Freddie had mentioned that there was a former National Steam Car Company bus lying derelict in the Ashford running sheds grounds, her hopes had shot sky-high, and she had had no intention of letting go of them without a struggle. The bus had been pressed into emergency service during the rail strike of 1919, and being obsolete was then never used again. That was only five years ago and the bus had presumably been in full working order then. It must have passed through hard years though, for even Jennie was forced to admit she was a sorry sight. It was a nineteen-seater single-decker Clarkson steamer, just right for them. Most such steam buses had been double-decker, but what use would an open top deck be to them? It was true that there were signs of rust, it was missing a tyre, some of the seating had been ripped out, its white livery paint cried out for renewal, and all of it was filthy—

But it was a bus. And it was free. Jennie loved it on sight.

Jennie drew a deep breath and turned to Freddie. 'Does she move?'

Freddie grinned. 'Have to see, won't we, Richard?' He turned to his brother-in-law. 'You don't stand a chance.

Jennie's always wanted to be on the footplate. Now she sees a dream come true, don't you, darling sis?'

'Wouldn't you?' Jennie retorted. 'Anna went on the footplate in France. Why not me?'

'And why not me?' Richard put in.

Too late. Jennie cursed herself for being so stupid and assuming that Richard would not want, or not be able, to drive because of his leg.

'We can share the driving,' she offered quickly. 'I can do my share while you're doing the important part, selling books.'

He said nothing more, and Freddie hastily began to talk boiler technicalities, fuelling, mileage, and water supplies, until the awkward moment passed.

For Jennie having the bus was a foregone conclusion. Not only was it their only chance of being able to afford the venture, but life had suddenly opened out in front of her as an open road along which she would triumphantly be able to play her part by steaming along in their very own bus.

Richard still looked dubious. 'Have you given any thought to the kind of roads it will be driving on? If you can call our lanes roads. Lines of potholes are more probable most of the year. How's a steam boiler going to take to that? I gather they take a lot of looking after at the best of times. And we'd need lighting. And there's the police licence to consider.'

'It would give us a start,' Jennie pleaded, 'and if one can have steam tractors in fields why not potholed lanes on a steam bus?' This wasn't going to be easy, she realized. 'We could avoid the worst lanes by parking at the ends and hooting.' She began to think of the winter ahead, the snow-drift blocked lanes, the frost-affected mud and gravel, the dark evenings . . .

'Taking books *to* the people,' Richard reminded her gently enough. 'Doorstop deliveries. Remember?'

'We'll amend that to nearby deliveries in bad weather.' Jennie looked to Freddie for help.

He responded nobly. 'Let me get the old heap going at least. We can't do it up completely for you, but the men can put it in working order on the quiet.' Jennie was impressed. Freddie was now twenty-eight, but it was still hard to think of her little brother as having such seniority. No company crawler was Freddie. His distinguished war record had helped, of course. Before the war he would have waited another twenty or thirty years before he got to this point.

'We can paint and fit the shelves,' Jennie pointed out eagerly. Could they, she privately wondered? Richard was no handyman, and she wasn't much better.

'You could ask Tom for help,' Freddie suggested, to Jennie's amazement. The expression on his face was neutral and Jennie was not sure how to react. Did he want to heal the rift? It seemed unlikely.

She laughed uneasily. 'You know Tom. He never does anything for free.'

Freddie didn't comment, and Jennie thought for a moment that she'd put her foot in it.

Thankfully, her foot hadn't offended after all. Freddie had apparently merely been thinking. 'Offer Tom a carrot, Jen. Sugar-coated, you know his sweet tooth. Tell him you'll take round bottles of beer on the Flyer.'

'No,' Richard said mildly.

Freddie laughed. 'How about books about beer then? Jen, didn't you tell me Mary was writing a history of the brewery or a recipe book or something like that? Publish it for them and sell it on the Flyer.'

'Brilliant, Freddie.' Jennie grasped at this superb straw.

'Publish?' Richard's voice sounded odd, and to her surprise he began pacing up and down. 'Freddie, you've got something there. I've always wanted to – Jennie, *that's* the way.' It was his eyes lighting up with enthusiasm now.

Her turn to demur. 'The cost, Richard. Design, printing – where do we get the capital?'

Richard seized her and danced her round. 'What an old steam slowcoach you can be,' he cried. 'Tom will pay, of course. He can afford it, or the brewery can. I'll design it, illustrate it – get it printed. After that—'

'After what?' Jennie prompted, somewhat dazed. She hadn't seen Richard so excited for ages.

'We'll publish more books of course. More publications beautifully designed like those of the Kelmscott Press, and this new one, the Nonesuch Press. Francis Meynell has shown it's all possible, to have both beautiful books and have them printed by machines to sell at a reasonable price. The public are lapping them up – it's the way forward.'

'And the money?' Jennie asked again faintly, thinking this should at least be mentioned. And what, she wondered, was all this about illustrating?

'We'll find it.' He hugged her. 'Together we will, somehow.' A long pause. 'And sell them on this old heap,' he added. 'You can even sell a few of your precious detective stories.'

Jennie grew heartily sick of red paint, even if the colour had been her idea. 'People need to see us coming,' she had declared. She had a vision of a snow-covered Kent, the barren dark branches of the trees, and their scarlet bus ploughing indomitably through. Only a few more weeks now to Christmas when their new life would begin. She was determined to finish the painting today, so that Tom's signwriter could come tomorrow to do a professional job on the lettering; they had compromised on what this should be: The Applemere Flyer for the name of the bus, and Pencarek Books in larger letters underneath.

Tom, always one to strike bargains, had made sure he left some at least of the work to her, but with a mere ironic 'Anything to help Freddie out', he had coughed up for umpteen gallons of paint. With a bit of help from Fairsted's former blacksmith, now blacksmith-cum-garage mechanic, she had set to on the last lap this morning. The twins would be warmly tucked up in the cottage with Aunt Win looking after them, baking scones while she worked out here in the thickest of old clothes.

November was nearly over, but there was still no word from Sir Roger or Lady Fokingham. Not that she expected a picture postcard every day, but usually there was at least one to indicate when they would be home. There had been nothing on this visit. Jennie had taken the twins to Applemere House yesterday, while she checked the removal of plants to the greenhouses or conservatory for the winter, and there had been no news there either. Mr Stevens seemed unperturbed, pointing out gravely that they would be telegraphing only when there *was* news. His expression conveyed that it was not his place to expect anything – but sometimes Jennie suspected a much more voluble Mr Stevens existed when he was with the house-keeper at the supper table.

Jennie was still unconvinced that the Fokinghams' silence

was normal, and was still mulling this over, as she painted away, when there was a toot on a motor car horn, and Freddie drove up. The new Riley Redwing tourer was Anna's but like everything else they shared it, and he had driven over from Ashford. Typical of Anna to buy an essentially open-top motor car, wonderful in July, but late November?

'Look at this, Freddie.' Jennie stood back to display her work with a flourish.

He nodded approvingly. 'Glad Tom forked out.' There didn't seem to be any sarcasm in his voice, to Jennie's relief. Perhaps the distance between her two brothers was narrowing, so far as Freddie at least was concerned, but she wouldn't count on it.

'He was a dear about it,' she replied firmly, 'and Mary was thrilled.' Jennie had been amazed about that because it wasn't easy to please Mary, who as daughter of the brewery owner still bore a faint air of condescension in speaking to Tom's family. Jennie suspected she had some status in Mary's eyes, however, because of her friendship with the Fokinghams. Her 'book' had turned out to be neither history nor pure recipes, but Kentish recipes with hops and beer. People were losing touch with their roots, she had assured Jennie earnestly. They didn't roam the fields to gather wild edible food as once they did. Jennie had tried to keep a straight face. If Mary had such roots in solid earth, she would keep them very firmly out of sight. Mary's roots were firmly attached to Canterbury streets, and there was little wild food to be sampled there.

'Shall we steam up and take her round to Dad?' Freddie asked, clearly longing to have a go. 'How's the water situation?'

'She's ready and eager to go.' So was Jennie. They had taken her out regularly for the last two weeks, and the Fairsted villagers – though at first annoyed that they weren't a regular bus service – had become mildly intrigued. Whispers were flying around. Water for the boiler was a slight problem since Applemere Cottage only had a well, but the gardeners at Applemere had been cooperative. So had Dad. His pre-war attitude of 'the Company wouldn't like it' seemed to have mellowed considerably, and the Applemere Flyer had twice refilled her boiler courtesy of the SECR.

'Let's arrive on the footplate—' Jennie had decided it was a footplate even though it was a bus. 'He'll love that.'

Dad had been taken aback when he first walked over to Applemere Cottage to see the Flyer, which was now lodged in a hastily converted barn, fifty yards away (thank you, Tom!). Dad was so advanced in many ways – after all he'd encouraged Jennie to apply to be a booking-office clerk when this was solely a man's job before the war – yet so entrenched in others. 'A footplate's no place for a woman,' he declared, and still maintained it. To pacify him she'd told him that Richard and she would share the driving, which was true, though it made sense to her that she should take the lion's share.

'And the twins?' Aunt Win had asked grimly.

'In another year they'll be at school and in the meantime . . .' Jennie's voice had trailed off.

'You thought I'd look after them.'

'Oh no,' Jennie looked suitably shocked. 'I'll take them with me.'

'You will *not*,' Aunt Win had firmly declared to Jennie's relief. 'They'll catch their death, they will. They'll come to me, or I'll come round to the cottage and no arguments about it.'

'What's young Lynette going to think?' Dad had chimed in. 'You don't want her thinking a woman's place is behind an engine.'

Jennie wanted Lynette to grow up thinking she could follow her own path, not be limited by tradition, but had diplomatically refrained from saying so.

The Applemere Flyer triumphantly steamed the mile to the Station House, with the usual curious eyes upon it, and hearing it Dad came hurrying through from his office. The Fairsted loop had reverted to its prewar level of use and Dad was afraid the Company might deprive him of his ticket-taker, saying that a porter was sufficient. But so far the axe had not fallen.

'My,' he now said admiringly, 'She's quite a beauty, I'll say that for her. That steamer's a pleasure to hear. How's the paraffin working out?' Suspicious to the last, he'd been appalled to hear that the boiler was fired with liquid paraffin fuel.

'Splendidly,' Jennie and Freddie chorused. It was a familiar refrain.

Dad shook his head. 'You take care, my girl. I'm fond enough of steam, but it's coal—'

'No room for coal on a bus, Dad.'

'Wait till your aunt sees this. Win!' Dad bawled, giving up the argument. 'Look who's here,' and Aunt Win came hurrying out of the house with the twins on her heels.

Jennie jumped proudly down from the footplate to hug her, then stopped short at the sight of her face. 'What is it, Aunt Win? What's wrong?'

'Didn't you read the newspaper this morning, George?' Win asked.

'No, the seven o'clock was running late.' He looked alarmed.

'It's Montevanya, Jennie. The poor king's been assassinated.'

For a moment Jennie couldn't take this in. The king? But that was King Stephen, whom she knew, that gentle old man. So formidable before the war, and so changed now.

'King Stephen?' she repeated stupidly.

Aunt Win nodded soberly. 'On his way up to the castle, it says.'

Jennie closed her eyes in shock. She remembered Anna telling her it was there that the only attempt ever to kill a king of Montevanya had been made, on that occasion by a crazed peasant. King Stephen had often produced the joke that there was no closed season for killing kings, and now he had been killed himself. How could anyone do that after all he'd suffered during the war and after all he had done for his people?

'Who by?' she asked.

Even as she spoke, she thought of Viktor, King Stephen's elder son, who had seized power during the war when the Germans overran Montevanya. King Stephen had managed to escape and Viktor crowned himself as the Germans' puppet king. At the end of the war he had been forced by the Allies to yield the throne back to his father, and had then been exiled with his German wife and family.

Visions of Viktor arranging to kill his own father raced through her mind. No, surely even Viktor would stop short of that.

'One of the revolutionary parties, it says. The Socialist Republicans, they call themselves.'

Dad cleared his throat. 'How about a cup of tea, Win?' He

led the way, a twin by each hand. 'This will be a shock to young Anna. You'd best be getting back, Freddie.'

'I'll do that. A quick cuppa first.' Freddie looked as if he needed it. The king had been Anna's uncle, after all. Jennie rapidly ran through all the terrible ramifications there might be, especially one of them.

Tea was a marvellous restorative. Even the act of drinking it brought a certain normality. Aunt Win had used the best teapot, which held at least two cups each, and the twins munched away at her gingerbread biscuits with gusto. Then finally Jennie put into words the fear they all shared.

'What about Eileen? Is she there?'

'I hoped you'd know, Jennie,' Win said worriedly. 'No mention of her in the newspaper. There wouldn't be, of course.'

Aunt Eileen, Win's sister, lived with the dead king's brother, Prince Georgius, for part of the year, and the rest of the time travelled by herself. She could be walking the Himalayas, driving along the Silk Road or – a new passion – flying to Baghdad, perhaps on the mail run. Or she could be involved in her other life, which Jennie suspected was secret service work. She said she'd given that up, but Jennie wasn't sure she believed her. If she was still active, she would be far from safe in Montevanya now – especially if Viktor were somehow involved in this coup.

'It's much more likely to be Viktor behind it than politicians,' Freddie said gloomily. Viktor, although Anna's cousin, was far from popular with her, though she tolerated his brother Max. Ever since the Russian Tsar, his wife, family and servants had been assassinated by Bolshevik revolutionaries, Lady Fokingham had feared something of the sort happening in Montevanya. Queen Zita, King Stephen's widow, was a sister of the Tsarina, both granddaughters of Queen Victoria. Viktor had seemed the main threat, however.

Jennie had never heard of the Socialist Republicans, although she did know there was a republican movement within the Montevanyan parliament. The latter was small, however, and the majority of those in parliament seeking change favoured a constitutional monarchy with more power to parliament and less to the king. And there was Max of course. Jennie's thoughts were completely jumbled. If Viktor had been formally banned from the succession then his younger brother Max would now be the legal king – or would the throne go to Viktor's son? There was no mention of either Max or any other new king in the brief report that Aunt Win showed them.

When Jennie had visited Montevanya in early 1914 she had parted on bad terms with Max, but meeting him by chance during the war found that he had changed greatly, sobered by war's harsh realities. Lady Fokingham had told her that he had married after the war – the need for an heir, she had added casually. His bride was from the Roumanian royal family and he had a son.

The necessity for arranged marriages in royal households had obviously not changed, Jennie had thought wryly. Marriage was for money, property, position and heirs. Poor Lady Fokingham. She would for ever be convinced that Anna's children by Tom were not 'true' grandchilden. They could never be heirs and so they weren't grandchildren. Sometimes, Jennie thought, it was simpler to be penniless and please oneself. But then one couldn't do that successfully without money – although it was true her aunt Eileen pleased herself about her life. The Harkness girls were, she reflected, a surprising trio: her mother Alice, frail and loving, who had died over twenty years ago, dear Aunt Win, with her strict exterior and loving heart, and Eileen, the cuckoo in the nest, who flew away but never entirely left.

'So where's this travelling bookshop Freddie keeps talking about?'

The unexpected voice from outside the bus made Jennie jump in the delicate task of pasting category labels on to the shelves. She had spent all last evening typing them out in capital letters on their ancient typewriter. She peered out of the window in disbelief, and then rushed to the bus entrance.

'Anna!'

There she was, hands stuck nonchalantly in pockets and at the same time looking as though she owned the place. As in a way she did, Jennie reminded herself, since the cottage and land were Fokingham property.

'Where are Lynette and Jamie?' Anna asked. Never 'the twins' for her, Jennie had noticed. The word was too painful a reminder of her own lost twins. Nonetheless she got on reasonably well with them, which was a pleasure to Jennie, and Lynette and Jamie found her great fun to be with.

'At the Station House. I needed to get the work finished.' It was December now and time was perilously short.

Anna shivered. 'Won't the books get damp? It's awfully cold out here.'

'We'll keep the barn heated at night, to keep the frost away, and Freddie's rigged up some kind of piped heating from the boiler, as he did on the ambulance train, for when we are out on the road. It doesn't work very well, but it's better than nothing.' Jennie led the way into the house. 'What on earth are you doing here?' It was the first time Anna had ever come to the cottage. Usually Jennie went over to see her, now that Fairsted had a direct bus service to Ashford, and the twins enjoyed the bus ride. It annoyed her that Anna, who had had a car of her own (which Freddie also used) since the end of the war, wouldn't drive over to her home, though she realized the reason why. It was too close to Applemere House.

Jennie stoked up the fire, made some cocoa, and waited.

Anna gave her an awkward grin. 'I wondered if you had any news of Montevanya?'

She didn't mean Montevanya, she meant her parents, Jennie guessed. 'No more than is in the newspapers. Anna, I'm so sorry, your uncle—'

Anna shrugged. 'It's not my family any more. None of them cared a whit about me, only what I could do for The Dynasty and its continuance. Fat chance of it continuing at all now, I'd say.'

'You'd probably be Queen of Montevanya now, if you'd married Viktor.'

Anna paled. 'Good Lord, I hadn't thought of that. A merciful escape.' She caught Jennie's eye and laughed. 'Don't they know any more at the house?'

She couldn't even bear to call it Applemere, let alone home, Jennie noticed. 'I went there last night as soon as Freddie had left. They've heard nothing. Surely your fath— Sir Roger will let them know at least when they expect to be back.'

If they're coming back, she thought privately. Who knew what might happen now? Revolutions could spread, and Lady Fokingham was Stephen's sister. But all she said was: 'I

27

suppose it's now King Maximilian versus King Viktor or Viktor's son?'

'Or the Republic of Montevanya,' Anna pointed out.

She was speaking seriously, to Jennie's surprise. She turned the idea over in her mind. Even after all the bitter conflict of the Great War in that region, the idea of peaceful Montevanya descending into civil war was a terrifying one.

'You must be worried about Eileen,' Anna added with genuine sympathy.

'Eileen's resourceful,' Jennie said, more confidently than she felt. 'She and Max will look after Georgius.' Unfortunately Georgius was a delightful eccentric, and not young now. He would have no designs on power, but that might not save him.

'Let me know if you get any news, will you? And Jennie dear, if that soft look in your eye means you think I'm weakening towards my former parents you are wrong. My brother's caught up in this mess, don't forget.'

'Can't you try the Foreign Office – surely they must have some knowledge of what's going on, and he does work for them.'

'I could. And I suppose I might. But the official line is rarely the whole truth. I'd place more reliance on what they tell old Stevens at the house.'

'I'll go to Applemere every day and telephone you from the Station House,' Jennie said. There was no telephone in Applemere Cottage, although Richard had splashed out on one for the bookshop. A business expense that had brought more expense than business. Thank goodness travelling buses didn't need one.

She hesitated, but now was the perfect time to mention it. With all the work of closing down the bookshop and stocking up the Applemere Flyer, she'd have precious little time for running over to Ashford. 'Christmas, Anna. I gather you and Freddie will be there?'

'There' was the Station House, where for the last four years they had gathered. Jennie longed for a united Christmas but so far Tom and Mary had spent Christmas with her parents, and visited the Station House on Boxing Day when Freddie and Anna weren't there. Yesterday, Aunt Win had proudly announced to Jennie, they'd *all* be coming on Christmas Day. Which meant that Freddie and Tom would come face to face for the first time since August. Enough was enough, Win had declared. Everyone could behave like a civilized human being and forget the past. Aunt Win might be an optimist over this, and Jennie waited on tenterhooks for Anna's reply.

'Of course, Jennie darling. How could I miss it?' she cooed.

'I wasn't thinking of you so much,' Jennie shot back. 'I was thinking of Freddie and Tom.'

Anna donned her look of cool innocence. 'Ten years, Jennie, it's been *ten* years since Tom and I had our little fling. Time for the air to have cleared, don't you think? I did try in August, as you know, but it failed. This is the perfect opportunity to try again. Freddie's really looking forward to a family Christmas. You know what a rotten cook I am.'

Jennie did – chiefly in her opinion because Anna couldn't be bothered to learn. She often wondered what Anna did with herself all day. The house wasn't that large, the result of a compromise between her wealth and Freddie's wages, and although there was a garden Anna took little interest in it. Jennie had asked her once how she occupied herself. Never again.

'I pass the time, Jennie. Waiting,' was the quick reply.

'For children?' How stupid she had been to ask that, and was surprised to get any sort of reply.

A crooked smile. 'Let's say for birth.'

But you're happy, she'd longed to reassure herself, but she could not do it, faced with Anna's irony. If Freddie was content – and he seemed to be, that had to be enough.

Christmas should be a straightforward happy day, Jennie hoped, longing for those of her youth, which – perhaps through hindsight – appeared to have been an endless succession of delights to warm her for the coming year. The church service, the carols, the dear faces round the table, presents such as they were, the family games, Aunt Win's turkey, gathering round the tree. Had that happiness been an artificial creation or had it been real? Did the fact that family tensions were forgotten for the day mean Christmas was artificial, or did Christmas mean the tensions of the rest of the year were only superficial hitches? Whichever it was, she was determined to enjoy it this year.

And so she did. The twins had chiefly books for presents – from stock of course. Beatrix Potter, *Alice in Wonderland,*

Edith Nesbit's *Book of Dragons* and a wonderful Old Mother Goose. Even Jamie, bless him, was struggling with a book. His interests were mechanical toys, but this year economy was essential. Out of the blue, Richard had remarked this morning, watching them pore over their acquisitions, 'Illustrations are the key to books.'

'Children's at least,' Jennie agreed.

'No, adults' too. We're all children at heart.' He said no more, but she felt he wanted to. No point urging him.

As they walked to the Station House after church service, Richard whispered to her, 'It'll be all right, Jennie. This is a blessed day, we're going to have a new life on the Flyer, publishing our own books, illustrating them, selling them as well as others, and it's all going to begin in the New Year.'

'Probably in the snow and ice. When people will have bought all the books they need at Christmas. Are we crazy, Richard, to start at such a time?'

'Yes.' He smiled at her. 'Does it matter?'

'No.' She felt deep thankfulness for all she had. Nothing would go wrong, not today. Aunt Win had bustled ahead, ready to rush in to check that the turkey was cooking properly and to put on the vegetables. When they heard a loud scream, Jennie feared the worst, though her rational self told her it was only a domestic crisis.

'We're needed,' she joked. 'Run, Richard, run, twins. It's burnt turkey for lunch.' She burst in through the door after Jamie, and stopped in sheer shock. It wasn't burnt turkey.

It was Eileen, clad in a bright blue dress with matching bandeau round her bobbed hair, looking as wonderful as the fairy on the Christmas tree. It was hard to believe she was fifty years old now. Her face was wrinkled by her travels and war experiences, but her eyes were so lively and laughing that one saw only those. Jennie felt a great surge of love at seeing her again. Everyone seemed to be babbling together, and Jennie was only vaguely aware of Tom, Mary, their children, Freddie, Anna and the twins, all squeezing round the small dining-table and Dad beaming his head off. His whole family was united once again. A bottle of sherry had appeared – from Eileen? – and even Aunt Win had a glass. The rest of the day passed in a daze and that night, falling asleep in Richard's arms, Jennie could only pick out two distinct memories.

The first was Eileen talking of Montevanya, of how Max was now king and no sign of Viktor. The second was a fleeting image of Anna smiling at Tom, as Freddie pumped his hand in reconciliation. Nineteen twenty-five, Jennie realized, was indeed going to be a marvellous year.

Three

The expected snow failed to arrive in time for the launching of the Applemere Flyer. Instead, they were faced with rain, floods and gales. True, they weren't quite so severe as those on Boxing Day evening, but from where Jennie stood at the door of the cottage, the outlook looked bleak. Richard had laid duckboards along the path to their gate, and the lane to the barn was just about passable, despite the mud. Who, Jennie said despairingly, would come out on a day like this, even to step into the Applemere Flyer?

'Laugh, Jennie,' Richard intoned solemnly. He was pulling one of his 'faces' and today's was Aunt Win in a grim mood. 'Are we going to wait until the weather's better? We are *not*.'

She obediently agreed. 'Then let's go,' he finished.

Gathered in the kitchen was a whole party that had nobly made its way here. Aunt Win (*not* in grim mood), Eileen, Anna, Mary (no Tom, alas), and Michael Fokingham were warming themselves by the range, ready to brave the outdoors again to see the Flyer in working mode. The twins were equally eager, obviously aware that this was an exceptional day.

The Flyer was still in the barn, superintended by Freddie, who had volunteered to come early for the water cart delivery, get steam up and drive it forth. Anna was here, Jennie realized, because Sir Roger and Lady Fokingham were still away, and it was a chance for her to talk to Michael, who had returned from Montevanya. Fortunately Tom hadn't accompanied Mary for whatever reason. Anna appeared to be talking amicably to Michael, as though there were no rifts at all in the family tapestry. Jennie hadn't seen Michael for some time, and was surprised how he had changed. His former gaunt, rather snake-like features had filled out, he had lost his haunted look, and was a good-looking man –

every inch a London society habitué. Very urbane, Jennie thought, whatever the weather.

The wind was driving hard against them as they struggled up the lane to the barn, galoshes slipping and sliding where the wind was worst. It was essential that the Applemere Flyer should keep to its timetable because she and Richard had printed posters to announce the launch, and placed an advertisement in the Ashford and Canterbury newspapers about their route. Even at the last moment there had been a hitch when the licence failed to come through. Recent regulations had prohibited too much unladen weight for buses, which was a problem for steam vehicles carrying heavy boilers. Finally Richard had persuaded the reluctant police authority that they were not a public bus, and not carrying passengers. The public would only be aboard when she was stationary. The panic was over.

The doors of the barn were open as they approached, and Jennie's heart lurched in pride at the sight of the Applemere Flyer, decked out with flags and paper chains to celebrate the day. All their hard work after the closing of the Canterbury shop was rewarded by the sight of it. Posters were fixed at jaunty angles to some of the windows, and inside were the racks of books they'd so carefully arranged to catch the eye. Richard had hopefully made a prominent display of *Precious Bane*, but he had graciously allowed Jennie a whole rack of detective novels, as well as one of romances.

Jennie was proud of her work. She had lovingly arranged Freeman Wills Crofts, Austin Freeman, Ernest Bramah, *Trent's Last Case*, an American writer called Mary Roberts Rinehart, G. K. Chesterton of course – how she adored the Father Brown stories – and a new writer, Dorothy L. Sayers, who had introduced an interesting detective called Lord Peter Wimsey. Richard's favourite, if he had one, was G. D. H. Cole, for he was a good socialist, but even Richard admitted that Dorothy Sayers wrote better. And of course there were the novels by Agatha Christie. Jennie had just read *The Man in the Brown Suit*, even though it didn't feature the Belgian detective Hercule Poirot, who had appeared in three of Mrs Christie's other books. She was convinced that this was an author here to stay, even though no one bought her very much at present. Agatha Christie was a challenge to Jennie, just as *Precious Bane* and Mary Webb were to Richard.

They had stayed up late on New Year's Eve, listening to the church clock strike midnight; they could just hear it across the fields.

'What do you dream of for nineteen twenty-five?' she had asked Richard, 'apart from the Applemere Flyer?'

She had thought he might say another baby, but he didn't. That was taken for granted between them. 'Painting,' he'd answered. He hadn't mentioned illustrated books again, and she thought he'd forgotten about them. 'I always wanted to draw and paint. Mary's book is a start.' Mary had handed the script to Richard on Christmas Day, with the air of one bestowing a precious gift – as indeed it was, to both of them. It could be the beginning of something new for Richard, and was the reason that Tom supported the Applemere Flyer venture. 'I've already begun the drawings,' he had told her. 'Kentish fields, hop-pickers, oast-houses, farmhouse kitchens; just sketches to get my hand in for the colour paintings.'

'That's wonderful,' she'd said, though taken aback that he had not yet shown them to her.

'Mary's found a possible printer; he's eager to expand into books and has a flatbed machine that could cope with irregular sizes.'

But that was for the future. Today, they celebrated the Flyer's first day of operations. Because of the driving rain, the party gathered in the barn, rather than await Freddie's emergence outside. Aunt Win had brought flasks of tea, and Eileen flourished a bottle of champagne, an odd, but enjoyable mixture.

Just as Freddie finished his champagne and leapt up on the footplate to drive the Flyer out, another vehicle drew up outside. It was a farm wagon, with George Overton holding the reins. Sitting in grim state beside him, clutching his briefcase with one hand and doing his best to hold on to an umbrella with the other, was a familiar figure.

Albert Hodge in bowler hat and mackintosh climbed down, touched his hat to the ladies, and shook out his umbrella:

'I regret my late arrival, Mr Pencarek.'

'Oh Albert.' Jennie ran to hug him, the informal name slipping out by mistake. She and Richard had both been worried about Mr Hodge, who had taken his last wage packet before Christmas and departed, with merely a formal good wish for the new venture. They could not afford to pay Albert, and yet they both felt not only unhappy but guilty at the parting. 'How good of you to come all this way to see us off.'

He removed his mackintosh to reveal the old frock coat beneath, and looked surprised. 'But I am here to work, Madam.'

'Work?' Richard repeated feebly.

'Certainly, sir. How are you to manage alone?'

'Not alone. Jennie will be with me to help.'

Albert looked disapproving. 'And who is to sell the books when you are in Canterbury, Mr Pencarek?' This would be essential, she and Richard had agreed. One day a week he should see travellers, pay accounts and keep up with the trade generally, and he had been offered free of charge a room in a neighbouring shop in Sun Street.

'I shall,' Jennie said uncertainly. 'After all, the bus will be stationary then.'

She talked to the air. Albert was already aboard inspecting the stock. He was, it was clear, a fixture.

It was a good omen. For when the Applemere Flyer finally got under steam, and Freddie handed over the wheel to Jennie, they did well. Their tour had taken them, despite the stormy rain, over to Elham, back through Marsham and Fairsted, past the outlying Fairsted farms and thence to Applemere, with only one boiler refill necessary.

'Two *Green Hats*, a Bible, two Agatha Christies, eight Everyman classics, and a copy of Olive Schreiner's *Story of an African Farm*, and quite a few children's books.' Richard counted up the total as they packed up for the night. 'Not bad considering the weather.' It continued raining heavily, but curiosity had brought people tramping out in their Wellington boots to see the scarlet monster steaming up to their doors.

'Perhaps it is *because* of the weather.' Jennie ripped her galoshes off, before tackling the revival of the fire. 'People can't get out so much in the winter. They want to read.'

'Or to listen. More and more people have wirelesses now.'

'Not the same,' Jennie said scornfully. 'There'll *always* be books.'

'Well done, Jennie.' Eileen had volunteered to come on the bus with her a few days later since it was Richard's Canterbury day. Albert's disapproval was obvious, despite the fact that

35

Eileen had done her best to conform to the dress code of an English lady. How could she know that Albert didn't approve of ankles, let alone knees?

'It's Richard's hard work.'

'I see your hand all over the Applemere Flyer. Richard is a dear, but he couldn't have put this dream into practice.'

'He wants to publish his own books,' Jennie told her proudly.

'Really?' Eileen looked very interested, and Jennie spent some time telling her all about the hop farm illustrations and showing her one or two sketches. That done, she could hold back no more. Eileen clearly wasn't going to mention it, so she had to.

'Tell me about Montevanya,' she pleaded. 'And the Fokinghams. Michael told me everyone's safe, but I want to know *more*.'

Eileen grimaced. 'Where to start? It happened out of the blue. Everything seemed business as usual, but suddenly Stephen was dead, and every Balkan monarchy was quivering in its boots as to what might happen next. Bolsheviks streaming down from Russia was the most likely prophecy.'

'So,' Jennie pondered, 'if you didn't pick up anything unusual before the assassinations, then it can't have been discontent fomenting in Montevanya for a long time.' This seemed obvious. If its parliament had been storing up opposition there would have been comings and goings at the Várcasá, as they argued it out with the king. Assassination would have been a last resort.

Eileen smiled at her. 'Exactly. We think alike, Jennie. No Bolsheviks, no resentful populace. Viktor's hand is behind this.'

'Then why has he peacefully allowed Max to become king without pressing for the crown, either for himself or his sons? Did you see Viktor there?'

'He was at the funeral of course. Too obvious to stay away. But I don't have to see him. I smell him, Jennie. I hear the rumble of Austro-Germany in his belly. The Kaiser wants a peaceful life in Doorn, now he's remarried, but his sons are still a honeypot for those of unpeaceful intentions to gather round.'

'So what do you think Viktor's plan is?'

'I suspect it's a waiting game. He underestimated the

strength of revulsion over Stephen's assassination. Both he and his descendants are formally barred from succession, so he'll let Max ascend the throne and then strike.'

'Does Max think that too?'

'No one knows what Max thinks. He has time on his side at the moment, and I believe he'll use it. Of course,' Eileen added, 'there's always Zita to reckon with. She's still ensconced in the Várcasá, though if Max's wife has her way she won't be much longer. It's the battle of the titans between them at present.'

'What's she like?' Jennie asked curiously.

'She's glued to her new throne, and doesn't want to share it with Zita. Otherwise she's amiable enough.'

'You don't like her.'

Eileen grinned. 'Liking isn't relevant in such circles. Doing her job properly is. And she does it. As does Max.'

'Does he love her? He told me once about his ancestor who actually did marry for love.'

'Ah yes. Well, I doubt if Max has been so lucky. But then he didn't expect to be. And as for Zita—'

'But she has no power now, even if she is Max's mother?' Jennie caught sight of Eileen's face. 'Has she?'

'Those who seek power, have power. Zita seems to want to remain in Montevanya which, considering her first love is Viktor, apart from herself and her royal status, is strange. I can't believe she conspired with Viktor to kill her own husband but if she went to join Viktor in Holland it would look as though that's exactly what she has done.' Eileen glanced at her, then said airily, 'I had a word with Michael.'

'And?' Jennie waited, seeing exactly where this was leading.

'I think it's time I paid a visit to Holland. I'd like some Delftware for Georgius' house. And who knows I might even see Viktor while I'm there.'

Jennie knew perfectly well what she had in mind. A snooping mission, either on her own account or on the Foreign Office's account – or her former employer's account. Who this had been Jennie wasn't quite sure, but she suspected King George came into it somewhere. Not to mention a gentleman who since the war had always been referred to as C.

'Do you blame me, Jennie?' Eileen's face was grave. 'Georgius's life might be at stake here. My home and my—'

Jennie thought she'd been going to say love, but for Eileen love was a word that tied you down, and Eileen would never admit to that.

'Favourite walking stick,' she finished casually.

'Then,' Jennie agreed solemnly, 'you must most certainly visit Holland. You can't leave Grannie's stick behind in Montevanya.' She remembered it. Incongruous in its plain woodenness, no silver handles, for Eileen could look like a tramp or a queen and the stick served for both. Grannie Harkness, whom Jennie dimly remembered, had died shortly after Jennie's mother. She had been a dour old lady with a heart of gold. Rather like the Persian king whom she read about in Sunday School, whose queen Esther only dared approach if the king's golden sceptre were extended towards her. Death was the punishment otherwise. Grannie Harkness used her stick the other way round. If she lifted it as you entered her room you ran for your life. Jennie wondered if she'd ever grow to be like that with her grandchildren. She couldn't imagine it, as she heard Lynette and Jamie shouting at each other in the kitchen. She loved them so much that the idea of their children being anything other than little angels was inconceivable. No stick raising for her.

'What makes you travel, Eileen?' Jennie asked impulsively, wondering why she'd never dared ask before.

Eileen looked hunted, then resigned. 'I suppose I should give you an answer.'

'You should.'

'New horizons are one reason. The other, more important, one is that in strange countries and among different peoples a traveller from the outside becomes everyone and no one at the same time. No one, because no one knows you, so one has to *make* oneself known, and everyone because by travelling at random there's no division in whom I meet. I have no place in their society, and therefore I could meet peasants one day, artists or shopkeepers the next, and emperors the next, or all of them together. I like to believe a united world might lie ahead.'

'But even in a united world peasants wouldn't mix with emperors,' Jennie pointed out dubiously.

'Ah, but they *might*. Around the next corner, I could come across an Italian countess chatting to a laundry maid, or an

38

Indian maharajah speaking to an Untouchable. Who knows? That's what takes me forward. I'm travelling in hope – like your Flyer. Is that how you see it?'

Jennie laughed. 'Hope of sales, at least.'

'That's your only goal?'

She felt under scrutiny, with Eileen's keen eyes brushing away her superficial response. 'Richard wants to help everyone, make their lives easier, happier if possible through books.'

'And you, Jennie, what do *you* want?'

She had all she wanted, hadn't she? She had Richard, she had Lynette and Jamie, she had her wonderful family – and she lived next door to Applemere.

'I used to want to rule the world,' she answered Eileen seriously. 'The war showed me it wasn't possible.'

'Not with a golden sceptre, but think of the Flyer, Jennie.'

She concentrated. 'I suppose it connects,' she began. 'It visits farms, manor houses, and cottages with the same books. Manor House folk might buy romances, cottagers classics, or vice versa. Nevertheless I don't see Queen Mary chatting to Mrs Overton in our bus, when she drops in to buy the latest Poirot mystery,' she laughed. 'If buy is the relevant word. She'd expect it to be given.'

'Regardless of Queen Mary, the Flyer is changing the world,' Eileen said firmly.

'Perhaps just an inch,' Jennie conceded, 'but Richard thinks now we've a conservative government once more, the world will inch right back again.'

'Nothing inches *back*,' Eileen said decidedly. 'By the way—' she called out as Jennie, hearing the sound of the altercation in the kitchen rising, went rushing in to investigate, Later that day it occurred to her to wonder what Eileen had been going to say, but by then it was too late. Eileen had had to leave.

The 'by the way' was not explained for several weeks, by which time Eileen had long departed, presumably to Holland. Jennie was reading a bedtime story to Lynette and Jamie from Beatrix Potter when Richard came to join her, sat down at her side, peered over her shoulder and took over the reading, to Jamie's great delight. Jennie loved these quiet moments, all together as a family.

Jennie was relieved Richard had come. He often didn't as he was frequently out of spirits when they returned home after a day on the Flyer, and had been so this evening.

'The doldrums of February,' she had said sympathetically. She knew what was troubling him. The sales of the cheaper books were going well, but the books in which his heart truly lay were not.

'Remember why you began bookselling,' she told him. 'Because you could sell all types of books. You weren't going to judge which books could help which people, whether by educating or entertaining or both. Your old professor's maxim, you told me. Yet here you are trying to impose your choice on others.'

'I see that. It's just that it's frustrating when I see such wonderful words lying unread.'

'But people buy what they *need*, and only they can judge what that is.'

He grinned shamefacedly. 'I know you're right, but starting off with ideals isn't the same thing as seeing them turn out in practice differently from how you planned it.'

He looked so woebegone her mouth began to twitch, and as usual that cheered him up. Jennie herself hated not to be taken seriously, but fortunately with Richard it was the other way around.

'What would I do without you, Jennie?'

'Starve?' she enquired politely. The trouble with living with an idealist was that he had to be reminded of the practical need for survival. When this was pointed out, Richard would join in with a guilty start, but otherwise would live in a dream-world of his own.

'I've something to show you,' he said proudly, watching her preparing for their supper.

'Can it wait?' She was in the midst of scrubbing carrots.

'Of course.' He was very polite, and so she did.

How could she have done so, she wondered when later in the evening he took her to his 'den', the tiny boxroom where he kept his accounts, and reference books. There, spread out over the table, were pencil and crayon sketches and some beautifully executed colour paintings of landscapes, buildings and market scenes, with people clad in exotic robes.

'What are they?' she asked, excitedly. 'They're wonderful.

Are they—' she hardly dared assume it, especially since they were in a different style to the sketches for Mary's book, '—*yours*?' As Richard nodded, almost shyly, she looked more closely. 'What's that?' She pointed to a sketch of a magnificent desert-ruined temple with colonnades.

'Palmyra,' he replied.

'And that's the Valley of the Kings in Egypt, isn't it?' she asked, moving on to the next, 'where Tutankhamen's tomb was discovered?' That had been two years ago, but there were continuing discoveries there, and the craze in Britain for all things Egyptian, including jewellery and dresses with scarabs, hieroglyphs and lotus flowers had still not diminished.

'Have these drawings anything to do with Eileen?' she suddenly asked him. Eileen had talked a great deal at one time about the glories of the tombs.

'Yes. She's publishing a book on her travels. A sort of diary cum travel book. She's asked me to illustrate it and left me her photographs.'

'Isn't she using them in the book?' So that's what Eileen had been going to tell her.

'No. They're too grainy for good reproduction. And anyway she thinks that good illustrations will give more atmosphere than bad photographs.'

'Who's publishing it?' For a moment she feared Richard might say, 'we are' because she knew a book of this complexity would be beyond them. Eileen deserved wide commercial marketing.

'Macmillan.'

'These are good, Richard. Even better than the hop scenes for Mary's book. I never realized—' She broke off, ashamed that she had not known her husband had such a gift.

He understood. 'Don't worry,' he told her. 'I didn't know myself. I used to draw when I was young, but after my mother died—'

'Your father stopped you. The work of the devil, I suppose.' Richard's father lived in Helston in Cornwall, and was a strict puritan. He had even refused the polite invitation to their wedding. He had, it was true, acknowledged the birth of the twins, but his letter had upset Richard for weeks. It had ordered him to turn from the devil (her?) and bring up his children in the ways of the Lord, or they would surely perish.

These ways were only as determined by him, Jennie had to point out time and time again to Richard. His aunt, his mother's sister, still lived in north Kent, however and they saw her regularly which was some compensation for his lack of family. Moreover, the Station House had adopted him wholeheartedly – a mixed blessing, Jennie observed, since family love brought family tensions, of which Freddie and Tom's estrangement was one prime example. Anna was another. The only person in the family who wholeheartedly approved of Anna was Mary – and that was because of her lineage. It was ironic that Anna could not stand Mary.

In March the Fokinghams at last returned to England. From the daily newspapers' pictures of the coronation in Montevanya Jennie hardly recognized the sombre-faced king as the fun-loving Prince Max she had met before the war, or even as the haunted wartime soldier. Queen Marta was a beautiful woman, Jennie acknowledged, with one of those calm oval faces that seemed impervious to the outside world. Perhaps it was. She certainly looked as if she could be another Queen Zita. She wasn't old enough yet to be a Gorgon, as was her mother-in-law, but she looked as if she might easily grow into one. Their son was called Stefan, a natural name for an heir apparent. Jennie studied *The Illustrated London News*, too, which had a sepia double page spread of the coronation, but it told her no more.

'Good luck, Max,' she whispered to the photograph. He certainly needed all the encouragement he could get.

At the first opportunity she went to Applemere House to welcome Sir Roger and Lady Fokingham home. Sir Roger was in London, for he had a post at court, but his wife was there. Jennie told her sincerely how sad she was at the death of her brother, King Stephen, and then remembered somewhat belatedly, 'And my sympathy for the Dowager Queen too, of course.'

Lady Fokingham gave her a twisted smile. 'No need for that, Jennie, but thank you. My sister-in-law, as you know, is a strong woman.'

Jennie did know. Queen Medusa Zita would most certainly not be found chatting to a farmer's wife on the Applemere Flyer.

'Have you heard anything more from Eileen?' Lady Fokingham asked.

'Not since she left after Christmas to go travelling.'

'She is back in Montevanya now,' Lady Fokingham told her to her relief. 'She came to visit the King just before we left, and plans to return to London again, I understand.' She looked straight at Jennie as if implying there was more to this than she could express.

So the situation was not so simple, Jennie realized.

'Eileen told me about the Applemere Flyer.' Lady Fokingham smoothly switched subjects. 'What a good idea, Jennie. I hope Applemere House is included on its route.'

It could hardly avoid it, being next door. But this would be another mixed blessing for Richard. The Fokinghams would undoubtedly buy some of his best beloved books, but on the other hand he would always suspect that this would make him beholden to them. That they were offering another kind of charity. Oh well, it would all come right in the end, Jennie tried to convince herself.

'Of course,' she replied. 'We'll be delivering a cheque for the rent tomorrow,' she added proudly.

'Everything is going well then. I'm so glad.'

'It is.'

Jennie spoke too soon. Everything was not going well. Richard and Albert had been alone in the bus today. Richard, she suspected, found the driving difficult though he never confessed to it, and by tacit agreement Jennie had been giving Albert driving lessons. He made a splendid sight, driving in his frock coat with which he insisted on wearing his bowler hat, tipping it to every lady he passed. With Albert a laundry-maid received the same courtesy as Queen Mary would, if she did manage to pop by one day. There was no laundry-maid in Fairsted, in fact, though there was a laundry *lady*. Widow Corby had been taking in laundry since Jack's death. Even now the thought of her childhood sweetheart had the power to upset Jennie.

'I said you'd leave a cheque at Applemere House tomorrow.' Jennie called out to Richard, who suddenly appeared home early.

'I hope you also said it would be the last for a while,' he muttered savagely.

'What do you mean?' Jennie was astounded. 'The sales are good.'

'It's that blasted boiler playing up again. I told you there would be high maintenance costs.'

Jennie knew the boiler had been steaming erratically, but they had put that down to bad roads and cold weather. It must be bad, for it was unlike Richard to swear.

'Have you asked Freddie to look at it?'

'No telephone,' he snapped.

'I'll cycle over to Dad, if you'll look after the children. It's still light enough. He'll ring Freddie.'

In fact Dad insisted on walking over himself. 'Plenty of steam in me yet,' he grunted. 'I'm not out to pasture.'

Jennie mentally sighed. Dad thought he knew steam, but this was a bus, not a train.

George Trent strolled up to inspect the errant boiler, as Richard demonstrated its lack of power. 'What water are you using?' Dad asked. 'Don't see you at the Station filling up very often.'

'Water cart.' They had set up this regular arrangement after the first few days of the Flyer's operations.

'Old Tyson's?'

'Yes.'

Dad nodded slowly. 'Chalk,' he pronounced with great satisfaction, having run some water off. 'That lazy old rogue's been using cheap local supplies of surface water, I'll be bound. Furred up good and proper, this boiler is, us being near chalk downs. That's why the old Southdown buses in Sussex went off steamers and changed to petrol.' The word came out as if it was the devil's own produce. 'Should have come to me, like I said. We use the Company cart, filtered reservoir water, see. We gets some chalk but not like this.'

'We couldn't come to you every day,' Jennie said despairingly. 'We need to fill up here.'

'How about using God's method?' Dad asked gravely.

'Praying?'

Dad snorted. 'God helps those who help themselves, so your Aunt Win's always saying. So why don't you help yourselves to some of His gentle rain. That's what Southdown did for a while. Underground rain storage tanks.'

Jennie could see Richard's face growing longer and longer.

44

Any minute now she'd hear those words, 'I told you so' again. And it had all seemed so simple.

'If I were you . . .' Dad said thoughtfully, 'I'd have a word with that Applemere gardener pal of yours.'

'Rain butts!' Jennie broke in instantly, seeing Richard's face grow thunderous. 'We could have our own, Richard. Outside the barn.'

She could see the muscle working furiously in his face.

'And snow, ice, drought?' he asked ironically.

'Then . . .' she sought desperately for an answer, 'we'll use Dad's supply as a second line of defence.'

'And now? We've a busted boiler.'

It took a week off the road for the boiler to be cleaned, and the new system set up for the Flyer. A week when Jennie prayed hard for rain and none arrived. Richard said nothing, but that was almost worse. It was her fault, she'd wanted steam and look what happened, was the message. Dad turned up trumps though, and lo and behold, one day the butts were full.

She told Richard that it was Station House water brought round by the Company cart, an explanation he accepted without query. In fact Jennie knew full well that Dad had called at Applemere House and had a word first with Lady Fokingham, and then with the gardeners. The house supply would be full of chalk but the gardeners would keep regular reserves of rainwater. This had taken courage indeed for Dad, since between him and Lady Fokingham lay the shadow of Anna. But so it did for all of them.

'I didn't know you knew so much about buses, Dad,' she joked.

'I know about a lot of things, Jennie,' he said darkly. 'We older folks might just sit by, but we notice all right.'

Jennie kicked off her shoes, and decided to make tea for herself and the twins. Richard wouldn't be home for a while. His spirits had picked up now, and this was his Canterbury day, when he was placing his order for Eileen's new book, among others. This would be published at the end of May and was called *Travels with a Walking Stick*, a title that pleased Jennie, and Richard was excited at the thought of seeing his illustrations in print.

She had had a good day on the Flyer. In spring it would have been hard not to have enjoyed steaming through the lanes, with the trees and green land bursting open with crops for summer. Not to mention the hint of apple blossom and the haze of blue from what would soon be a sea of bluebells. She and Albert, whom she had insisted on paying, were becoming well known in the Kent countryside. Every day held surprises. Who would have thought the prim and proper Miss Clifford would be an addict of Bulldog Drummond, or that young Tommy Dobbs would devour World Classics from Dante to Palgrave's *Golden Treasury*. Eileen had been right about the Flyer. They *did* help connect, and that's what Richard and she wanted most.

It was exciting to sell something new to customers, and then see them come back for more next time. In the cold weather, when people could not so easily travel to libraries or shops, she had thought the Applemere Flyer would do better than in the summer, but the weather was fine now, and still people came to buy. Amazing. Lady Fokingham said it was because of Richard's and her enthusiasm, which was encouraging. She was so enthusiastic she wanted to sell customers everything. She had been reluctant at first to encroach on the selling side, but people seemed to like consulting a woman's opinion, and she had found herself a niche on the Flyer with the detective stories. She had begun on romance too, but astonishingly Albert, who was quite a hit with the ladies, had suddenly taken these to his heart. Not *The Green Hat*, of course, or *The Sheikh*, but the safe stories of love and romance by Cecil Roberts, or Jessie Champion's *Vagabond Love*. Only seven shilling and sixpence for a journey into Elysium.

It was usual for Richard when he returned from Canterbury to discuss the day immediately, and she was even more eager now to hear about it today, with Eileen's book on the verge of publication.

'Oh, here's one to please you,' Richard teased her, after he'd told her about his main purchase. 'A steaming romance to shock you to the withers. Do we have withers, Jennie? It beats *The Green Hat* and *The Constant Nymph* put together, so the traveller said.'

'How does he know it will sell as well?' Jennie was always suspicious.

'He's read it.'

'Did you get a sample?'

'No, they've all been snapped up. The word's already gone round about this one.'

'Did you even see it?'

'Yes, of course. It's written well, but it's a shocker all right.'

'What's it called?'

'*Forbidden Fruit.*'

'That *is* good,' Jennie said approvingly. 'Nothing like going all out to make your point in the title. I take it this isn't a book on the law of gardening then.'

'No. A rip-roaring passionate romance. A lot of "pagan bodies" and "Chislehurst minds".'

'Whose are the latter?'

'A vicar.'

'Gosh!' Jennie was impressed, once she'd stopped laughing. 'That's really beyond the pale.'

'And the pagan body belongs to the vicar's wife.'

'*And* it's well written?' Jennie could hardly believe it. 'Who does she give the body to?' she asked, agog for more.

'Who do you think? Look at the title. It's the gardener.'

Jennie burst out laughing again. 'Seriously?'

'Very. The novel's all about freedom and sexual passion. The lady eyes up the gardener as his muscles move on his sweating back in the hot sunlight.'

'When can I read it?' she asked promptly.

'I shall forbid you to. Our only copy shall remain behind locked bookcase doors, to which only I hold the key.'

'Then I'll fling myself on our gardener—'

'We don't have one.'

'Lucky for you.' She swooped on Richard to kiss him and was firmly clasped in his arms, as Lynette wandered in.

'What are you doing?' she asked curiously.

'Loving,' said Richard, sitting up.

'Love me too.' She held out her arms, and he obliged with a kiss and hug.

'Who wrote the book?' Jennie called as she went out to get the twins' tea. 'Sounds like another *Garden of Allah*. Does the gardener go back into a monastery like Count Androvsky?' That exotic novel published over twenty years earlier was about a woman who fell in love with and married a passionate count, who unfortunately turned out to be a former Trappist monk.

'Don't know. Only saw the first thirty-two pages.'

'Who wrote it?'

This time Richard came out into the kitchen. 'I can't remember.'

'Oh Richard,' she said in exasperation. 'It could be Queen Mary writing it.'

'If it really matters I'll check my copy of the official order. I took a chance,' he admitted sheepishly. 'I ordered a dozen. That means I'll get thirteen as it's being specially pushed.' He disappeared into the living-room where he had left his briefcase and re-emerged waving a piece of paper and laughing.

'What have you been doing, Jennie? It's by someone called Trent.'

An awful foreboding swept over her, and she rushed to seize the copy order from him. The foreboding had been justified. It wasn't just any old Trent. It *was* their family.

'It's Anna,' she told him, appalled.

Four

'I want to talk to you, young lady.'

Aunt Win bore her grimmest look, and the young lady could be none other than Jennie herself, since the twins were at school. It must be serious, Jennie realized, if Aunt Win had come all this way on her old boneshaker of a bicycle. Aunt Win made great play nowadays of her 'rheumatics' when she was in a bad mood. As she clearly was today.

'Why don't you sit in the garden,' Jennie suggested, 'and I'll bring you some tea.' Their garden, beautiful with May greenery, would surely calm her down.

'We'll do our talking first. Richard is on the Flyer, is he?'

'Yes. I needed a day to prepare for the twins' birthday. Anyway, Mr Hodge can drive just as well as I can.'

'You rely too much on that gentleman. You take advantage.'

Jennie was indignant. 'We do not. We pay him.'

'Not enough for what he does.'

'He enjoys it.'

'Just as I enjoy looking after the twins when you're late back. Like it, but an imposition all the same.' The twins would be seven tomorrow, and 'a real handful', as Dad constantly put it.

This looked really bad. Jennie took the bull by the horns and sat down in the deckchair next to Aunt Win. 'What's wrong?' she asked quietly. 'Dad playing up again?' Dad was getting on for sixty now, and had his depressed periods, just as Richard did, though for different reasons. Retirement was only five or six years away, and then he and Aunt Win would have to leave the Station House. He'd hate that, because if he couldn't afford to rent a property, he'd have to choose

49

between living with Tom, Freddie or herself. Aunt Win was more robust about it. 'The Good Lord will provide,' she assured Jennie, and refused to discuss it.

Win bristled at the idea that Dad was being awkward. 'Your dad's looked after by me. He's happy enough. It's others that aren't.'

Jennie went pale. Aunt Win couldn't be talking about Tom and Mary, and so:

'It's Anna, I suppose,' she said resignedly. Who else?

That really upset Aunt Win. 'No Jennie, it is not. It's Freddie. Can't you ever forget that girl for a minute even for your own brother?'

'What's wrong with him. Is he ill?' Jennie flushed, aware there was some truth in this. She was also alarmed.

'I don't know, Jennie, and that's a fact. But something is, and I have my suspicions.' She cast a dark look at Jennie. 'We'd better have that tea now, girl. We need to discuss delicate matters.'

No one could forget Anna, Jennie thought in self-defence as she warmed up scones and got the remains of the cream out of the pantry. One sniff told her it was too late. The cream was off, so it would be jam alone. Ah well, once upon a time it would only have been 'jam tomorrow', she thought philosophically. At least now it was 'jam today', even if it was only her own damson conserve from last year. And the 'jam today' situation was partly due to Anna – or rather her novels.

Once the news had come out that the scandalous *Forbidden Fruit* was by Anna Fokingham, who used to live at Applemere House and was now married to the famous wartime engine driver, the novel sold like hot muffins. It was not only a local success, but a bestseller in the rest of Britain and even America. Everyone in Fairsted wanted not only to read it, but to buy it to revel in at their leisure. What they found whetted their appetites for endless gossip: they struggled to identify the vicar's wife of the novel with the meek fifty-year-old Mrs Martin at the rectory, and old Joe Stebbings who looked after the rectory gardens was eyed with great interest, as the possible object of Mrs Martin's inflamed desire.

1925 had therefore been an extremely good year for the Flyer, and Anna had obliged local appetites by providing another equally shocking tale in 1926. *Adonis Resurgent* was a title that deterred many buyers until they heard about the contents. They were not disappointed. It was the story of a country squire's wife who had a double life when she periodically visited London to go on the razzle in Mayfair for a series of brief liaisons. When her husband became an invalid, she abandoned Mayfair to look after him and the estate, but the final paragraph of the novel left it open as to whether her former life was entirely behind her. There was something about the way she greeted the young farmer at Home Farm that suggested it was not.

Anna's new book, *Out of Bounds*, about a woman MP torn between duty and illicit love, was due to be published in late May this year and it promised – Richard told her gloomily – to be just as successful as the first two. He wasn't entirely gloomy however, for the books made a lot of money, but he was torn as usual between the desire to put his own choices before the public and their determination to buy other titles.

What could be so wrong with Freddie that Aunt Win had come here specially? Aunt Win never went to visit Anna and Freddie at Ashford, partly through shock at the novels but also because Anna had never taken to housewifery. Though she and Freddie employed a maid and a cook, the results were less than perfect since they had no caring eye upon them. This pained Aunt Win, who maintained – despite her own sister's departure from grace in this respect – that a woman should be a housewife first and foremost. Sometimes Jennie was glad the Station House was a mile away.

She set down the tea tray, and waited in trepidation for Aunt Win to launch forth.

'He's not happy, you can see that,' Win pronounced, as the scone hovered between plate and mouth.

Could she? Jennie was forced to admit that recently Freddie no longer seemed the cheerful youngster he used to be. 'He's getting older, that's all,' she reassured Win. 'He's a family man now.'

'Getting disillusioned, if you ask me. And where's the family?'

Jennie could have kicked herself for falling into this trap. 'There's time yet.'

'It's been eight years since they wed. She's no spring chicken.'

Jennie protested vigorously. 'She's only my age, thirty-one.'

'If she's still able. It's my opinion,' Win lowered her voice in case the trees were listening avidly, 'she's *done something about it*.'

Jennie sighed. 'We can't know that. And,' she added firmly, 'it's not our business.'

'Moreover, it's my belief something's going on with that young lady.'

Jennie blinked. 'You mean you think she's in love with somebody else?'

'That's one way of putting it,' Aunt Win agreed.

Sometimes Jennie wondered which of them was the more modern of the two. This had never even occurred to her. She had assumed the novels were Anna's outlet for the frustrations of everyday life, and as for sexual passion she had Freddie for that. Anna loved Freddie – didn't she? A terrible doubt crept over her. Because she loved Richard, had she falsely assumed that Anna's marriage had turned out so well?

'But who could it be?' Jennie had a complete blank as to who Anna's friends were nowadays. Ashford was a railway town through and through. Had Anna found herself a gardener? A vision of Anna's mocking face flashed through her mind. 'Try again, Jennie,' she seemed to be saying.

'London,' Aunt Win supplied darkly. 'It's these books, I'll be bound.'

'Writing novels isn't necessarily a pathway to sin.'

'They give people ideas.'

Or perhaps, Jennie thought, where Anna was concerned, ideas sparked the novels. Novels could not only be read out of need but written too.

'What about that publisher of hers?' Aunt Win continued. 'Mr Finch. He was at that party, remember?'

Jennie most certainly did. It was one of the worst occasions of her life, barring of course the war. Anna had decided to throw a party at their Ashford home to celebrate the publication of *Adonis Resurgent* last year. It had been a dismal failure from the inedible canapés to the disgusting trifle and warm white wine. Although the food hadn't been the cause of the problem, it had contributed. Freddie had certainly looked unhappy there, Jennie agreed. Fancy trying to mix Aunt Win,

Dad, Tom and Mary (now that the brothers were on speaking terms again) and Anna's new friends from London in one room. She remembered Nicholas Finch as a rather supercilious forty-year-old, who raised an ironical eyebrow if addressed by anyone he did not already know.

Added to this pot-pourri of guests, Michael had been present, bringing his own impenetrable circle of society friends. If Nicholas Finch represented the bohemia of Chelsea, Michael represented society, at its supposed best, excluding the extravagances of Mayfair, which Anna seemed to patronize. His circle was drawn from gentlemen's clubs, the ex-royalty of Europe, and the higher echelons of the military and peerage. There had been more need of levelling that evening than ever aboard the Applemere Flyer. And it didn't happen.

There was also, Jennie remembered, a quiet good-looking man in his thirties whom Michael introduced her to. He was the younger son of a duke (very Dorothy L. Sayers, she had thought, amused), Lord Anthony Hart. Jennie had talked to him briefly before Anna had intervened and taken him over. She had danced with him and, as she watched them, Jennie could see he was an excellent dancer. Could it be that Anna was now attracted by the way of life she had previously shunned? Jennie shivered. No wonder Freddie had looked so bewildered, if he had seen Anna's dancing, and he could hardly have missed it.

'If you're right, Aunt Win,' Jennie said, 'I hate to think what might happen.' Freddie and Anna divorced? Impossible, Freddie would never divorce her, and Anna would have no grounds to divorce him. Was Freddie doomed to a life of watching Anna having affair after affair? Steady, she reminded herself. This is all speculation.

'We might find out.' There was a note of grim pleasure, Jennie noted, in Aunt Win's voice. 'Freddie tells me Anna's set on having another of those parties for this book of hers. In London this time. You'd best have a word with that young lady.'

'I could have millions of them, but she'll take no notice.'

'If you don't speak, who can?' Aunt Win softened. 'It's your own fault, Jennie. You would run with both the hounds and the fox at the same time. And see where it's got you.'

Where it had got her was that the hounds (the Fokinghams)

had disappeared from her life, or were at least keeping at a distance. She and Richard still lived in the cottage, and maintained a formal relationship with the Fokinghams, but there was no denying that the former friendship had cooled to the point of ice. The days of tennis parties were over – at least for them. It had been inevitable after the publication of *Forbidden Fruit* and the bitter interchange that had preceded it. The novel had placed them in an impossible situation as regards Applemere House. If they sold Anna's book locally in the Applemere Flyer, then Sir Roger and Lady Fokingham would be furious, seeing it as a personal betrayal. If they did not sell it, not only did they stand to lose a lot of money they couldn't afford, but they would seem to be taking a stand against the book on moral grounds. As that was not the case, they had had no choice.

Nevertheless Jennie had decided to warn Lady Fokingham about the publication and had called on her, only to discover she already knew. Naturally enough, Jennie supposed, since the news would be buzzing round London. She had felt foolish, particularly as Lady Fokingham's attitude seem to be that Jennie had something to do with it.

'How could Anna do this, Jennie?' Lady Fokingham tossed the copy of the novel that Jennie had brought her on the floor. No matter that it had cost Richard over two shillings to buy.

'She needs something to fill the time,' Jennie replied. It was a weak answer, even though it was true.

'To write this obscene muck is to betray all she was brought up to believe in. What is wrong with the girl? First she marries—' Lady Fokingham broke off.

'Freddie.' Jennie's temper had frayed. 'Freddie's a good man, if you'd ever cared to meet him.' The Fokinghams had not attended the wedding.

Lady Fokingham apologized. 'I'm sure he is. But Jennie, such different backgrounds. Could you have married Michael for instance? It would have come to the same thing.'

Jennie had tried to keep back a nervous giggle. Not the same thing at all. No one would ever marry Michael, at least in a true marriage, but Lady Fokingham still didn't realize it. 'The war was a great leveller,' she offered.

'It can't level out what Anna is.'

'Anna *is*,' Jennie had retorted, 'what she chooses to be. Which is Freddie's wife.'

'I can't agree. And now this trashy novel. A disgrace to our name.'

'*Our* name in fact,' Jennie snapped. 'Her name is Trent. And it's well written; it makes a point.'

'Why can't she fill in her time some other way?' Lady Fokingham moaned. 'If only she'd married one of her own circle she could have had a normal life.'

'You mean had babies?' Jennie cut in sharply.

Lady Fokingham fixed her with steely eyes, but Jennie didn't regret speaking out. 'Yes.'

There was no point in saying Anna had had babies and that her parents had taken them from her against her will. Both were well aware of this. One side thought it justified, the other did not.

'This novel is her baby,' Jennie had replied.

'Nonsense. It's the outcome of an unsuitable marriage – and I mean unsuitable for both Freddie and for Anna.' She picked up the book and handed it back to Jennie, adding: 'You won't be selling this rubbish, of course.'

Jennie braced herself. 'We will.'

Lady Fokingham had been even more shocked than Jennie had anticipated. 'Around here, to our friends?'

'To whoever wants to buy it,' Jennie said steadily. 'It's a good novel.'

'It's filth.'

'To you perhaps, but not to others.'

'Have you no standards, Jennie?' Lady Fokingham's face was white with fury. 'I understood Richard had. To make money out of this is disgusting.'

'You're wrong. It fulfils what we set out to do. To provide what people want to read, whether it's fact or fiction, classical or modern, entertainment or food for thought.'

'People only buy filth if it's offered to them.'

'But what is filth to one person is not to another. Who judges that?'

Lady Fokingham had risen to her feet. The interview, and friendship, were over. 'I am sorry it has come to this, Jennie. I realized that you were still friendly with Anna, but I had hoped that you also felt some loyalty towards us. I see now that your need to make a living has blinded you to the immorality of what you are doing.'

'And I see, Lady Fokingham, that your upbringing has strait-jacketed you from the needs of others.' She saw Lady Fokingham blench, but had no regrets. For once, she was wholly on Anna's side.

Jennie told Richard a little about Aunt Win's comments on Freddie that evening while she was icing the twin's birthday cake. He had been relieved at the cooling of relations between Applemere House and themselves two years ago, even though it had caused difficulties. Although the Fokinghams hadn't been so petty as to turn them out of their cottage, extra help, including the supply of rainwater, was denied to them. Lynette and Jamie had missed their visits to the gardens, but school had provided a new preoccupation, and they had long ago stopped asking when they could go to the big house.

'Win may well be right,' Richard answered. 'The success of the novels is bound to have had some effect on Anna, and therefore Freddie.'

'But an affair? And she doesn't seem as though she's going to turn into an arty bohemian or even a society dope and dance fiend. She appears just the same.'

'How short are her skirts?' Richard asked practically.

Jennie giggled. Skirts were at their shortest ever, in fashionable society at least. They were way above the knee and where society led even Ashford and Kent were following, albeit more demurely. Even so, Albert averted his eyes when he climbed on to the footplate with her at the wheel.

'High,' she answered, 'but rarely a glimpse of stocking top.'

'Sounds suspicious to me.' Richard paused. 'If she's daft enough to take a lover, it wouldn't be here, it would be in London. But it's my guess that these novels are born of sheer devilry mixed with boredom.'

Perhaps he was right, but Jennie was painfully aware that she would have to take this up with Anna. She was in no doubt that if there *was* trouble in the marriage, Anna was the stirrer, not Freddie, whatever the cause.

She sighed. 'Perhaps we should offer her a job on the Flyer.'

'Nix to that. Nothing doing.'

The Applemere Flyer *was* doing well, however, and not on the strength of Anna's novels alone. Other more meaty fiction was booming, not only British writers, but American too.

Scott Fitzgerald's *The Great Gatsby* had sold well last year, and a newcomer, Ernest Hemingway, with a novel called *The Sun Also Rises*. The Flyer even had some success with prestigious books such as those by the Sitwells and it seemed that, far from diminishing an interest in reading, the popularity of the wireless and the cinema had created a thirst for it.

The Flyer had established routes and customers now, and even those who had hitherto refused to buy from a travelling shop were being won over – if only to buy the latest Edgar Wallace or Agatha Christie. Thank heavens for prolific writers, Richard had observed. Wallace was said to write his books in days, and there was a joke flying round about a man asking at a London news-stand for the 'midday Wallace'. Anna did at least allow them some breathing space with one a year. The steam boiler was still going well, and every so often the Flyer paid a visit to the Ashford sheds for Freddie's maintenance men to check it over on the quiet, but so far it hadn't let them down again.

'I want a book for my birthday,' Lynette had insisted. Richard had bought her *Peter Pan*. They had taken the twins to see the play in London last Christmas, a trip that had resulted in Lynette attempting to 'fly' over the back of the sofa until a painful fall had put an end to that adventure. Jamie was no reader; he had to be coaxed away from the Hornby train set that the family had clubbed together to buy him last Christmas. Richard was an addict too. 'You can't complain,' he pointed out to her, after a long session with Jamie in the attic room where the train track was laid out. 'You're from a railway family.' His birthday present was a branch line for the track.

If only Anna were so easily pleased with life, Jennie thought crossly, as she caught the bus to Ashford to carry out her mission from Aunt Win. Anna made her so welcome when she arrived, however, cooing with appreciation at her having made the journey, that it made her motive in coming seem less and less necessary. Nevertheless, she knew Anna well enough to suspect from the glint in her eye that she was all too well aware what had brought Jennie here. No point in beating about the bush, therefore. This bird could fly at the slightest sign of trouble.

'What's wrong between you and Freddie, Anna?'

'Nothing,' was the instant retort. 'Heaven just goes on and on. So I do need a little touch of hell every now and then.'

'From Freddie?' Jennie asked sharply. She couldn't imagine it.

'Oh no. Freddie is pure bliss. My novels are my contribution towards creating hell, of course. Now darling, do tell me how Mary's books are selling.'

Jennie sighed. A swift change of subject, and the end of her task so far as Anna was concerned. 'Be careful, Anna. Please.'

Anna smiled. 'I always am, darling.'

When the invitation to Anna's party arrived, Richard confessed he wasn't eager to go. Jennie had mixed feelings, however. This party could be as bad as last year's but on the other hand she felt they should be there, even though it was in London. 'Freddie will need support,' she pointed out.

He shot a strange look at her. 'The Fokinghams won't be there though.'

'Of course not.' Jennie was surprised he'd even mentioned it.

'No,' he agreed. 'They couldn't be. Not after your affair with their gardener.'

'*What*?' She stared at him, but he seemed entirely serious.

Then seeing her amazement, he looked first bewildered, then managed to laugh. 'I don't know what's happening to me, Jen. I've got *Forbidden Fruit* on my mind, I suppose. I've got to reorder.'

'Just so long as you don't have a liaison with the rector's wife,' she tried to joke, but the incident had made her uneasy. Richard had had several such absent-minded spells in the last year, saying odd things, and seeming very depressed. He said it was because he was dreaming about illustrations of wicked witches for children's books, but now she began to wonder if he wasn't making himself ill with overwork.

Eileen had published a second book on her travels and again his illustrations won critical acclaim. He had also published several books himself now, using the printer that Mary had found. So far they had been children's storybooks of flying exploits. She had written the text, and he had illustrated them. They were doing well, since the public had a fascination with flying. Odd, she thought, when one thought of what flying

58

had meant during the war. It had brought bombs, death and destruction. The war was behind them now, however, and all was safe.

Or was it?

Jennie was listening to the wireless, a recent luxury after splashing out on the ten shilling licence fee. Until recently news programmes had only begun at six p.m. in order not to compete with newspapers, but that rule had been relaxed, thank goodness, and it was a lunchtime treat to listen if she were at home. She suddenly caught the words:

'Montevanya, moving towards . . .' and then the reception faded. She twiddled all the knobs but when the sound came back some other item had replaced it. She wondered whether she dared dash round to Applemere House to enquire what had happened, but what would she say? She would receive a frosty reception, even from the servants. Jennie was forced to contain her impatience until the evening news, which confirmed that King Maximilian had announced that he was moving Montevanya towards being a republic and would abdicate in favour of an elected president in due course. It had apparently caused consternation all over the Balkans, as Montevanya was surrounded by monarchies in Bulgaria, Roumania and the Kingdom of the Serbs, Croats and Slovenes. Even Hungary under its regent Admiral Horthy was a virtual dictatorship.

'Why?' she asked, when she met Eileen in London a week later. Jennie had treated herself to the theatre as an advance birthday present from Richard in order to meet Eileen at the Criterion to see the new Noel Coward play *The Marquise*, with the delightful Marie Tempest in the leading role. The play was superb, but in the interval Jennie took the opportunity to pin Eileen down on Montevanya.

'It's a nest of vipers out there, and Max fears they might come crawling out of their lairs. He wants to forestall them,' Eileen answered.

'Kaiser-type vipers?'

'Not he himself, but remember he has sons, not to mention grandsons, though they're not all eager to follow in father's footsteps. And there's darling Viktor and his two sons.'

'But the Kaiser's descendants can't go marching back into Germany.'

59

'There are other ways of stirring the pudding till it cooks the way one chooses. And there are plenty being stirred, gently or not so gently, all over Europe.'

'What will Georgius do if Max abdicates?'

Eileen looked intently at her cocktail, replying after a while, 'Wait to see what Max does. Poor Georgius, he'd hate to leave his beloved Tellestin House.' The 'House of the Jumping Spirit' was the nickname for his home in Montevanya, devoted to every magical trick under the sun.

'And would you want to?'

'I can make my home anywhere.'

'Even England?' Jennie asked daringly.

'Who, my darling Jennie, knows?'

'But if you give up travelling?'

Eileen looked amused. 'You sound just like Win, Jennie. Why should I give it up? I'm only fifty-three. I can gallop over the deserts for a few more years yet. What would you want to be doing at fifty?'

'What I'm doing now,' Jennie replied promptly.

'Precisely. And so shall I. I'll continue to travel – and other things of course.'

'Novels like Anna perhaps?'

Eileen smiled. 'Not, I think, like Anna. And, Jennie, if you have any influence over that young woman do rein her in.'

'I don't have any influence,' Jennie muttered. Her failure with Anna was a sore point. She had even tried broaching the subject with Freddie, but he too had stonewalled her. Whatever was wrong – if anything – was being kept firmly to themselves.

'You underestimate yourself.'

'Experience tells me I don't.'

Eileen sighed. 'Then I fear for her, and more importantly for Freddie.'

'She's holding a party in London to celebrate her new book, so I could have another word with her then.' All the words in the world would avail nothing with Anna.

'Where's she holding it?' Eileen asked. 'Some arty place in Chelsea drinking wine out of Toby jugs and using prehistoric flints for knives?'

Jennie laughed. 'No. Aunt Win's safe from that. It's a place in Regent Street.'

60

'Not,' Eileen asked, 'the Silver Slipper Night Club by any chance?'

'Yes, that's it. Do you know it?'

'*Of* it.' Eileen burst out laughing. 'Poor Win. It's the most outrageous place in London at the moment. Another of Mrs Meyrick's little ventures which has only just opened.'

Even Jennie had heard of Mrs Meyrick. She ran the notorious but fashionable 43 Club, was perpetually in trouble with the police for breaking the out of hours drinking rules, and the social crowd was drawn to it like a magnet for its champagne drinking, its dancing and even for the dope gangs that operated there. Mrs Meyrick had spent some months in prison for flouting drink laws, but had bounced back. Jennie's heart sank. She was appalled at Anna's taste in dragging Freddie and his family through this ordeal.

'I almost wish I could be there,' Eileen said.

'Can't you?' Jennie longed to have her support for Aunt Win.

'No chance. The government's so split between its pro- and anti-Soviet factions and seeing Reds in every bed, including India's, that they've taken their eyes off Europe. Some of us believe eyes are needed there, and mine are two of them.'

Anna never did anything by halves. It would be too late to return home to Fairsted after the celebration party which did not begin until ten p.m. So Jennie, Richard, Anna, Freddie, Tom and Mary, not to mention Aunt Win, were staying at the Ritz. Of course. Where else? This was Anna. Dad had flatly refused to attend, saying he'd look after the twins, but Aunt Win was determined to confirm her worst suspicions. Even more amazingly Mr Hodge had accepted Anna's invitation. He sold her books, why shouldn't he come too? Anna had reasoned. Jennie admired her for it. Anna saw people as they were, not as they were born.

'Your aunt needs an escort in a den of iniquity,' Albert had explained seriously to Jennie, with which she had gravely agreed, with visions of Aunt Win being whisked off for the White Slave Trade. She hoped Albert was enjoying the Ritz's luxury as much as they were.

'Can you see me?' Jennie called to Richard from the far side of their enormous room.

'Just about. Make sure you find your way to the bed tonight.'

'I could jump in now,' she offered.

The invitation was promptly taken up, and they luxuriated in bed secure in the knowledge that for once time was on their side.

Rather to Jennie's disappointment, they dined not at the Ritz but at a small Italian restaurant in Soho. A friend owned it, Anna told them, and it was only a stone's throw from the Silver Slipper. Judging by the conversation Anna had with the owner, a dark-haired flamboyant Italian she had met during the war, it fleetingly passed through Jennie's mind that this might have been while Anna was searching for her lost babies. They would be babies no longer of course, but twelve years old now. When Jennie thought of her own twins, and how much their loss would have meant to her, she was ready to forgive Anna anything and everything.

Aunt Win and Albert Hodge valiantly attacked their spaghetti with knife and fork, as though they ate it every day, but Jennie couldn't see it arriving on the Station House menu, though the delicious desserts might well do so.

When they arrived, Jennie was relieved that the Silver Slipper seemed the height of elegance, even though the glass dance floor raised her eyebrows in these days of short skirts; the club was beautifully decorated with the walls covered in painted murals that would have little place in a real den of iniquity. Not that she could see much of either the floor or the walls. The floor was packed with dancers, the men all dinner suited and bow-tied, and the women fashionably clad in flimsy short evening dresses and heavily beaded. If Jennie thought the Fairsted party might look out of place here, she was wrong. No one had time to look at other people. They were all too busy admiring themselves and wanting to be seen.

Exotic-looking drinks of extraordinary colours appeared, and one was put in Jennie's hand by Tom, but before she had more than a sip it was removed and he whirled her on to the floor, and she was astonished to see that Mary and Richard were already dancing. He rarely danced, so Mary must have hidden powers. It was a dance she'd never heard of, though fortunately Tom seemed well acquainted with it. The Black Bottom dance seemed to consist of stamping up and down loudly (which Richard could do admirably, he pointed out later that night). It was fun, though hardly romantic, and she was happier dancing with Richard for the blues number that followed.

'Tom's talking to Freddie,' she whispered to him, seeing her brothers standing together at the bar.

'Is Freddie talking to Tom though?'

Jennie craned to see through the jigging crowd. 'Yes, he looks glum though. Where's Anna?'

'Dancing with Albert.'

'Good for her.' From what she could see, Albert seemed a surprisingly good dancer, so she hoped that he would remember Aunt Win in due course.

'They make a good couple, don't they?' Michael came up to join her a little while later, while Richard went off to dance with someone else. Jennie saw with dismay that Anna was now dancing with Nicholas Finch. Of course he was her publisher but they seemed to dancing very closely, and her misgivings came back.

'Who are all these people?' she asked Michael, to take her mind off Anna. After all, she was here to have a good time too.

Michael grinned. 'That's Winifred Harkness, famous star of stage and—'

'Be serious,' she pleaded. 'I'm dying to know.'

'That—' he indicated a debonair moustachioed man '—is Ex Crown Prince Carol of Rumania, and the woman he's dancing with—'

Jennie caught her breath. 'Not the famous Madame Lupescu? His mistress.' Their escapades were well known. Forbidden to see her, let alone marry her, by the King, the Prince had jumped ship, or rather train, when returning home from Queen Alexandra's funeral eighteen months ago, and now was always with her.

'The very same, Jennie. The lady with whom he preferred to spend his life rather than the throne. Quite something, isn't she?'

Not to Jennie. This woman was too flamboyant, too imperious, even on the dance floor, with rather coarse features and flaming red hair. Magnetic, yes, attractive, no.

'And that is Noel Coward, and that—' a dark-haired lively looking young woman '—Elsa Lanchester, taking leave from her own club, the Cave of Harmony and that—' he pointed to a rather nondescript woman in a far from fashionable dress '—is Mrs Meyrick, who runs this club and several others.'

'She doesn't look extraordinary at all.'

'Tut tut, Jennie. You set too much store by looks. That lady buys champagne at twelve shillings, sells at thirty, and at two pounds after hours. There is a lot of champagne drunk here, which means that she is a most extraordinary woman in wealth alone.'

Jennie could hear the pop of bottles whenever the band fell silent, and could see his point. Amid this fashionable crowd she began to feel a country mouse. Her pale pink dress and beads, which had felt so smart when she left their room in the Ritz, had already felt dowdy by the time she reached the hotel door in Piccadilly. Now she felt worse, although the champagne was helping her fight back. She remembered the last time she had drunk it – at the launch of the Applemere Flyer, and the time before that, in Montevanya when Max had tried to get her drunk and succeeded only too well.

'And this,' Michael indicated the man walking towards them, 'is Lord Anthony Hart.'

She remembered their earlier meeting and so did he for he smiled, as they were formally introduced again by Michael. 'Mrs Trent and I are old friends, are we not. We met a year ago at Anna's delightful party.'

That wasn't quite how Jennie would have described it, and she had a feeling he was really of the same mind, but he smiled at her in a way that made her feel they were sharing a delicious secret, so she smiled knowingly too. He began to chat to Michael and then Anna arrived.

'Darling Anthony,' she greeted him, winding her thin arms round his neck. Dressed in ivory satin, with so many beads sewn on it she glittered with every move, she swept him on to the dance floor.

'She dances even better with Anthony than Nicholas, don't you think?' Michael asked, watching them closely.

They did, and it confirmed all Jennie's fears. Perhaps it confirmed Freddie's too, for immediately the dance ended he walked on to the floor to ask Anna for the next dance, with barely a word of apology to Anthony, whom he almost elbowed out of the way. They were quite close, and Jennie could hear exactly what Anna was saying: 'Oh darling, it's the Charleston. You can't do that. I'll stay with Anthony for this dance.' Anthony obediently moved forward, but Freddie didn't budge. Suddenly the dancers on the floor were still as the music began. Anna looked slyly from one to the other, and laughed: 'Oh, very well, you silly darlings. I'll dance it alone.'

She began slowly at first, then as the music speeded up, was suddenly all flying feet and flurry of skirts. The other dancers stopped, mesmerized by her glittering solo. There was no one for anyone but Anna now, radiant, as her skirts flew, and arms, legs, eyes harmonized to the music. It was a sight Jennie was never to forget. Anna was both aware and unaware of the two men before her, and Nicholas too had come to join them. She saw Tom standing with Mary, come to join Freddie in support, as Anna continued to dance, a spellbinding figure on the glass floor.

As the dance ended the rapt audience began to applaud, first slowly and then excitedly. Anna stood there, her radiance slipping from her and suddenly at a loss as if she didn't know which way to go or whom to join, Anthony or Freddie. Jennie solved it for her, by walking across, taking her hand and leading her off the floor. Someone had to break the spell, and there was only her.

'Anna, you sparkle. You light up the room.'

'Do my novels?' Anna asked in slurred voice.

'Your novels are you.'

She meant that Anna poured her life spirit into them, but perhaps to Anna it meant something else, for she said: 'You think I'm a vicar's wife or a woman MP torn between duty and love?'

'No. I mean you . . .' Jennie was flustered, and Anna laughed. 'Have some more champagne.' She seized two glasses from a passing tray, and handed one to Jennie, who drank it eagerly, delighted that all was well between them.

'Here's to *Out of Bounds*,' she said giddily.

Anna lifted her glass. 'Just wait till you see the next one, darling.'

Five

1928

The Applemere Flyer was bowling along splendidly today, Jennie thought, as they turned the corner into Elham. Elham was a favourite stop for Albert, since he had a sister living here. They timed their arrival for one o'clock, so that Albert could take lunch with her, while she and Richard ate theirs in The Square. This usually proved a great draw, for no sooner would they open the packet of cheese and pickle sandwiches than customers would mysteriously appear from nowhere, usually demanding 'the best' of the new fiction.

Most of their regulars used to trust only the word of Mr Pencarek or Mr Hodge. Increasingly, and flatteringly, however, they would trust the word of Mrs Pencarek, especially on detective or romance novels. Such discussions, which often necessitated tact, intuition, and downright obstinacy, took time. She had to work out whether by using the word romance the would-be buyer was looking for another *Wuthering Heights* or a novel such as those of Georgette Heyer. Jennie liked these stories of the Regency period, which in style and wit were far removed from the average romance. To buyers of Jane Austen she always recommended trying Georgette Heyer as well.

'I ordered Anna's new book yesterday,' Richard remarked. It was raining and so the Applemere Flyer was quieter today. However eager, buyers would prefer to wait until the bus steamed up to their homes.

'And you didn't tell me?' Jennie cried.

'I forgot. I'm sorry.'

How could he, Jennie fumed. This was the novel that Anna had referred to at her memorable party. Had she been joking? Knowing Anna, the answer to that was no, and therefore both Jennie and Richard had been agog to know what was in this yearly offering for 1928. It was already March, and Anna's novels were usually published in the summer. It hadn't been a good winter, and bad weather was continuing with a vengeance, peaking with the terrible gale at the end of last month when winds of over a hundred mph had battered Britain, and trees fell like ninepins. They had tried to take the Flyer out, but after a near miss with a falling branch, and several lanes blocked, they had turned round and steamed to the barn. Not good for business, so Anna's new novel was even more important to them.

'What's it called?' she asked, avid for every titbit of information.

'The Dishonourable Miss Sheringham.'

'Oh I like it – at least,' Jennie caught sight of Richard's face, since Richard was still occasionally rather odd about such remarks, 'the bookseller's wife in me does. It's a wonderful title. You don't have a sample, do you?'

'They're not giving them out for this one.'

Jennie was puzzled. 'That's strange, isn't it? Why not?'

'I suspect so that it will make all the more clamour when it does appear. Sixth July is publication day.'

'Her thirty-third birthday. Anna must have arranged that. I suppose they're expecting the title alone to sell the book, plus her established reputation.'

'Yes. All Finch's traveller said was that the novel was about society life in England, which hardly surprises us, does it?'

'No. Especially if Anthony Hart's the model for the hero.'

'Surely not. Anna wouldn't stray so near to the truth.'

Jennie thought about this. 'I think Anna would do anything she pleases. Suppose she's decided to spell all her frustrations out, and this novel is the story of her affair with Anthony, with some thinly veiled Freddie in the background.'

The likelihood of this made her fear the worst. Since the party last year they had seen little of Anna or Freddie. At the few family gatherings, including Christmas, he still maintained his cheerful outward self, but his gaunt face and lines of strain round his eyes and mouth told a different story. When Jennie did visit Ashford, they were never there together. Both Anna and Freddie seemed to be playing the same infuriating game, which came down to: Jennie darling, lovely to see you, let's talk about anything except what really matters. Freddie's defences were noticeably up; Anna used her usual verbal portcullis which she could drop or raise in an instant. Mostly when Jennie saw her it was down. She'd talk vaguely about plans for future novels, perhaps doing something 'more serious', as she expressed it, but never said a word about the 1928 volume. This hadn't struck Jennie until now, but looking back she realized how skilfully Anna had skipped round the subject.

'We've got four months to wait to find out. Less, if the publishers distribute the books in good time,' Richard said. 'You'll have to make do with Edgar Wallace and Virginia Woolf in the meantime.'

Jennie laughed. 'I don't think Mrs Woolf would like being mentioned in the same breath as Mr Wallace.' Virginia Woolf's name seemed to crop up everywhere nowadays, and not only in connection with her novels, which Jennie tried hard to like. She had all but failed, although she could see they were *good*. She did like *Mrs Dalloway* but *Orlando* left her struggling. Like the Sitwells. The two brothers and their sister Edith were almost like film stars in the way they attracted attention to themselves. She had read Osbert Sitwell's *England Reclaimed* about a housekeeper and servants in a large house and the nearby villagers, but it bore little resemblance to Mrs Johns of Applemere House or to Fairsted. The adventurous 1920s through which she was apparently living were for the fortunate few, she decided. The vast majority of folk, including herself and Richard, just worked on to earn the money to live, enjoying it on the way if they were lucky enough. She and Richard did, fortunately.

'Our mission,' Richard intoned gravely in answer to her comment, 'is to provide pleasure for all.'

Jennie aimed a mock blow at him with her sandwich. 'You're just an old money grabber,' she told him affectionately.

'Your pimp, you mean.' Richard's face hadn't changed, and the shock of his language first startled, then terrified her. It was getting worse. Should she reply? *How* could she reply? Seriously, that she loved no one but him, or treat it as a ludicrous joke? She decided on a compromise.

'Not a pimp, darling,' she replied easily. 'You make the money from selling books and I drive the bus.'

'What do you do with the money you make from your liaisons with other men?' His face did change now, contorted into fury. He really meant it. He did. She struggled to keep calm, so as not to enrage him further. 'There are no liaisons. When would I have had time for them?' she tried to joke.

Reason did not work this time. 'My day in Canterbury. You arranged for me to be away every week.' Even his voice was quite different, a rasping hoarse tone that was new.

'I'm here with Albert on the bus, darling.' She felt her restraint ebbing, and used all her willpower to hold on.

'Oh.' He looked puzzled but then: 'It's Albert,' he cried. 'Why didn't I realize? You've conspired nicely to get me out of the way. What a fool I've been.'

Dear God, what was this? It was madness. It would be pointless rebutting this. 'You're not yourself, sweetheart. You're ill,' she said gently. Then, when he stared at her: '*Ill*. We'll go to see Dr Prince.' The Fairsted doctor was on the point of retirement now, but Richard liked him and refused to see the new doctor.

'I'm not—' Richard shook his head. He was so white she thought he would faint. But he rallied, and colour came back into his cheeks. 'Have I been talking nonsense again, Jennie?'

'Yes.' Now the crisis was over she felt trembly and sick. 'We'll go to see Dr Prince tomorrow.'

'There's no need. I've just been overworking, that's all. Quite funny really. I'm getting Anna's books and real life mixed up. I'm all right now.' He smiled, obviously seeing her anxiety. 'Truly.'

Richard did see Dr Prince, who put it down to overwork, to her relief. There was no recurrence and as the weeks passed she put her fears to the back of her mind, as a new worry replaced it, this time over Eileen. They were taking water from the station supply for the Flyer, when Aunt Win emerged from the Station House waving a newspaper, as she had done once before, and instantly Jennie's mind flew to Montevanya again.

'He's done it,' Aunt Win was shouting. The news hadn't made the front page of the *Daily Mail*, but inside there it was: 'Abdication of King Maximilian.'

'I hope Eileen's going to be safe.' Aunt Win's face creased in worry.

'Why shouldn't she? It seems a peaceful transfer of power

69

to parliament.' Jennie scanned the article. Indeed almost *too* peaceful.

'But there's nothing about Eileen and that prince of hers.' Aunt Win always had difficulty in referring to Prince Georgius as he and Eileen had not married. Paramour hardly seemed to fit two middle-aged respectable people. 'It's all about republics and presidents, not the things that matter. That's the trouble with newspapers.'

The things that matter. Aunt Win was right. For them what mattered was the Tellestin House, Eileen and Georgius. Jennie hopped off the Flyer at Bossingham to buy *The Times* and *Daily Telegraph*, hoping for fuller details, and took them back to Richard. There was no mention of Georgius here either, but there were plenty of political details. There was already unrest in the Balkans, for the Croats were threatening to pull out of the Kingdom of the Serbs, Croats and Slovenes, popularly known as Yugoslavia. Roumania had a volatile monarchy to say the least. Prince Carol had had a sudden hope of power last year, when his father the King had died, but the Roumanians had had other ideas. Only a few weeks ago, he'd planned another coup but had, to the great excitement of the press, been stopped at Croydon airport. No Queen Madame Lupescu for the Roumanians.

Bulgaria was still a monarchy and so was Greece, but to the north of Montevanya lay Soviet Russia run by the dreaded Bolsheviks, and the new republic would need to be stable. For this reason, *The Times* announced, King Maximilian had chosen to remain in the country for the time being at least.

'That sounds odd,' Richard commented. 'What do you think is the real reason?'

'He's waiting to see if Viktor strikes a blow.' Jennie read on. 'Look at this. Queen Zita has decided to make her home in London, and is travelling here with ex-Queen Marta and Prince Stefan. What do you make of that? Aunt Win would say a woman's place is by her husband.'

'But Queen Zita is pro-Viktor. Even if he's sniffing around, she wouldn't need to leave the country.'

'Darling, if she stayed she would be seen to be supporting the faction that murdered her husband.' Jennie shivered at the very thought of Queen Zita in England however.

She heard little more about Montevanya as the summer wore on, except for a picture in *The Illustrated London News* of a sour-faced Queen Zita arriving in London. Her time was taken up by her work on the Flyer and at home. She heard little from Anna or Freddie, and nothing from Tom, though Mary seemed to have struck up a friendship as well as a business relationship with Richard over the children's stories they were publishing together. He saw Mary every week in Canterbury, and it occurred to her to ask why, since there were no current work issues outstanding.

'Jealous?' Richard raised an eyebrow.

She laughed. 'No. I don't see you and Mary as a couple.' Mary was far too pretentious, and had brought her children up in the same manner.

'I think she's lonely,' Richard offered.

'How can she be?' Jennie asked incredulously. Not only did Mary have two children and a large house to run, even if she did have several servants, but her spare time was filled in with her children's writing, and she was also patron of various charitable organizations in Canterbury, a fact of which she was extremely proud.

'Being busy doesn't always make one less lonely,' Richard observed, and Jennie made a face at him for being sanctimonious. She supposed it was true, however. Richard's company, the Flyer, the Station House, the children and darling Albert were the engine that kept her wheels spinning.

'The children are at school,' Richard pointed out, 'and Mary doesn't see a lot of Tom. He always seems to be at meetings, or travelling.'

Tom had told Jennie that he travelled to Belgium and Holland quite frequently on brewery business, and to meetings in London, so she supposed Mary had a point. Freddie must feel much the same with Anna so often in London nowadays. He'd cracked a joke that she went so often now she wrote her novels on her knee in the train. *The Lady*, *Tatler*, and *The Illustrated London News* all had plenty of photographs of Anna, usually drink in hand, cigarette holder elegantly poised and chatting to Lord This, That or The Other. Sometimes Jennie recognized her companions, such as Nicholas Finch, apparently heir to a baronetcy, or her brother Michael. Jennie knew Anna saw a lot of him, yet he was still closely in touch with her parents, which meant that he too was running both with the hounds and with the fox. A dangerous game, as she knew full well.

In the last week of May, Jennie saw another photograph of Queen Zita, this time together with 'her late husband's sister Lady Fokingham, formerly Princess Marie of Montevanya', and she studied it with great interest. It was strange to see people she had known in the newspapers, where they seemed so remote, and odder still to think that neither could affect her life now.

Or could they? The answer came very quickly.

The following day she was just leaving the barn and the Applemere Flyer for the night to return to the cottage, when she looked up to see two stately cars, a Daimler and a Rolls-Royce, coming along the lane. She promptly moved on to the grassy bank, assuming the cars to be carrying the Fokinghams. The first car, the Rolls-Royce, did indeed contain Sir Roger and Lady Fokingham, with Michael driving; the latter grinned out at her, but the Fokinghams did not. The chauffeur-driven Daimler behind had two passengers in the back, a man and a woman. Surely that was Max? Jennie gaped. She had a fleeting glimpse of the dark-haired, bearded middle-aged man, and then of the woman and their eyes met. It was Queen Zita, who stared frostily at her through the window. Flummoxed, Jennie stared right back, wondering whether to smile or curtsey. Neither seemed appropriate and in sheer shock, therefore, she did neither.

She watched the cars turn into the gates of Applemere House. In the old days when motor cars weren't so reliable visitors invariably arrived by train; the Company then ordered the train to stop at Applemere Halt, which meant someone going up to the Halt to man it. She used to love as a child walking to the Halt to see all the grand people arrive. Now a queen, or rather ex-queen, chose to arrive by car. How stupid, she thought. Why bring a motor car all the way from London, when you could take a train? Because, she belatedly realized, it would be a common train. For Queen Zita it would once have been a *royal* train, but now that she was queen no more, she would have to mix with the common folk. Get used to it, O Great Former Queen, she thought to herself. The times are changing. Then she reproached herself for her lack of charity, and ran back inside to give the twins the exciting news that ex-royals were at Applemere House.

The twins' eighth birthday was celebrated in great style on the Saturday just after their real birthday, with a party half in the garden and half in the cottage. Friends from school attended, together of course with Aunt Win, and even Dad managed to slip in for half an hour. Mary brought Alfred and Arabella, who for once joined amicably in the games and treasure hunt. Aunt Win had made a cake, and Anna and Freddie had sent Jamie more Hornby train accessories, and an elegant dolls' house for Lynette. By the time the guests had departed, Jennie and Richard were exhausted, especially Richard, since he had been working on the Flyer right up until the party began. He looked very white, and when she came downstairs from putting the twins reluctantly to bed, she found him slumped on the sofa.

He looked up as she came in. 'Sorry,' he managed. 'One of my headaches.'

'That sounds as if you're having them regularly,' she frowned.

'No, only the usual nightmares. Oh, and I had funny turn with Mary at the party – I thought she was Anna for some reason.'

He laughed, but she didn't. All her fears came racing back. 'Richard, you really must go to the doctor again. It can't just be overwork.'

He shrugged. 'What do I tell him? Bad dreams and headaches?'

'And oddities of speech.'

He looked at her. 'All right, I'll go on Monday.'

She was surprised that he had agreed so easily, and then realized that he must therefore be seriously worried too. She waited on tenterhooks, and since the twins were still at school, she decided to run up the lane to meet him. When she did so, she was relieved to see him looking happy and relaxed.

'Mild shell shock,' he told her. 'Dr Prince says it's all to do with the war, and particularly the train crash. As well as losing my leg, it's probably started off all sorts of inner worries and things. I could have had a bang on the head during the crash, I wouldn't know.' Richard had never recovered his memory of the crash itself.

73

'But it's ten years since the war.' She was puzzled.

'I've been having these dreams for years. Dr Prince said it's quite normal.'

A vast weight rolled off her, and she took his hand. 'So I just get used to your thinking I'm Anna too, yes?'

'No,' he joked. 'You can tell me I'm really off my chump. Just say "shell shock" to me, and I'll shut up.'

Sundays were the best days, Jennie thought. Today Richard had some discomfort with his leg so he hadn't come to church with her. It happened from time to time and he would travel to Roehampton to sort it out. He volunteered to cook the lunch instead, and she was enjoying her moments of freedom. As she walked back across the fields, she found herself looking towards Applemere House, and remembering all that had gone on in the past. It crossed her mind to wonder where Queen Zita was now. She hadn't seen her leave, although Michael had told her it was a fleeting visit. Good. The more fleeting the better.

She ran into the cottage, calling, 'I'm back!' She could smell the meat cooking in the range but there was no sign of Richard. Then he appeared, and she knew instantly that something had happened. He was followed by a familiar figure who looked so out of place in their cottage she didn't instantly recognize him. Then she did. How could she have been so stupid?

'Max!' she greeted him without thinking, then realized she was out of order and stammered. 'I'm sorry, King – um—' or should it be ex-King? she wondered, and compromised on: 'Your Majesty.' And curtsey, she told herself.

She had only got a little way down, when he interrupted, 'Please not, Mrs Trent. And not Your Majesty. I am formally Maximilian Deleanu, and, if you please, still Max to you.' Still Max – yet she hardly recognized the youthful Max of pre-war days, or even the soldier he became. His dark hair was slightly receding, his beard had a few strands of grey in it, he was sturdier than before and his face was lined, looking somehow defeated. That was the chief difference. The Max she had known had been confident, optimistic, outgoing.

'And I'm Jennie,' she stuttered. What a stupid thing to say. Of course she was Jennie. She hadn't been Imogen for ages, and there could be no Mrs Trent between them. She pulled herself together. 'This is my husband, Richard.'

'We have introduced ourselves, while we have been waiting in your beautiful garden.'

'It is nice, isn't it,' she replied, well pleased. Then she realized they were all standing up. 'Would you like to sit down?' she asked awkwardly. 'We could go into the parlour.' There was no fire there, but it was warm enough at this time of year.

'Perhaps. I have some unpleasant news. I would not wish to tell you in that peaceful garden.'

'Eileen?' she asked sharply.

'No, forgive me. Nothing like that.'

She glanced at Richard, who shook his head. So he didn't know what this was about either. Max clearly found difficulty in speaking so she had to break the silence:

'Is Her Majesty with you in England, both Her Majesties?' she added.

Max managed a smile, and looked more like the old Max. 'Both are here in London and well, thank you. I return there today. On your steam train, Jennie. I remember your telling me about the steam trains years ago, and now I am a commoner again, I too can travel by train.'

Jennie was impressed and so, she hoped, was Richard.

'Tell us what you have come for,' Richard suggested. 'Although I can guess.'

Could he? It was more than Jennie could.

'My aunt would have come herself, of course,' Max began, 'but I volunteered to speak with you. To explain.'

Explain what? This was becoming ominous.

'My mother Queen Zita will be living in London for the moment but she wishes to come eventually to live in Applemere to be near Lady Fokingham, and to stay here from time to time in the meanwhile.'

'Of course.' A horrible pit in her stomach was forming.

'She has, I'm afraid, taken a liking to this cottage,' Max continued steadily, 'and naturally since it belongs to my aunt and her husband, they have no grounds for refusing her. That means—'

'They're throwing us out,' Richard cut in sharply.

'Richard!' Jennie said warningly. No point antagonizing the messenger, even though the story was rubbish. Queen Zita hadn't even bothered to set foot in the cottage. How could she have developed a liking for it? She swallowed. 'When does Sir Roger wish us to leave?'

'At the end of this month. He hopes that will give you time to find another place to live.' Max hesitated. 'In fact Aunt Marie had one idea—'

'No thank you, but thank her,' Richard said, calmer this time. 'We'll find our own home. I'll not be indebted to the Fokinghams any longer.'

Max bowed his head in acquiescence, though he looked anxious, Jennie noticed. Her heart had sunk to the bottom of her boots. Where on earth would they find a cottage to rent that they could afford? And then it hit her with painful force: 'The barn, Max,' she said, suddenly. 'What about the Flyer?'

'I'm sorry,' was all he could reply. 'That too will be needed.'

She could see the muscle working in Richard's cheek. He said nothing, however. It was clearly untrue that the barn would be essential for Queen Zita, and they all knew it.

Jennie swallowed and rose to her feet. 'Thank you for telling us, Max. We'll leave at the end of June, as Sir Roger wishes. And the Applemere Flyer too of course.'

'I have heard about the travelling bookshop from Michael. You have done well.' Max looked almost wistful.

Richard did not comment and almost banged the door shut behind the departing visitor. 'To hell with The Fokinghams,' he snorted. 'Thank heavens we'll be free of them for ever. No more betrayals.'

'I gather you haven't found anywhere to go to yet,' Michael said, perching on the edge of the only chair with any space left on it.

He was right. They'd been looking for weeks without success. Everything was either too small or too expensive, and to buy a house was out of the question for a year or two yet.

'Nowhere.' Jennie tried to smile. 'Of course we could always live in the Flyer. Very educational with so much to read around us.'

'I've a suggestion that might interest you. You remember Anna's friend Anthony Hart?'

'Yes,' Jennie agreed cautiously.

76

'He has property near Bossingham. It's not that far away, and it has a dower house in the grounds, lying empty. You could rent that. He'd accept at the drop of a hat.'

Jennie swallowed. Bossingham was a small village some miles away between Stelling Minnis and Canterbury. It was true that it lay in their area for the Applemere Flyer, but nevertheless, 'I'm sure we couldn't afford a dower house, Michael, though it's good of you to suggest it.'

She could see Richard's lips were tight. He hated the idea.

'You don't understand,' Michael continued. 'Tony needs someone there whom he can trust. He'd take anything in rent, or nothing. Let's say what you're paying here. He needs someone to check the old pile doesn't fall down. There are a couple of servants there, but who guards the guards, and all that. Eh?'

Jennie hesitated. It sounded too good to be true, but Richard would never agree. She could sense he was willing her to say no for him. 'We have the Flyer, you see, Michael. That needs to be parked and maintained somewhere.'

'There are the old stables. No horses there now, so you might be able to do them up. Think about it.'

'It's not for ever, Richard,' Jennie pleaded after Michael had left. 'Only until we can buy somewhere of our own.'

'I won't have the Fokinghams feeling sorry for us. I *won't*.'

'It's not the Fokinghams. It's Anthony Hart, and he has no reason to feel sorry for us. You're being irrational.' The moment she used the word she regretted it, for he flinched. 'Where else could we go?' she finished.

'Bexley?'

'Then we'd have to start the business up all over again in a new area. If we're to buy a cottage for ourselves we can't afford that risk. If Anna's next book makes us a fortune we could buy one next year.'

Richard gave a guilty start. 'I forgot to tell you. The books came in yesterday.'

'The Dishonourable Miss Sheringham?' Jennie shrieked. 'Richard, how *could* you have forgotten? Have you read it yet?'

'Hardly. I'll get you a copy.' He went out into the hallway, and she heard him scrabbling in cardboard boxes. Then he reappeared, book in hand and gave it to her.

77

The cover was arresting. All vivid colours, sharp lines, and a girl with dark shingled hair, peering sideways at the viewer with a knowing look in her eyes, and a half smile on her lips.

'I'll read it this evening as soon as the twins have gone to bed,' she told him. 'After all, if it's the story of Anna and Lord Anthony,' she laughed, one eye on Richard, 'we might as well know what our future landlord's like.'

Later that evening, she heard Richard wiping his feet on the mat as he came in from mowing the grass, the sound of his footsteps approaching, and then he came into the parlour where she had been curled up in an armchair with *The Dishonourable Miss Sheringham.*

'Well?' he asked, as she swung her legs to the floor.

'Not well. Richard, this novel isn't about our future land-lord at all. But it *is* Anna's own story.'

'Isn't that partly Hart's?'

'No.' She heard her voice quivering. 'No, it's Tom's.' She burst into tears now she'd told him, and the first shock was over. 'This novel gives the story, thinly disguised as fiction, of her passion for Tom as a girl, and of how they were parted by her parents. Worst of all, darling—' Richard was staring at her aghast, '—if the novel is accurate in this respect too, she's *still* in love with him.'

Six

Now that her words could not be retracted, the horror of what she was saying came home to Jennie, and was instantly translated into what this could lead to.

'Are you sure?' Richard asked. 'It's late in the evening and you know how easy it is for fantasies to get transformed into fact.'

Jennie grimaced. 'Make your own mind up. Listen to this: "Across those desolate snow-covered fields lay Harcourt Manor and the small cottage where Jack lived. Soon he would be home from the brewery. Hungrily, she imagined his taking off his boots, shaking the snow from his damp golden hair, then stripping off his clothes to towel his naked body dry. In her mind's eye she followed each movement of that towel, seeing his skin glowing from the rough rubbing, and gleaming in the light of the oil lamp, his body afire and desiring her. With each movement of that towel, her own senses were aflame, unable to bear the distance between them. She was less than a mile away, but trapped within the walls of Sheringham House by a barred door that existed only in her mind. She felt blinded by a cocoon of white snow, unable to reach the light of paradise in Jack's arms. The snow stifled her, holding her back from running to him for ever. Here she was slowly being murdered by her prison, the hell of torment that spelled death for love. I will be free, I *will*."

'You want more?' Jennie asked, glancing at Richard's face. 'Believe me, it gets better.'

'I suppose,' Richard said glumly, 'I'll have to read it. If you're right, you're not going to be the only one to interpret it correctly. What about Mary? Did she know about Tom and Anna?'

'I don't know. I doubt it.' Miserably Jennie tried to think back to Tom's wedding. She had been away from home during most of the war and what little time she had spent in Fairsted had not been spent worrying about Tom and Anna. She was too relieved that Tom had married and, so she'd assumed, put Anna out of his mind. And his two children by her too? At least Anna had had the decency not to mention that in the novel. Did Tom still think of them? He never talked of them, but that was not the same as forgetting them. Her brother and her friend. How little she had known about either of them.

'Mary will know soon enough now.' Richard sighed.

Jennie was appalled. If Mary did not know about Anna's place in Tom's life, the shock would be enormous. She could see that Richard was beginning to take this as seriously as she did, but that hardly cheered her up. She longed for him to tell her she was dreaming and the novel was no more about Tom than its predecessors. He had been skimming through the book, however, and all he said was: 'We'll have to discuss whether we ought to sell this or not. We're depending on it, remember.'

Another problem – and at this of all times. 'We can't not do so,' she pointed out practically. 'Everyone will know it's being published, so it would only make matters worse to announce that it can't be bought from us. It would make people all the more eager to read it.'

'That's true, but this novel is going to cause real distress. Doesn't that make a difference?'

Jennie wrestled with her conscience, trying to think it through. 'It's the same moral problem we had before, except that it's worse because of our family being involved. To brazen it out and sell it as the other novels might be the best way of dealing with it. People would gossip but nothing would be said openly. It might with luck then die down, whatever readers may privately think. Wouldn't that be best for Mary?'

'That's a lot of woulds and mights. I don't like it, Jennie.'

'And you think I do?' she answered angrily.

He flushed. 'I agree that your plan is probably best, but I dislike the thought that Anna comes out triumphant yet again. She has a reason for publishing this, and I don't like being her pawn. So we don't go to her party, and so far as I'm concerned I'm happy if we never set eyes on her again.'

*　　　*　　　*

The Dower House at Goreham Court was a fairytale castle, or so the twins thought. Jennie, carting their cottage furniture into these Georgian rooms, felt more like Cinderella than the queen, but once the worst of it was done she began to relax and appreciate the beautifully proportioned rooms and windows – and the garden. It wasn't like her Applemere garden, but it was 'theirs'. Even better, outside its fences was a whole park, which they could use to their hearts' content. The twins had had to change school for the last two weeks of the school term, which caused some friction. Lynette liked the new school, but Jamie did not, sulking because his Fairsted friends were far away. In vain did Jennie explain this was just a temporary move. A year meant nothing to an eight-year-old.

Richard had pulled a face when he saw the stables. There was a lot of work needed before the Applemere Flyer could have an inside shelter again. At least there were plenty of water butts in the grounds, and if the bus took in the Station House on its route there would be an extra supply there. The old steamer was faithfully chugging on, but even Jennie was beginning to admit that its days might be numbered, and it would soon be time to change to a petrol bus. Another expense, which meant they would again be beholden to *The Dishonourable Miss Sheringham*, her predecessors and successors.

Jennie tried to divide her life in two: the part that belonged to the Applemere Flyer and the part that belonged fiercely to her family. Now it seemed they would be in head-on collision, even though they had reluctantly agreed that not selling the book would be worse than selling it. Nevertheless, she had doubts about what they were doing. Even she played a small part in the book, as Norma's best friend Alice, who of course was Jack's sister. How dared Anna do this to her?

Jennie remembered declaring her goal for the Applemere Flyer was for it to unite people through the power of the written word, whether this was through political polemics, Jane Austen, or, she supposed, the novels of Anna Trent. The goal would now be attained at the bottom level.

'If anything can be guaranteed to appeal to virtually everyone in Fairsted,' she remarked to Richard, 'it will be this wretched novel.'

Publication day for Anna's book was Friday, July the sixth, her birthday and also the day for Anna's party. This time fortunately it was once more in London, since Richard was still refusing to attend. It wasn't to be at the Silver Slipper, however. Mrs Meyrick's career continued to bounce up and down with so many police raids that apparently it was easier to open up a new club than sort out the mess of the previous one. Society still flocked to her doors.

'The party's to be at the Hotel Cecil,' Anna had told her when she last saw her.

It was a clever choice. The most respectable of hotels for the most unrespectable of books. Jennie was relieved that Anna hadn't elected to hold the party at the Plough in Fairsted. She was quite capable of it.

She worried that as yet she and Richard didn't know whether the theme of the book was public knowledge. Aunt Win, for instance, wouldn't know, so should Jennie break the news to her? Did Tom know? Did Mary? And worst of all, did Freddie? The thought that he would the last to know gave her nightmares. If only she could be a complete ostrich and hide from all the results that would inevitably stem from this book, unless they were very, very lucky. Why on earth had Anne decided to do this? Was it just to exorcise ghosts from her own mind? If so, could she not have hidden the truth behind a thicker cloak of fiction?

Perhaps it was simply another stage in her battle with her parents, but why drag Tom into it? The novel left it in no doubt that Norma Sheringham married the younger son but yearned for the elder one; even worse, it implied that the marriage was a mere nod towards convention. The last sentences had Norma in the kitchen preparing her husband's tea, a deliberate and clever bathos after the highflown farewell to love of the preceding text. The implication was that love was over, only duty remained.

Jennie threw herself into making a start on the overgrown garden at the Dower House. The grass and weeds had been hewn down from time to time over the years, so the housekeeper explained, but it had not been tended and loved for many years. The physical effort took her mind off her other worries, at least until the Thursday before publication day for Anna's novel when these paled into insignificance.

'Mummy!' Lynette came racing through the kitchen door into the garden. 'It's Uncle Tom and Auntie Mary.'

Her bright-eyed excitement contrasted with their strained faces as they followed her. Tom had his smart business suit on, suggesting they had come on the spur of the moment. What did that imply? Jennie was instantly wary.

'Not a bad old place,' Tom observed carelessly. His rubicund face looked cheerful enough, but this often bore little resemblance to his true feelings. 'Where's old Richard?' he asked.

'In the stables. I heard the Applemere Flyer come back ten minutes ago.'

'I'll stroll up there,' Tom announced.

In order to leave her with Mary, Jennie realized wryly. Thank you, Tom. One look at Mary's face, and she realized they had seen the novel. She tried to put a stopper on the wild thoughts that rushed through her head. Had they come to ask her not to sell the book? No, please not that. Mary's usually calm assured face was strained and white, and she didn't glance once at Tom as he promptly strolled away.

'Let's go inside,' Jennie managed to say cheerfully. 'I'll get some tea and this—' she looked deprecatingly around '—is hardly a pleasure garden yet.'

'It's a lovely house,' Mary said dutifully, though there was no life in her voice and she looked on the verge of tears.

'What's wrong?' Jennie asked quietly, as soon as she had ushered her to the more or less tidy sitting room and shooed Lynette and Jamie away. Tea could wait.

Mary's hands were clasped tightly around her. 'I – we – wondered whether you would change your mind and come to Anna's party tomorrow.'

'We can't.' Jennie hadn't expected this, the one thing that Richard had been adamant about. 'You can see how much we have to do here.' Weak, but it might pass.

'Please, Jennie.'

If Mary was reduced to pleading, then there was no doubt she knew the whole story, and that it had been a terrible shock for her.

'Why do you need us there? Can you tell me?' she asked gently.

'Tom insists we go. I don't want to, oh I *don't*,' Mary burst into tears. 'How can I, Jennie? You've read . . . that thing?'

No escape was possible now, and nor should she seek one, Jennie knew. 'Yes, I have. It was over a long time ago, Mary. He's been happily married to you for eleven years.' Useless words. What did time matter in a case of what Mary obviously saw as betrayal?

'But it isn't over. It's there in the book. That woman sent Tom a copy and I found it. I *hate* her. She's still in love with him, and they've been making a fool of me.'

Jennie ran to her side, putting her arms round her. 'It's all over for Tom and that's what matters,' she reassured her, cursing Anna for her selfishness.

'Is it?' Mary asked bitterly. 'He says it is, but how can I know he's speaking the truth? Tom can lie and lie and lie. He told me *all* about his past, so he claimed, and it didn't include Anna Fokingham. All I want to do is crawl into a hole when I think of all our friends tittering. And Tom actually insists we go to the party. Both of us.'

'Does he say why?'

'He *says* that if we stay away it would seem to confirm everything in the novel. I can't bear it, Jennie. I can't – unless you come too. And what about Freddie?' she cried.

The worst situation had come about. There was nothing Jennie wanted less than hypocritically to attend the party, but Mary was clearly desperate. If Tom, Freddie, herself and Mary were all present, Jennie supposed, that might, just might, cast doubt on the rumours.

'I'll talk to Richard,' she agreed, but her heart sank at having to do so.

'You go if you have to, but leave me out of it,' Richard had reluctantly agreed.

The Hotel Cecil proved comfortable and sedate compared with the Silver Slipper, but once the guests were assembled and the band playing, there seemed little difference between the two to her. These exotic birds of paradise and dinner-suited escorts twittered and frolicked like the grasshoppers in the Aesop Fable that Richard had illustrated for one of his publications. Ants, lowly creatures such as she and Richard, preferred preparing for winter ahead, and she longed for the Dower House, which now seemed home compared with this alien hotel.

She was standing, with Tom and Mary, at the doorway, feeling somewhat bemused when she saw Anna sparkling her way towards them in a pale green chiffon tulip-skirted gown, swathed round the waist and pearls tumbling over its low-necklined bodice. More adorned her short curly hair. She looked as fragile as a petal blowing in the wind, but her smile was that of a Medusa.

'Darling Mary, and Jennie. How wonderful. And Tom *too*,' she cooed. They were kissed and hugged, passive puppets in the hands of the puppeteer. Then Medusa changed into a siren, promptly claiming Tom as her dancing partner. He stayed her partner, for dance after dance, while Jennie grew increasingly desperate. There was no sign of Freddie, though Michael was here, and so was Anthony Hart.

'Look at her,' Mary moaned bitterly. 'She thinks she's Mata Hari.' Her own brown dress was expensive and suited her, but its dowdiness marked the difference between her and Anna. Finally after the fifth dance Jennie could stand it no longer, and walked over to Tom at the end of the dance, informing him gaily that the next dance was hers. Anna merely laughed.

Tom grinned at her, as he whirled her away. 'Thanks for coming tonight, sis. I appreciate it.'

'No doubt,' she retorted. 'After all, Mary needed a companion if you were to spend the whole evening with Anna. You should be dancing with her, not me.'

'You're a good little thing, Jen,' was all he said, as he spun her round.

'I am *not*,' she retorted crossly. 'I'm your sister. I'm yoked to you throughout life. And,' she added meaningfully, 'yoked to Freddie as well, so don't you forget it.'

'I'm hardly likely to,' Tom murmured, and she glanced at him sharply, catching a look of real pain on his face. As so often, she had rashly assumed there was at least an armistice between her brothers, if not peace. Anna's novel might end it with a vengeance.

'It really is all over now, isn't it, Tom? Anna is just exercising novelist's licence when she implies she's still in love with you.'

'Alas, yes. Would that I were such a dashing fellow as this Jack seems to be.'

'Don't joke, Tom,' she snapped. 'It's too serious.'

He didn't reply, but he did ask Mary for the next dance. For a moment Jennie thought Mary would refuse, but at last she rose to her feet and walked stiffly on to the dance floor. They had danced one whole dance together, before Anna took a hand. She floated over to them, tapped Mary on the shoulder, and announced loudly for the room to hear, 'This is the Hostess's Excuse Me dance,' and took Tom over once again. Jennie, dancing with Michael, was powerless to intervene, because he stopped her from doing so with a firm hand on her arm.

'There's nothing you can do, Jennie,' he said seriously.

He was right, but, oh, how much she wanted to try. She could see the crisis coming. Even Michael couldn't have expected what happened next.

Mary was fighting back, physically pulling Anna away from Tom, and shouting out, 'And this is the Wife's Excuse Me!'

It availed poor Mary nothing. Tom, his cheerful grin for once wiped from his face, stalked off the floor leaving Anna to laugh in his wife's face, with the entire company of guests watching in great amusement. This kind of scene was probably commonplace for London, Jennie hoped, and might be forgotten tomorrow. They couldn't know how serious it was in Fairsted terms.

Michael was still holding Jennie back, as Mary stood her ground like a tigress, yelling at Anna to leave Tom alone. Anna shrugged, turning to join Tom, and Mary acted. She slapped Anna's face so effectively that the sharp sound stabbed through the air, shattering Jennie's hopes that this altercation would be swiftly over and little regarded. Anna's face was white as she held her hand to where it must be stinging from Mary's blow.

It was Mary who walked off with the victory to join Tom. 'We'll go to our room now,' she announced clearly, with a faint emphasis on the *our*. Surprisingly Tom went with her, leaving Anna staring after them.

'Go to dance with her, Michael,' Jennie pleaded impulsively, seeing her there alone in the middle of the floor. Not as she had at the last party, glorying in her triumphs, but stripped of her defences. 'Or ask Anthony to dance with her.'

'No, Jennie. Neither of us. Anna's got to learn manners someday.'

Jennie took a deep breath. The morals of the situation went completely out of her mind. Anna needed help. She was still the girl she had first known and pitied, so Jennie disciplined herself to walk slowly to Anna, gabbling the first thing that came into her head.

'No one's dancing,' she seemed to be addressing the whole room, 'and I'm tired of being a wallflower, Anna. Dance with me please.'

Anna, with a look of amusement, let herself be guided, as the band took the hint and began to play again. She and Anna danced a stumbling Charleston, with Jennie near to tears. Whom was she betraying: Freddie, Mary, Tom, Richard, herself?

With a semblance of normality restored, the dance floor filled again and the evening regained some vitality. Jennie seemed to have signalled that this was a private problem, nothing to do with the mad bad world of Mayfair, whose rules on freedom only went so far, it seemed. Anna had stepped over the line, even for Mayfair.

The rest of the evening passed in a blur and afterwards she could only remember dancing with Anthony Hart. She had taken a liking to him, and wondered how he was feeling now that the novel's subject matter was private property. After all, he had been Anna's escort and presumed lover for some time. He looked rather like Michael with his fine sharp features, only he was fair where Michael was dark. His straw-coloured hair and fresh complexion, and greater height than Michael made him look very . . . she searched for the word . . . patrician, but a comfortable person to be with. There were shades of Lord Peter Wimsey about him.

'I'm sorry,' she managed to say, 'about all this. And Anna.'

He seemed to understand for he laughed. 'Don't worry about me, Jennie. Look after your own. How's the Dower House?'

'We love it – or when we get straight we will.' Normality was restored.

'I'll be down some time soon.'

'Still?' she asked.

'Yes, still. I shan't go and blow my brains out.' He began to roar with laughter. 'Don't worry about me. You'll have enough to cope with.' The laughter stopped and he looked quite serious. 'Watch Anna, Jennie, if you can. She doesn't mean to be but she's dangerous.'

'Not now. You don't know her as I do,' Jennie said stoutly.

'It's your family, Jennie, but if I were you, I'd think about that novel quite carefully.'

'Not sell it in our flying bookshop, you mean.'

'No. Selling it makes no difference. It's what's written in it worries me – for your sake. The ending.'

'She's accepted marriage. That's how I understood it.' Could there be any other explanation? Seeing Anthony Hart's amused face, she began to feel uneasy.

'So where's Freddie?' he asked.

'He doesn't like these social parties. He often stays at home.'

'Tonight? I think not. Look at this.' He took her hand, and led her to the table where free copies of the books were available. He picked one up and turned to the last paragraph, reading out: '"Norma spread the butter on the bread slowly and deliberately. The egg was on the stove. She could wait for it to cook. She had all the time in the world. It might take three minutes, or four or five. But it would boil. It could not be stopped. Oh take heed of that egg, Norma."'

Jennie froze. Was he right? Was there another explanation of those lines than the one she had seen? No, she refused to believe it. 'She's accepting that she's married,' she said steadily.

'Is she?' was all he replied; he gave her a quick kiss and was gone.

There was no mention of the *Dishonourable Miss Sheringham* in the newspapers, to Jennie's relief, except for a brief paragraph that a lively party had been held last evening for Anna Trent's latest novel. London society obviously kept its secrets to itself.

The newspapers did have another bombshell to drop, however. They had more important events to report to the world than scandal. The unrest in the Balkans had come to a head, not in the Kingdom of the Serbs, Croats and Slovenes as expected, but in Montevanya. There was civil war raging – in so far as it could rage in such a tiny country. The fledgling republic that Max had created had taken a sidestep, and Viktor, instead of plotting to become president, was aiming to be elected as king.

This didn't make sense to Jennie, after she'd scanned the paper for news of Eileen or Georgius. There had been none.

Kingship meant inheritance, not election, and furthermore if Montevanya wanted a king again, why not choose Max? Why not indeed? The newspapers agreed wholeheartedly with Jennie, it seemed. With growing concern she read the news that Viktor had been behind the revolutionary party now trying to force the country to 'elect' him as monarch. He would not, the newspapers considered, rule as Max and his father had. He would be more like Benito Mussolini, the dictator in Italy, and that was an appalling prospect for a hitherto easygoing country like Montevanya.

What of Max, Jennie worried. Was he safe? All he had tried to do was turn his country peacefully into a republic, and what he and Eileen had feared most had come about. There were discreet mentions in the newspapers of the prospective King Viktor's popularity with the army – it was news to Jennie that Montevanya had one, apart from ceremonial guards. Perhaps this was the result of their occupation by the Central Powers during the war, under Viktor as a puppet king. Viktor had learned to live with military rule then, but would he do so now? Now he would be in charge of the army, not answerable to it.

All this and having to worry about Anna and Tom as well. What was she going to tell Richard, she wondered. The orders for the novel must have been distributed now, and Aunt Win would have demanded her copy straightaway. Lady Fokingham – no, Jennie realized; she was one worry she could dismiss. The Applemere Flyer no longer called at Applemere House.

When Richard met her at Fairsted railway station, he had no great news to report save that he and Albert had delivered all the orders and in addition the novel had sold several copies. Perhaps, she thought hopefully, the storm would be deferred until after the weekend.

It was not to be. Aunt Win had a piece of her mind ready to bestow on them, when they called to collect the twins.

'A fine kettle of fish,' she stormed, as though the book was their fault.

'You've read it then,' Richard said.

'Enough.' Aunt Win broke off to attend to Lynette's latest tale of woe, and then came right back to them. 'That young madam needs a good talking to. And since you won't do it, I'll have to.'

Jennie felt an insane desire to giggle at the thought of Anna chastened by Aunt Win. 'I did try, Aunt Win. Anna has her own ideas, though.'

This was brushed aside. 'And Tom too. I've told him his father's going to speak to him. Disgusting, I call it.'

'When he's coming?' Jennie asked in trepidation.

'Tonight.'

Richard glanced at her in relief. They could be gone before he arrived, on the excuse that Lynette and Jamie had to be in bed. No more was said in the interests of the party, but Dad had a word with her as they left. 'I've told her not to do say anything, Jen. Least said, soonest mended. We all ignore it, and Freddie can hold his head up again. After all, it were all years ago.'

Trade on the Applemere Flyer on the Monday was brisk, even more than they had expected. Whereas the novel had only sold half a dozen copies on Friday and Saturday apart from the orders, suddenly their entire stock of fifty was cleared in a day, and Richard had to order some more as soon as they were home.

'The news went round quicker than we anticipated,' Richard said wryly. 'I don't know whether to be pleased or sad.'

As soon as Richard disappeared into the garden on their return home, Jennie telephoned her father, suspecting something had happened that they didn't know about. Sure enough, his voice sounded glum.

'Good job you missed it all, Jen. There was a fight in the Plough and Jacob had to be called.'

'Who between?' she asked, alarmed. If Jacob Parsons, the village policeman, had to be called in this was trouble indeed.

'Tom and Mr Michael. Your aunt would insist on my having a word with him, so I took him to the Plough so we could talk about it man to man. And who should come in but Mr Michael. He always goes there when he's down here, and it's my guess he was here to discuss this novel of young Anna's with his mum and dad. His Nibs went for Tom like he was a poacher after his pheasants, and Tom wasn't much better. Two grown men fighting it out. Tom wouldn't listen to me. I'll never be able to have a peaceful pint in there again. Mr Michael was shouting about the disgrace to his family name from a – well, I won't tell you the word he used, and Tom was yelling at him to keep his toffee-nosed self out of it. He knocked Mr Michael clean out he did.'

Jennie couldn't make sense of this. Michael had wanted to keep out of the crisis at the party, so why seek trouble out now? Could it be because this was Fairsted, not London? There'd always been animosity between those two, so it was hardly surprising it should erupt over the novel.

No wonder it had sold well today, though.

Jennie went wearily to the door. It must be Lynette and Jamie coming back. It had been a hot sticky day on the Flyer, the school holidays had just begun, and Mrs Grant, the house-keeper at the Big House, as they called Goreham Court, was looking after Lynette and Jamie, in so far as they needed it. They tended to amuse themselves, playing the Duchess of Guggle and Mr Wallowby (butler) in a series of playlets concocted by Lynette.

'Jennie, may I talk to you for five minutes?' It wasn't the twins, it was Lady Fokingham. Her chauffeur sat in the car waiting to drive her home. She looked distraught, and Jennie quickly forgot the coolness between them as she showed her into their drawing room. Parlour was too cosy a word for this elegant room, even if their ancient Chesterfield didn't exactly do justice to it.

'It's good of you to see me, Jennie, after all that has happened. I—' Lady Fokingham swallowed, 'I beg you to listen to me, to try to understand.'

'What's wrong? Is it Prince Georgius or Eileen? Surely not even Viktor would harm them?' Jennie's imagination leapt ahead.

'No, it's nothing to do with Montevanya, though God knows the news is bad enough. Poor Max.'

'It's Anna's novel then. I heard about the trouble in the Plough,' Jennie rushed on. 'Tom has behaved badly to Mary, but there's nothing between him and Anna now. It's her fantasy.'

'It hardly matters,' Lady Fokingham said. 'The damage is done. Anna lacks all restraint. I understand now just how ruth-less she is. I used to convince myself that Tom had seduced Anna, and that all that happened after that was therefore his fault. I no longer do.'

91

Jennie flushed. 'What has happened?' Obviously something had. Lady Fokingham couldn't just have found out about the novel. She would have read it immediately it was published.

'I went to see Anna to ask her how she could drag our name and reputation through the dust. I can understand she might want a different kind of life to that we wished for her, but she has deliberately set out to damage us. It's sheer vindictiveness. And why now?'

Lady Fokingham seemed about to cry, the unthinkable in someone usually so poised and assured.

'She's destroying Mary and Tom's lives too,' Jennie pointed out, 'Not to mention her own and Freddie's.'

Lady Fokingham looked at her. 'You are right. Freddie at least cannot be blamed for this.'

'For what? What happened?'

'I went unannounced. It was . . .' Lady Fokingham paused, 'a terrible mistake,' she ended simply. 'I thought she would slam the door in my face, but she invited me in. Foolishly, I went. Your brother was not there, and I was glad of it, I would not like him to have heard the dismissive way she spoke of him.'

'Of Freddie?' Jennie's anger grew. Did Anna take his love so much for granted?

'I'm afraid so. She saved the vitriol for my husband and myself, however. Freddie seemed more an irrelevance. She blamed her father and myself for everything that had gone wrong with her life – or rather, *right* with her life, as she confusingly then claimed. She appears to see her relationship with your brother Tom, whether past or present, as "the real life" and the way we brought her up as a degrading and artificial prison.'

'Was she hysterical?' Jennie tried to conjure up the scene. If Anna had been calm she would have been playing one of her games.

Lady Fokingham burst into tears, obviously reliving her ordeal as she spoke. 'She spat full in my face. I had stolen her babies, forced her into a loveless marriage in order to escape the bondage we had apparently decreed for her, we have in some way prevented her from having more children. In short, we ruined her life. Does she not understand that we are influenced by our upbringing too, and that though we may also wish to escape its constraints from time to time, we know that we cannot. It is the same problem but, alas, with far different solutions. I fear for her future, Jennie. I even fear for her sanity.'

'How can I help?' Jennie asked, with growing concern not only for her family but for Anna herself.

'It is too late, I believe.'

'Is there nothing I can do?'

'No. Anna is fully bent on her own destruction, or at least that of her happiness. Your brother Freddie may love her but he is obviously no match for Anna's wilfulness. He has my sympathy.'

They all needed sympathy. Jennie was shaken after Lady Fokingham had left. Lady Fokingham was wrong, however. There was something that Jennie could do, and it stood out a mile. She must go to see Anna herself, on behalf of her family. She would go tomorrow.

She decided not to mention Lady Fokingham's visit to Richard that evening, but to leave it till the morning when he would be less tired and more likely to think rationally. The timing was still wrong, however. Richard was quite clear that his views on the Fokinghams had not changed. Nor those on Anna.

'You realize Freddie and Tom will probably never speak again? What will that do to Aunt Win and your father? Not to mention poor Mary's life blown apart.'

'Poor Mary,' Jennie repeated exasperated. 'She's the only one you think about.'

'She's in trouble,' Richard retorted. 'You're quick enough to defend Anna. Mary needs comfort too.'

Jennie was furious with herself for having mentioned Anna or the Fokinghams at all. She could see all the signs of one of Richard's headaches coming on, and she knew to her own cost that once started, it would not shift for at least two days. She tried hard to put it right. 'It was stupid of me to have talked about it when you're tired.'

'I am not bloody tired,' he shouted at her.

She tried to take his arm to lead him to a chair, but he swung round, punching her full in the face to make her let go. The blow caught her on the cheek and mouth, and she had to cut off a scream of pain in case the twins upstairs in their bedroom heard. She staggered back, and sat down, nursing her cheek.

Richard loomed over her, dragging her upright again. 'You know it's all your fault, don't you?' Her lip was cut, and as she looked at the blood on her hand disbelievingly, he added, 'It's not much.'

Jennie was scared, terrified not only for herself but, because of the crazy look in his eyes, for him too. What was happening? Surely the increasing violence of these turns could not just be the results of shell-shock, whatever Dr Prince had said. She could understand it if the headaches were late at night after he'd been working, but they tended to be in the mornings.

Then, as usual, his anger left him as suddenly as it came. He slumped deathly pale in a chair, and she rushed to bring him some tea to revive him. She put the cup to his lips to ensure he drank it, and after that he seemed a little better.

'Did I do that?' he asked, looking first doubtfully, then horrified, at her swollen lip.

'Just one of your turns, not you,' she comforted him.

'I *hit* you?'

'Let's go to the doctor again. And this time we'll go to the one in Bossingham.'

'I like Dr Prince.'

'This one is nearer. You won't miss so much working time.' She knew that would convince him. She wasn't going to be told it was shell shock this time.

She decided she should go on the Flyer too today, so that Richard could rest, after they had been to the surgery. It was Albert's day off fortunately, and she could manage the Flyer alone for once. All thought of Anna flew from her mind, until she picked up the post from the doormat. At first it looked like Eileen's handwriting to her, but then she saw it was posted in Ashford. *Ashford?*

In sudden fear she ripped the envelope open. Of course it wasn't Eileen's writing. It was Anna's:

Darling Jennie,
Now don't be too shocked, will you? I'm afraid dearest
Mama and Papa will be. You see, Tom and I have decided
to elope. Won't that be fun? In fact, by the time you read

this, we will already have left. Elope is a silly word of
course, since there's no Gretna Green for us, but it's
the sort of word I should use, according to my upbringing.
Darling Tom, no one but him, ever. I know you'll look
after Freddie. He means well, but it just wasn't to be.
Tom and I plan to live not far away, so I doubt if you'll
lose touch with the untouchables.
Our love, Anna

'Jennie, where are you?' Richard was calling. 'I thought we
were going to the doctor.' She pushed the letter quickly back
into its envelope. Bad news could wait.

Seven

1929

'Too late, why does everything come too late? We've actually made a decent profit. Another year like this and we could have afforded to buy a cottage.'

Richard sat at the table hunched over their annual sales figures for 1928. Not only had Anna's novel (hardly surprisingly) outsold its predecessors by many hundreds, but amongst their other successes was *Precious Bane*. At last Mary Webb's book had had due recognition, after the prime minister Stanley Baldwin had publicly recommended the book last year. Suddenly the demand for the book all over the country was insatiable and the novel had been reprinted five times according to the country traveller.

'So much for literary prizes,' Richard had snorted when they sold out just before Christmas. The novel had won a prestigious prize as early as 1925, but sales had remained at the same rock bottom level. 'One word from a public figure, which no doubt served some political purpose, and sales boomed.'

'Who cares why?' Jennie had tried to cheer him up. 'It's sold, and all your belief in it was justified.'

Richard had remained silent. Nothing she could say convinced him that it wasn't his fault that the novel hadn't sold earlier. If only he had explained properly to customers ... if only he had had the right words ... If only, if only ... Those words haunted them all the time now.

If only they hadn't believed Dr Prince when he said Richard's headaches were the result of shell-shock. If only she'd forced Richard sooner to see another doctor when her suspicions deepened that Dr Prince might have been wrong. Now it was too late. The tumour in Richard's brain was too large to operate on. The new young Bossingham doctor had diagnosed it quickly, but too late. The headaches were coming agonizingly frequently and were increasing in intensity: Jennie forced herself to face the fact that soon Richard would die. They both knew it, and sometimes they talked of it, when Richard was lucid. When the pills the doctor had given him to lessen the pain failed to work, Richard could do nothing but lie rigid in a darkened room, with wet rags on his brow, facing the end of his hopes, the end of their dreams. He was often so violently sick that the effort would exhaust him and make the terrifying headaches worse.

The first shock had now passed, and she could hardly bear to remember those agonizing days in which she had had to force herself to break the news to her family. She'd told Aunt Win and Dad first.

'We don't know how long he has to live,' she had said, trying to sound matter of fact.

'Oh, Jennie girl.' Dad got up slowly from his chair and she could see his eyes moist with tears.

Aunt Win had scarcely been able to speak. 'I'll put the kettle on,' she said automatically. 'We'll have a nice cup—' She broke off, and Jennie found herself comforting her rather than the other way round. Shakily, they laughed together at the stupidity of that, and Aunt Win blew her nose. 'No, we'll need to make plans,' she began.

Plans! Jennie had felt oddly peaceful, as though the horror she faced could indeed be reduced to such practical proportions.

Dad had coughed. 'Your aunt's right, Jennie. Those children will need to be away from the house at bad times.'

Once Dad and Aunt Win knew, it had been easier to try to explain to the twins that Daddy would not be with them much longer. Now, they had accepted it, though how they would react when it happened might be a different matter.

Somehow the news had spread. Plans were indeed made, Freddie was miraculously the rock she had always found him, the village as a whole combined to smooth her path, and the Station House became an extension of her home, always there, always a help – except when she was inevitably alone to face her future.

So much still lay unspoken between herself and Richard,

for his periods of normality were growing fewer, and with looking after the twins and the Applemere Flyer, she could not tackle issues head on. Time was running out for closeness. Some days he hardly seemed to know her, sometimes the manic fantasies would consume him and then she would take the twins to the Station House for Aunt Win to care for, or if time were short up to Mrs Grant at Goreham Court. Jennie was half nurse and half money earner with little time for anything else. No one knew for sure how long Richard had to live, but her instincts, confirmed by the doctor in this early spring of 1929 said that it could not be long.

'I have to go now, Albert will be waiting,' she said gently. Each morning she had to tear herself away from the painful sight of Richard still struggling to bring the records up to date, despite being ill much of the night.

Albert, dear faithful Albert. If it wasn't for him she would have to run the Flyer alone. He had come with her every day since Richard's illness incapacitated him, faithfully turning up to an agreed railway station, according to the day's route. She had insisted that Pencarek Books should pay for a telephone to be installed at his home; it was an instrument he had always regarded with deep suspicion, preferring his own elegant letters, penned in immaculate copperplate, as a means of communication.

'The word on the page is good enough for me,' he would declare.

With Richard's health so precarious, which meant that the Flyer's route or even appearance could be altered at the last moment, he had reluctantly agreed, however. The sound of his voice bawling down the telephone as though he were shouting at her from his Canterbury home rather than speaking down a wire always made her laugh – and Richard too, when he felt well enough.

'How is Mr Pencarek today, Mrs P.?' Albert asked as usual one day when she drew up at Chilham station and found him bowler-hatted, briefcase in hand, patiently waiting. The boiler had played up this morning and she was late, because she had wrestled with it herself rather than disturb Richard. Albert had not said a word, probably because her flushed face told the story of the battle itself. Calling her Mrs P. was the closest Albert got to informality, even though he took it as a compliment that he was now Albert to them and not Mr Hodge.

'Not at all well.'

Albert put his briefcase down on the small reading table they used in the Flyer for writing receipts and orders, and inclined his head. What did he keep in that briefcase Jennie wondered, or was it just part of the uniform?

'Then we must make it a good day for Mr Pencarek,' he replied. 'Shall we say twelve copies of *Precious Bane*, twenty *All Quiet on the Western Front*, thirty *Goodbye to All That* – and no copies of *The Dishonourable Miss Sheringham* or *Ulysses*?'

Albert making a joke? Jennie was ridiculously grateful to him. Normally books were definitely no laughing matter to Albert, and so a joke was another sign of how upset he was about Richard.

'Thank you, Albert,' she replied in suitably grave tones. 'And perhaps we won't mention how well Sapper, Dornford Yates or Michael Arlen are selling either.' She could no longer tease Richard about her detective stories selling well because ever since the publication of *The Murder of Roger Ackroyd*, he had become an admirer of Mrs Christie and even admitted that there were other detective stories that might just pass muster as readable, even if Sherlock Holmes reigned supreme so far as he was concerned. After Mrs Christie's mysterious disappearance at the end of 1926, her books had sold like hot cakes, although she and Richard had argued as to whether the current Agatha Christie, *The Seven Dials Mystery,* was as good as its predecessors. After all, it did not feature Hercule Poirot, so in her view was less gripping, but Richard said it caught the mood of the times and that it should remind Jennie of their brief look at the 'bright young things' at the Silver Slipper Club.

She didn't want reminding. The less she heard about Anna and Tom the less she need worry about the tug of loyalties they had presented. Least important of these was that the rekindling of friendship between herself and the Fokinghams had been abruptly terminated, but this time Jennie was furious at their attitude, rather than regretful. The Fokinghams' coolness to them, just when they needed all the friends they had, suggested that they thought Jennie was somehow approving of Tom's behaviour, and even of Anna's.

Jennie and Richard's main concern was for Freddie. Tom had left his job at the brewery of course, but financially Mary was well looked after, since her father was its owner. Anna and Tom had been gone several months now, and since these were winter months, it had not surprised Jennie to get a post-card from Provence, in the south of France. Not Nice or Cannes, she noticed. At least Anna had the sense to avoid the fashionable venues. The postcard had displayed a Roman theatre, but its reverse merely wished them: '*Salut*, Jennie. *Salut*, Richard.' It was signed by both Anna and Tom. There was no address (not that she would expect one) but it showed an infuriating lack of concern on both their parts, especially Tom's. Suppose one of his children were taken ill? Or Dad or Aunt Win? And, Jennie thought miserably, what about her and Richard? Elder brothers were supposed to be comforters and supporters, not debauched lovers gadding about in some foreign country.

Mary on the other hand was recovering fast from the shock of Tom's disappearance. When she last visited them, she seemed solely preoccupied with the children and her books. The latter had given her a new role in life and she was as involved in it as ever Tom had been at the brewery, even if it were not so financially rewarding.

She had shown the text of her new children's book to Richard in great excitement. 'It's the first in a new series of books for children,' she explained. 'It's about a brother and sister who are whisked back in time by a magic train set; they enter the train, off it puffs, they descend at a particular station, walk through the door – and there they meet all sort of famous historical people and get involved in battles and magic and goodness knows what.'

'Like Nelson?' Richard had immediately asked, his interest caught, and immediately his hand had reached for his pad and pencil.

Jennie blessed Mary for this brilliant idea, as it not only gave Richard something to occupy himself and to think about when he was not well enough to work, but also involved her, since she became the 'expert' on the railway trains and stations involved. It was something they could work on together, while the important issues lay resting awhile.

Freddie seemed to have withdrawn into himself, and no

wonder. No longer a fresh faced youth, he looked gaunt and sunken in the face. He steadfastly refused all invitations to move back to the Station House, preferring to stay on alone in the Ashford house. It was his home as well as Anna's, he pointed out with asperity, as though he had been accused of living off her earnings.

When asked tentatively what his plans were, Freddie had just replied, 'I don't have plans. I have a job, and that's it.' He'd looked at them belligerently. 'And don't you go feeling sorry for me. I'm all right. Now I know where I am.'

But where was that? Still wondering how his elder brother came to run off with his wife? Jennie longed to be able to talk to him as a sister should, but all Freddie would say was, 'Tom's her dancing shoes, but I'm her old slippers. She'll be back, you'll see.'

She couldn't penetrate this armour. It was almost as though he blamed her for bringing Anna into their lives, and yet she, Tom and Freddie had all met her on the same day, the day of her twelfth birthday when they had walked to Applemere Halt. Since then Anna had touched all their lives, at first with excitement but now with sadness.

The number of days when Jennie was on the Applemere Flyer without Richard at her side increased, and her struggle to interest customers in books grew harder, for all Albert's help. What pleasure could she take in the new titles coming out from Somerset Maugham, Hemingway and Priestley, when Richard was not at her side to enjoy them? She dutifully went into Canterbury every so often to see travellers and place orders, trying to follow Richard's instructions, but she hated this side of it.

The former enjoyment she had had taken in seeing farmers' wives mixing with solicitors' and doctors' wives, and young with old, as they browsed or talked together in the bus, was fast vanishing. There was a small area at the back of the bus where people could retreat with a book to browse through its contents, and during the winter months particularly, they had vacuum flasks of soups and hot drinks for customers to enjoy while they did so. It had been a delight then to hear the chatter. They were also used as a centre for information, for local knowledge, or the latest news for those who had no wireless. Some people climbed aboard to enquire about something and

101

stayed on to buy a book. She put this down to Albert, who adopted a particularly benign expression as he stood at the exit. They would turn, bookless, to leave the bus, see his formal black-suited presence and courteous smile – and turn back to buy, suitably abashed. They would then receive a solemn:

'We are grateful for your custom.'

Although spring had come, it brought no hope, only fear. Jennie hated seeing the fresh sprigs bursting out in rebirth, while Richard was slowly dying in agony. It wasn't fair, she railed against fate to herself. He had so much to give to the world, he had survived so much, only to have this torment come upon him.

At least they could afford to pay the doctor now, and each time he came he would say that Richard should go hospital, but always he refused.

'There's nothing can be done,' Richard pointed out, 'so why not stay at home?'

Jennie had mixed feelings. She either had to keep the children away or see them suffer at the sight of Richard's deteriorating condition. She hoped desperately that Richard would never realize what he was putting them through, as he could not think clearly for himself as the days passed. All he thought of was the Applemere Flyer, her and illustrations for Mary's book.

'The train, Jennie,' he would murmur. 'The magic train to the past. And the future, the future too . . .'

Then he'd fall silent, and she'd put his pad into his hands so that he could draw. And he did. He drew constantly, producing brilliant sketches for Mary's stories. He drew not just for the two she had so far written but for other ideas that he had himself, of a mystical magical land that lay somewhere only Richard could enter.

'Over the hills and far away . . .' he murmured when she asked him where his dreams were taking him.

One day when he was feeling better he decided to go for a walk round the grounds of Goreham Court. 'To get strong again,' he said wryly, 'so that I can have my last trip on the Flyer.'

She watched him go, and the house felt empty, for the twins were at school. 'It will be like this when he has gone,' she told herself, trying to accustom herself to the chill of emptiness, to make the nightmare more real. No, she decided, she would go into the garden where she would not have these walls closing in on her. She had only just left the house when she heard voices, and a car draw up. Then came a ring on the bell. She ran back to open the door, expecting it to be the milkman coming to collect his money. But it wasn't. There on the doorstep were Anna *and* Tom.

She was speechless, staring at them as if they were apparitions from another age. They looked just the same was her first thought. How could they?

'Darling,' Anna said warmly, stepping inside uninvited with Tom following her. Tom hugged her, as he casually asked: 'How are you, sis?'

Any thoughts Jennie might have had that they had returned to say it was all over and that it hadn't worked, were quickly doomed to disappointment. Freddie had been right: Anna was back, but obviously not to return to him. Tom's cheerful face looked as self-possessed as ever, and Anna was blooming. She had put on a little weight, and although it didn't fit her usual waif-like image, it certainly suited her – or was it the effect of the elegant short-sleeved skirt and top she wore, with the flared skirt actually covering her knees?

Thank heavens Richard is out, was Jennie's next thought, standing aside as they passed by her. Anna looked incredibly fashionable, and she must have noticed Jennie's admiring look for she said airily, 'Coco Chanel, darling. Heard of her?'

Jennie nodded, even though she hadn't. She wasn't going to be patronized as a country bumpkin by Anna. Tom was clad not in country wear but in a splendidly cut suit.

At the thought of poor Freddie's anguish, her anger rose. Be blowed if she'd offer them coffee and biscuits. She'd wait until she knew what they had come for.

'Are you here for long?' she asked formally as she showed them into the drawing-room, just as though this were merely a family visit by her elder brother and her best friend. If only that was the case!

'Oh.' Anna mimicked Jennie's careful voice, 'I don't know. For ever perhaps.' She and Tom broke into giggles, which annoyed Jennie even further.

'Whatever are you doing here?' she demanded. 'You can't just come walking back as though nothing had happened. I take it this is just a flying visit?' Please, please, say yes, she silently pleaded. She couldn't cope with Anna here, not now.

'No,' Anna replied sweetly. 'We really are planning to stay. Why not?'

Why not? Jennie was appalled. 'You can't.'

'I see no reason not to.' Anna sounded cool.

'You hurt a lot of people,' Jennie flashed back. 'They're still reeling from it. You can't inflict more hurt, as you would by your presence here.'

'No one cared much about our hurt, I notice,' Anna hit back.

'She's right, Jen,' Tom chipped in.

'There happens to be a difference,' Jennie retorted. 'You're married not to each other but other people. Don't they have a right to be considered?'

Anna shrugged. 'Let them work it out. We're happy as we are, aren't we, Tom?'

Jennie felt sick. Trouble was on its way, or rather it had just arrived. Then an even worse thought struck her. 'By coming back, you don't mean into this area?'

'Yes, of course. I told you you wouldn't be losing us. Not Fairsted, or Ashford, or Canterbury however. So society won't be too disgusted at our presence.'

'You don't think the news might leak out?' Jennie retorted furiously.

'Of course it will, but we won't go out of our way to flaunt ourselves.'

'Where do you plan to live?'

'Here,' Tom told her blithely.

For one terrible moment Jennie thought they intended to move into the Dower House with her and Richard, but Anna quickly dispelled this particular nightmare. 'I've bought Goreham Court from Anthony Hart. It will suit us very well, and you and Richard will be our tenants. Won't that be nice?'

It seemed to Jennie that never, ever would she be free of Anna's schemes. She despaired. To have her so close, and Tom too – it was too much.

'We can have jolly times like we used to,' Anna continued, apparently highly amused.

Misery flooded over Jennie. 'Richard's dying,' she blurted out.

Anna stood very still, and for a moment Jennie glimpsed the friend she used to have. She watched Anna swallow, then move towards her. Anna hugged her, just as she used to when they were young. 'How long, Jennie?' she whispered.

'Days, weeks, I don't know.' All her resolve left her. This was one complication she didn't need, and she broke into racking sobs. Not even during the war had she collapsed so utterly.

Tom went to get some tea, while Anna talked to her. All Jennie took in was, 'We'll help you, Jennie. Would warmth help? We could take Richard to the south of France and you too. You'd like it.'

'Too late,' Jennie said. Anna meant well, but how could she appreciate the reality? Richard could hardly get up in the mornings, let alone travel. And other help? What could Anna, what could anybody do? Somewhere she found the strength to say, 'You can't do it, Anna. You mustn't move back here.'

'Why not?' Anna asked, sounding surprised, rather than defensive. 'We like it here, and I can be with you again.'

Be with her? It was a temptation to roll away the years, but could the past come back? And even if it did, that didn't take away the problems for others, or for Anna. Her reply came out of nowhere, 'You'll be hurt, Anna.'

Again she saw that unguarded look. 'Me?' she answered ironically. 'Not Freddie, not my parents, not Mary. *Me*?'

'Yes.' Jennie began to see more clearly. 'All of you.' Nothing was black and white, things seldom were in life. Now she thought she understood Anna's point of view. Anna always hoped that things could turn out right for her if only she were bold enough, and that the hurt she had suffered as a child could be put right by action on her part to strike back.

To move back here, however, where not only those who had been hurt by her behaviour would ostracize her, but the whole of society, was one step too far. Couldn't Anna see that? She and Tom weren't married, they were living together as man and wife, and there was no acceptance of that even in London let alone in rural Kent. Clearly Tom was so besotted he couldn't see further than Anna, but Anna's eyes were fully open. If they went elsewhere they could pretend they were married, which in society's eyes, would be acceptable. Here it would be impossible for them to be happy. It occurred to

Jennie that Anna always did gallop after the impossible, and often she got it – but at what price? Freddie, what about poor Freddie?

Anna grimaced. 'Thank you, Jennie.' She was about to add something else but the doorbell rang. Tom sang out that he'd answer it, and Jennie was so preoccupied with the problem of Anna that she did not even wonder who it was. Tom would deal with it. This time, however, he could not. Despite her throbbing head, she could hear a familiar voice although she could not remember whose; then Tom was talking.

Anna's mother, Lady Fokingham, came into the room. For a moment, Jennie realized with horror, she would have been the only person Lady Fokingham could see, since Tom was behind her and her daughter hidden from her view by the door.

'I'm sorry to arrive unannounced,' she began, 'but I have heard a terrible rumour that Anna—'

'Yes, Mama?' Anna appeared to confront her mother, eyes glittering. 'I imagine you have heard,' she said coolly, 'that I'm moving to Goreham Court. Rumour is correct, as in my experience it usually is. Tom and I have bought the estate.'

Lady Fokingham's face drained of colour. 'To live in?' she whispered.

'That is usual with houses.'

'Together?'

'That too is usual. I suppose Tom could sleep in the stables. I'll ask him – Tom!' Anna called, and he strolled in from the hallway looking as though nothing were amiss, though he could scarcely have failed to hear Lady Fokingham's words.

Jennie watched impotently as Lady Fokingham realized who Tom was. In other circumstances Jennie would have laughed at the expression on her face. Although Tom had ushered her into the house, Lady Fokingham had probably never met him, and even if she had seen him before, she clearly had not recognized him in his smart Paris suit.

Now, despite her earlier view that Anna was at least partly responsible for the situation, she was looking at Tom as if he were a monster, the seducer of her innocent daughter. 'You can't do this to me,' she half choked, as she turned back to Anna.

Oh, those last two words. How could Lady Fokingham have

been so stupid? Jennie froze, as she saw Anna's eyes blaze into life. She could foresee only too clearly what would happen now. And it did.

'To *you*?' Anna threw at her mother in her calmest sweetest voice, which was when she was at her most dangerous. 'Is your welfare of any relevance to me?'

'You're my daughter, alas, and a Fokingham. It is relevant to us, and you know it, Anna.' Lady Fokingham retorted. She had changed from the reasonable woman Jennie had known to the implacable guardian of her upbringing. For a moment Jennie saw what Anna had been up again in her youth. 'Have you no self-respect?'

'I do, Mama. My self-respect is intact, not that you have ever had any interest in that. Only in Fokingham self-respect.'

Lady Fokingham lost her temper. 'They are the same thing, you stupid girl. Can't you see that you're condemning yourself to a life of misery? As if it isn't hard enough that you marry a train driver and reduce yourself to writing trashy novels to pass the time – trading, of course, off the position which your father and I gave you.'

'Don't talk to her like that,' Tom roared, before Anna could answer. 'If people just let us alone we'll be quite happy, thank you.' Jennie was half appalled, half impressed at Tom's defence. He was usually all too apt to pretend he was invisible when fur was flying in family arguments.

'It's you, my man,' Lady Fokingham turned on him with contempt in her voice, 'who have ensured that people *never* will let you alone. From the moment you took a fancy to our name and fortune and pursued Anna—'

'Oh, Mama, he didn't,' Anna laughed. Actually *laughed*. How could she, Jennie agonized, seeing no way of stopping this free-for-all? 'I chased darling Tom. I pursued *him*, I placed myself naked in his bed where he could hardly fail to fuck—'

'Anna!'

The last taboo had been broken and Lady Fokingham blazed. 'Convention, my girl, is stronger than you. You'll drag yourself as well as this fellow to the gutter in your enthusiasm to ruin us.'

'I doubt it. Without any explicit reference to Applemere House or the dignity of the Fokingham name, I can now write wonderful novels on the life of the British aristocracy as it really is.'

'That filth hardly qualifies as either wonderful or as novels.'

'They were just my apprenticeship in writing. Dear Mama, you wait until you see what comes next.'

'I will have you hounded out of here.'

'This is my house.' Jennie had to make some sort of stand, not knowing how much more of this Tom, let alone Anna, could take, but she had to shout to make herself heard. Anna seemed in fact to be livening up for the battle but Tom was very white. He looked as he had when he was about ten and his favourite pet mouse was taken away from him. 'And, Lady Fokingham, no more references to "my man". You and Anna will never agree about the past—'

'No,' Lady Fokingham interrupted. 'There I agree with you, Jennie. This all stems back to those babies, doesn't it, Anna? When will you realize Anna, that we acted in your own best interests?'

Appalled, and before she could act, Jennie saw Anna launch herself to attack her mother physically; she flew to intervene, but Tom was first, catching her in his arms. Anna could only hurl a vicious:

'Really? How sweet of you to think of me, Mama. I only wish you'd given Michael and me away at birth too. We might have grown up reasonably well.'

Her mother did not reply. Jennie thought she was going to cry, but the Lady Fokinghams of this world never cried in public. She simply departed, casting a scornful look at Tom on the way. 'Goodbye, Mr Trent. I wish I could say it was a pleasure to meet you.'

'Phew!' Anna slumped down on the sofa, trying to smile. In fact, Jennie noticed, she was shaking. 'You'd better hurry up with that tea, Tom. And if there's any whisky around put a slug in, will you? After all,' she added disarmingly to Jennie, 'this is almost *my* house. We are your new landlords now.'

Jennie did her best to reply in the same vein. 'Please don't tell me Queen Zita might want to live here.'

'I won't,' Anna assured her. 'Though I suppose it might be possible that Eileen and Georgius might want it.' She giggled as she saw Jennie's expression. 'Joke of course. Poor old Uncle Georgius has had to leave half his blessed automata behind in Montevanya, and start again now that Viktor's more or less in charge of the country. General Deleanu indeed. Poor old grandfather would turn in his grave, if it wasn't for the fact that Viktor's dancing on it.'

'Are Eileen and Georgius really coming to England?' Jennie asked hopefully. If so, it was the best news she had heard for a very long time.

'Yes. They're in Paris at present, but Georgius is convinced that London in the place for him. He wants to join the Magic Circle and has some crazy idea of earning his living as an illusionist like Jasper Maskelyne. I ask you. Is it likely that any of that lot would have a clue about earning a living?'

'You did,' Jennie pointed out tartly.

'True,' Anna said smugly. 'Anyway, I'm sure Eileen isn't averse to living here half the year. She can still go off on her treks.' She paused. 'Something's just struck me as odd about Mama's little outburst. You too, Jennie?'

As always, Jennie followed her thoughts and unwillingly grinned at her. 'Yes. Your mother prophesies doom for you and Tom if you live here unwedded, but happily condones her brother living in unmarried bliss with your aunt. Except of course,' she added wryly, 'she makes her sit several places down the table at formal dinner parties.'

Anna laughed. 'Hear that, Tom?' she called to him as he appeared with a tray. 'You'll be sitting under the table, let alone beneath the salt, if ever we dine in style at Fokingham House.'

Tom shrugged. 'No surprise. Since I'm a peasant to your parents, why don't I make you eat in the kitchen, waiting on me hand and foot?'

'Darling,' Anna said earnestly, 'I'd *love* to be your slave. Shall we try it tonight?' flashing him a look that left Jennie in no doubt of the sexual pull between them.

Richard took the news about Anna and Tom surprisingly equably; indeed he welcomed it, perhaps because it would be some sort of support for Jennie. Here at Bossingham they were sheltered from the gossip that she knew was already flying round Fairsted village. It was inevitable, she supposed. Mrs Grant had a nimble tongue, and perhaps a gardener might be married to the sister of the Fairsted baker's niece – and, hey presto, the story was out.

Aunt Win had reported to her in grim satisfaction. 'Your father will never lift his head again.'

In fact Dad took it amazingly well, only concerned for Mary and the fact that they saw little enough of Alfred and Arabella, and would undoubtedly now see less. Jennie had insisted Tom should tell Mary himself, not leave her to find out from others, but she rued the day she did so, since Mary promptly arrived the next day demanding to see Anna. Not, it appeared, because she wanted Tom to return, merely to tell her what she thought of her, and assure her that thanks to her Tom would never see his children again.

Jennie bowed out of the ensuing uproar; she could not cope. She must think of Richard, who, even to her eye, was deteriorating and had at last bowed to his doctor's wishes. He went into the Kent and Canterbury hospital, where they could administer more relief than was possible at home. Jennie's heart broke as she saw Richard's last sad look at his den. That marked the end for her more vividly than anything else, especially when he made an effort to talk about new illustrations for Mary's book. Somehow the image of that magic train must be helping him, she realized, for it was on his mind constantly, every time she visited him in the hospital, and especially the last time she saw him. Through the window she looked down on the cloisters of St Augustine's College, willing some of that peaceful scene to make her calm and strong for Richard.

'We're taking a magic train together; that's all it is, isn't it, Jennie? We're just seeing what comes at the next station: I'm just going one station further than you. I think it's brighter . . .' His hand sought desperately for hers, and she clasped it between both of hers.

'I'm travelling with you, darling. Always. I'm coming with you.' Perhaps her prayer had worked for her voice sounded calm and confident, despite the surging waves of emotion within her.

'I don't want to leave yet. So much more to do.'

'I'll do it for you.' She fought back tears; she must remain reassuring. Convince him she could see what was in his vision.

'You know what to do?' he whispered.

'Tell me again, Richard . . . To make things better for people?' she added when she could see he was struggling to frame words.

110

'More. I want . . .' He stopped and tried again. 'I want it *never* to happen again.'

'War?'

'No – yes, but more. There'll always people like the Fokinghams, and there'll always be labourers. We can't all be the same, because it wouldn't work. But there's no reason we can't all meet on equal terms without Fokinghams feeling superior to farmers, farmers to labourers, labourers to tinkers. Do you think that's what Anna wants?'

The change was so abrupt she couldn't follow him. Beyond her freedom Jennie wasn't sure what Anna *did* want, apart from Tom.

'Perhaps,' she replied guardedly.

'That's what I want,' he said with a trace of his old animation. 'That's what Lynette and Jamie must want. It's what the Applemere Flyer is for, isn't it? Lady Fokingham reads Edgar Wallace. Billy Overton's son reads Ovid and Edmund Spenser. Books . . .'

She leaned over and kissed his blue Cornish eyes as they began to close. They saw a truth that she did not, but one day, she vowed, she would. The Flyer was only a beginning, but surely it was heading in the right direction? Somewhere at journey's end, Richard's dream might come true, and she could play her part in it.

Eight

1930

'It's the slump, Mrs P,' Albert said. 'Trade will pick up now the summer's coming.'

Would it? Albert's voice sounded cheerful enough, but his eyes told a different story. They weren't looking straight at her for one thing. Jennie had experienced slumps before; there had been one not long after Pencarek Books started in 1920. This slump was more insidious, however, and unemployment was growing. If people could not afford bread, they could not afford books, however much they might welcome the escape that they could bring. It was as usual the very poor who were hardest hit. Those with slightly more money were still buying books, but what if the slump grew worse? She wouldn't even have the dole to live on, since she was not employed. At least Albert would have that pittance.

The slump had begun last autumn with the crash of the New York stock exchange, and from what she heard on the wireless and in the newspapers the situation in America was much worse than here. But fear had quickly spread, not only amongst those who controlled the share prices but throughout the general population too. Superficially the grasshoppers danced on. Musicals, films, theatre, dancing and fashion were all thriving, and if the occasional grasshoppers slipped quietly out of circulation, they were either not noticed or ignored.

I'm being too pessimistic, Jennie kept telling herself. It was hardly surprising, since sales were certainly slipping. She hoped it was the slump in a way, because otherwise she would have to acknowledge that it might be that Mrs P. was no substitute for Mr Pencarek. And that meant she would have failed Richard, with no hope of even contributing towards his dream, however hard she struggled. And she would, she *would*.

112

As for Albert's confident hope that summer would improve matters, she had no such faith. It had been a year since Richard had died. A year that had passed in a blur of struggling to divide herself into three parts: the first was determined that she should do everything she could to keep life the same for Lynette and Jamie. They had been very subdued after their father's death, and she owed much to Tom for stepping nobly into the breach and becoming a substitute father. It helped that 'Uncle Tom' was so different from Richard and Jamie had responded very quickly. Lynette was slower, but had then followed suit. The second Jennie tried to wear a cheerful face on the Applemere Flyer and at the Station House; but the third wept silently into her pillow every night, reaching out in vain to the empty space.

'You're right,' she answered Albert. 'This is sometimes a dead season for sales.' It wasn't true and Albert knew it of course. Generally sales were good in January, decreased in bleak February and March, and then began to pick up quickly. At least Anna's new book, *Burning Bridges*, was coming out next week.

'How do you think it will go?' she asked Albert. Jennie knew she was too biased where Anna was concerned to be able to judge her books objectively.

Albert had obviously decided on truth. 'I don't know, Mrs P. It's different, isn't it?'

It certainly was. Anna had promised her parents a shock, and she had given it to them, as Jennie saw when their subscription order arrived three days ago. Unfortunately she had given her publishers and the booksellers a shock too, including Jennie, to whom she had said nothing more about the novel's contents. Anna and Tom had done as Anna had assured her they would; they kept themselves much to themselves, and they disappeared frequently on long or short visits. When they were at Goreham Court, however, Tom was generous in the time he gave to the twins. Occasionally he would disappear to Canterbury to see his own children, but they never came to Goreham Court or to the Station House, and Dad and Aunt Win missed them greatly.

Anna's new novel was a comic and satirical attack on the world of her parents – and to Jennie's amazement, on the bright young things of Mayfair too. Her style and approach

113

were completely different to the passion of her earlier novels. A devastating wit had replaced rebellion and might prove even more destructive than the onslaught on convention that had produced Anna's earlier plots.

The 'Dishonourable Miss Sheringham' had turned into Margaret Rackham, a former suffragette, who looked with disillusioned but comic eye on the world of today; accepted everywhere, she was not part of the social scene, but a visitor casting a disillusioned and ironic eye on it. Eccentric characters and outrageous caricatures leapt joyously through Anna's pages, which included an obvious reconstruction of life at Applemere and at Fokingham House in Kensington. Her parents, to anyone who knew them, were clearly recognizable, and so, Jennie was painfully aware, was she. In this novel, Jennie had the role of Margaret's best friend, Polly Brent, who was at least not too much of a caricature, but served as a stooge to those who were. Nor did Polly appear to have a brain in her head. Thanks, Anna, Jennie had thought wryly, but there were more important issues for her to contend with than analyzing yet again her friendship with Anna. It is, so let it be, should be her attitude.

It remained to be seen what the Flyer's customers would think of *Burning Bridges*. Jennie knew she would have to warn them it wasn't like its predecessors, but guessed they would probably buy it all the same. The question was: if Anna continued in this vein, would they buy the next one? She firmly subdued her instinctive thought that if only Richard were here, he would in his magic way *know* the answer to this.

But he wasn't here. Only his guidance, and her passionate wish to fulfil what he wanted kept her going.

'I've completed the figures ready for the tax return, Dad.' Jennie and Albert had brought the records over to the Station House. Aunt Win and Albert were playing Ludo with the twins in the parlour while she and Dad pored over the books on the dining room table in order to confirm the figures. Albert had tactfully withdrawn, even though he had done most of the work.

'How much do you think you've made, Jen?' Dad's brow was furrowed as he tried to pretend he was a master of tax affairs. Poor Dad, he had enough to cope with, with his own records for the Southern Railway, the renamed South Eastern and Chatham. Nevertheless he was determined to help her.

'Last year we made five hundred and ten pounds in profit. Albert and I think we've made three hundred and eighty-four this year.'

'How much tax did you pay last year?'

Jennie produced Richard's carefully kept books. This had been one of the last jobs he was able to do, and she could still hardly bear to see his handwriting. 'He paid three pounds five shillings and sixpence.'

Oh Jen, guess what, she remembered his saying. *We've actually earned enough to pay some income tax. Isn't that wonderful?* They'd had a quick dance round the room together to celebrate this magnificent event.

'Reckon you won't be paying any this year. You've two children, that helps. Mind you, there's the rent. That must be costing you a packet.'

Time and time again Anna had insisted she paid no rent, but Jennie would not have it. It was one thing to accept charity from Lady Fokingham, from Anna she just would not do so.

'It's a hard thing, Jen, being on your own. I've glad I've got Win,' Dad continued. 'Mind you, the way things are going . . .' He nodded his head significantly towards the parlour.

'What?' Jennie said incredulously, as she realized what Dad was implying. 'You're imagining things, Dad. Albert and Aunt Win? They're—'

'Too old?'

Jennie felt ashamed. That's just what she had meant, but she was old enough to know better. 'They're so set in their ways.'

Dad sighed. 'Suppose I'm right? Don't want to be left on my own.'

She knew what he was thinking. Left to himself, Dad would go on working for ever, but would the Southern Railway let him? She doubted it. Even the Elham Valley line, let alone its Fairsted loop, was a minor line again now that the Dover to Folkestone trains had a new link. The most direct line between the two ports was still closed because of a landslip during the war, and then trains had been diverted through Fairsted. That was no longer the case, and, worse, next year the line would be converted to single track only. Passenger numbers were down.

'It's those darned motor buses,' Dad would grumble, and Jennie felt as guilty as if she were running a passenger service herself. The days of steam for her were coming to an end, so Freddie had warned her, and she should look out for a decent old motor bus to replace the Applemere Flyer. It would be a wrench, and she was determined not to give up on steam before she had to. Albert loyally supported her, though she knew he hankered after the easier life that petrol might produce.

'You won't be on your own, Dad,' she said gently to allay his fears. 'No more than I will. We'll be together, whatever happens.'

'You're a good girl, Jen,' he said gruffly. No more was said. Nevertheless his chest was fully puffed out as he marched into the parlour after Jennie. 'We've done now,' he informed them. 'The work's over.'

Jennie looked at Albert and Win with new eyes. Seeing them bending over the Ludo, shaking the dice, she was forced to see Dad's point. They could have been married for years. After all, Aunt Win was getting on for sixty, and Albert must be about sixty already. She began to worry all over again about Dad, until she saw the way they were looking at him. No exclusion there.

'Come and sit down, George,' Aunt Win said. 'This gentleman is winning far too often.'

Jennie smiled. Aunt Win's eyes were sparkling, as once they must have shone for her lover killed at Omdurman. And here he was again, if Dad was right, in the guise of Albert Hodge.

She was surprised she had not noticed this harmony at Christmas, when on impulse she had suggested to Dad and Win that Albert join them. Aunt Win had been all in favour of the idea, and so Albert had come. He had proved the strength of the gathering, for Jennie was worn out with struggling to make Christmas 'the same' for Lynette and Jamie, and at the same time refrain from thinking about her Christmases with Richard. The year he'd dressed up as Santa Claus and suddenly marched in through the back door, crying Ho, Ho, Ho. The year he'd made crackers at home out of crepe paper and asked them all to shout Bang! She had to stop remembering, she told herself. The future was the more important now. She must build new memories for the twins.

Anna and Tom had not been invited for Christmas at the Station House, but Jennie doubted whether Anna, at least, had even noticed the lack of an invitation. Freddie had come on Christmas Day, but had hardly spoken to Jennie to her great distress. Did he think she was somehow responsible for Anna's being back in Kent, just because she lived in the Dower House? Did he think she was betraying him just as much as Anna had? She was so upset she decided to have it out with him later in the day.

'I understand you don't want to come to visit me at the Dower House,' she stormed, 'but this is Fairsted and the Station House. Why are you glowering at me here?'

He replied quickly enough. 'I don't want you reporting to her ladyship Anna how poor old Freddie is.'

'It doesn't occur to you I just want to talk to my brother and let Lynette and Jamie meet their uncle once in a while?'

'They've got an uncle, Jennie. He's called Tom.' Freddie's eyes met hers, but they looked less defiant.

'Yes, they have. But they're not part of your dispute, Freddie, so don't drag them into it. They can do with another uncle too – especially one that drives train engines.' This was true. Every lad in Fairsted wanted to do that when he grew up.

Freddie flushed. 'I'm not much good with children.'

'You've never tried.' She paused, deciding to risk going further. At least he was talking. 'Are you waiting for her to come back?' she asked gently.

He shrugged. 'I'm not waiting for anything. I'm just getting on with life.'

'You've shut off steam, Freddie. You won't get anywhere without it.'

He had the grace to laugh. 'I have my job and there's a grand life at Ashford. I'm out most evenings doing something with the lads at the social club.'

'You should—' Jennie broke off. She had no right to speak and perhaps it was too soon. How could she say to him that he should forget about Anna? Perhaps she was wrong, perhaps one day Anna would return to him. The 'old slippers' might still have attraction.

Pigs might fly, she thought later that night. Anna would never fly in accordance with anyone's dreams. She was a particularly obstinate pig.

Burning Bridges earned Anna admiring reviews – save in Fairsted. There, as Jennie had predicted, the sales were initially good, but then word must have gone round, for sales almost dried up, and she and Albert looked aghast at the pile of unsold copies. 'Good reviews—' Albert began ponderously.

'Don't always sell books,' Jennie finished for him 'Who in Fairsted reads the *Literary Review*?'

Answer: not many. Anna never asked her how the book was selling, to Jennie's relief, but she was over the moon with the reviews in the national press. Tom seemed less happy. He seemed to be enjoying his role as a sort of estate manager, though Goreham Court was hardly in the great houses of England class. It owned two farms, and six cottages, but Tom seemed happy enough, and he was doing Anna's administrative work too, which was considerable.

Burning Bridges had had one more startling effect. According to Dad, since Anna's return the Fokinghams had spent less and less time at Applemere House, and in early June Aunt Win reported that they seemed to be moving out for good, judging by the furniture leaving by Pickfords. Michael was taking the house over, and the railway van had picked up his furniture at Fairsted station to take to Applemere.

Anna was highly gratified to hear the news. 'I say,' she said. 'What a success for me. Notorious daughter triumphs.'

'It's a big house just for Michael to live in,' Jennie pointed out, puzzled. She wasn't surprised at the Fokinghams' departure for she knew that the gossip in Fairsted was considerable, and not always disapproving of Anna and Tom.

'I doubt if he'll move in alone.'

'He's marrying?' Jennie thought this highly unlikely, given Michael's sexual interests.

Anna laughed. 'Hardly. I expect Anthony Hart will move in with him.'

Jennie blinked as her head spun with conflicting thoughts. 'But he's only recently sold you Goreham Court. I thought he wanted to leave the district.'

'Darling,' Anna said gently. 'Do think. Anthony is Michael's friend. He has been for years.'

'I thought he was *your* friend?'

'No, dear. Anthony's not that way. Michael asked me to make it look as though we were together, that's all. It made it easier for them. So having established publicly that Anthony is *all right* by his apparent pursuit of me they can now share a house without fear of discovery by our saintly Foreign Office. Or our even more saintly parents.'

What would Fairsted make of *this*? Jennie wondered. She guessed the answer was nothing. It would never occur to Dad or Aunt Win or anyone in Fairsted that there was anything unusual in two friends living together. Jennie was truly glad for Michael's sake, for he too had suffered in the past. Considering the pressure there had been on Anna to get married, Jennie could only imagine how much worse it had been for Michael, who would have been told his role in life was to ensure the Fokingham name continued.

'Apparently,' Anna continued, 'Mama is telling everyone that they're living together until Michael finds himself a wife. She believes it, too. As he's thirty-seven, society no doubt thinks it high time he does marry.' Anna thought for a moment. 'In fact, I might write a novel—'

'No,' howled Jennie.

Anna smiled. 'Don't worry, it won't be about Michael. Or Anthony. I do need *some* friends,' she added casually. 'It's wonderful living here in isolation, now that neither Kent nor London speaks to me. Only my publisher does that, and even he's pretty guarded about what he says. He's mollified by the good reviews for *Burning Bridges*, but rather cross with me, all the same. Now look, Jennie,' Anna changed to a brisker tone, 'I want you to do me a favour.'

Jennie regarded her suspiciously. 'What is it?' Anna's favours tended to involve hard work.

'I want you to come to the Riviera with me.'

Suddenly Jennie was eighteen again, and envious of Anna's glamorous life – as she had thought of it then. *Jennie, I want you to come to Montevanya with me.* She wasn't eighteen any more, however, and she was more cautious.

'Are you telling me I need a holiday?' she asked.

'Yes, but more than that. I really need someone to go with. I have to go because of my next novel – I've had such a good idea. You'll love Cannes, not to mention Monte, we can go to the casino, all sorts of jolly things. There's a new summer casino opened in Cannes and now all those stuffy old Grand Dukes and Princes have vanished, all sorts of interesting people are going. You might even meet Douglas Fairbanks or Charlie Chaplin. The old winter season is dying out, and the hotels are opening for a new summer season on the Riviera. Who knows, even Herr Hitler might be there?'

'I doubt it,' Jennie said drily. 'It doesn't sound his sort of thing.'

Herr Hitler was head of the National Socialist party in Germany, whose followers were known as the Nazis; it was having more and more success in the German parliament. Eileen, who had paid a flying visit from Paris at Easter, clearly thought that this Hitler was a force to be reckoned with, though it remained to be seen whether it was one for good or evil. Eileen was inclined to the latter.

'Why can't Tom go with you?' Jennie asked Anna.

'He doesn't want to.'

'Why not?'

Anna shrugged. 'Not his thing. He says he feels out of place. He's happier alone with me here.'

This surprised Jennie, since the Tom she knew was not only highly sociable, but eager to mix in 'the best circles' as Aunt Win called them. 'I can't come, Anna,' Jennie said regretfully. 'There's Lynette and Jamie to consider.'

'Solved already. Tom wants to take them to north Cornwall.'

Events seemed to be going much too fast for her. 'Anna, please explain.'

She obliged. 'Tom always wanted to take Alfred and Arabella there. He and Mary were going to go, but then I came along, so it was – er – postponed. Mary won't let him take them now, so he wants to take the twins. Just think, Jamie would see the Brunel bridge over the Tamar.'

'I'll talk to them,' Jennie said dubiously, 'but I'm not sure about it.'

'So you *do* want to come with me.'

Jennie was taken by surprise. She'd given herself away. 'There's the Applemere Flyer to consider too.' The idea was beginning to grow on her however. 'I can't leave Albert to run it alone.'

'Suspend operations for two weeks.'

'One can't do that with a business.'

'Very well. Leave the problem to me.'

Jennie thought she'd heard the end of it, until Anna came strolling over to the Dower House one morning. 'Everything's solved,' she announced. 'We can go.'

'Where?' Jennie had forgotten all about it.

'Cannes of course. We're booked to sail on July thirtieth. You can start packing, and include a dress for your birthday.'

'But the Applemere Flyer,' Jennie cried, her mind still on essentials.

'Eileen is coming over from Paris. Georgius wants to take a look at Psycho, Maskelyne's famous card-playing automaton, so he can try to work out what made him tick. Eileen will look after the old bus for you.'

Jennie wavered. It was true Eileen was the one person in whose hands she felt the Flyer would be safe, but still she had to get the twins' approval. And of course Albert's. He proved no problem. 'You go, Mrs P.'

Lynette and Jamie were worried at the idea of her going to France without them but on mention of Cornwall all this was forgotten. Uncle Tom was the most marvellous person in the world. Cornwall was where Daddy had come from, where wonderful trains ran, and where King Arthur had lived. What greater excitement could there be?

The Carlton was a palace to rival the Várcasá in Montevanya, Jennie decided. Lynette would no doubt prefer Tintagel, with its ruined walls and glorious setting, but here was luxury and unostentatious comfort with its marble pillars and rose-pink carpets. How wonderful not only to have one's slightest need attended to, but so many needs she didn't realize she had. The need for someone to escort her up and down in the lift, for example, for someone to turn down her bedcover, for someone to place a rose in her room each day. Even in the Várcasá that didn't happen. Here she was a guest, and even if her clothes were hardly designed by Elsa Schiaparelli, she was treated as though they were. She had assumed in her innocence that she'd be sharing a room with Anna, but instead they were in adjoining rooms.

'Much better, darling,' Anna pointed out. 'I can stay up and drink or dance all night.'

Drink and dance? Was that part of Anna's 'research' for her new novel? Jennie decided not to enquire further. She was here to enjoy herself and pretend that she was in the Várcasá again.

Descending the sweeping grand staircase, her hand graciously poised on the stair-rail, it was easy to pretend she was not Jennie Pencarek but a duchess or film star. She felt ready to rule the world, just as long ago she had vowed to do. Was her enjoyment of this luxury betraying Richard, she wondered? No, he was here with her in the blue sea that lapped the golden shore before the hotel; he was in the glorious sunset each night as the sun slipped behind the mountains; he walked with her along the leafy Croisette, sunbathed on the beach, and applauded when the great Suzanne Lenglen played tennis on the hotel courts; he was both in the splendour of the restaurants and at the rear doors which the workers used.

The Carlton was in the middle of the bay, a magnet for those approaching by boat with its white walls, balconies and twin turrets. These fascinated Jennie, and at first she hadn't believed Anna when she told her that they were modelled on the breasts of a famous turn-of-the-century courtesan, La Belle Otero.

'I wish mine were that shape,' she said wistfully.

'They can be now,' Anna pointed out. 'Breasts are back in fashion.' To the left was the hillside of La Californie with its splendid mansions of last century, where the Grand Duke Michael had lived, and Prince Leopold, Queen Victoria's son, had died after a fall at the famous Cercle Nautique club. In the other direction lay the winter casino and to the port, and on one magic day they had taken a boat trip to the nearby island of Ste Marguerite, and the old fortress where the Man in the Iron Mask had been imprisoned.

'I know just how he felt,' Anna said. 'Looks like Applemere House to me.'

Jennie dutifully laughed, but how could this dour place be compared with the magic of Applemere, for all the beauty of the island around it?

On the day before Anna had said she had some research to do and hired a car, and Jennie had set off on her own to the hillside of Mont Chevalier behind the port where the old fishermen's quarters lay. She had lost her way coming down the hillside from the old church at the top, and found herself at the back of the town, where there was a very different Cannes to that of the Croisette. Washing hung from windows, small shops and restaurants vied with each other, houses and flats crowded together, housing those who supported the rich. The seafront was rather like Mayfair, but this, Jennie had decided, was London's East End.

As she had emerged on to the Croisette again, Richard had been saying earnestly to her: 'It's the same everywhere. The two don't touch each other, even though they depend on each other.'

I'll make them do so one day, Richard. I am trying. I am.

On her birthday they dined in splendour in the larger of the two hotel restaurants. Jennie had brought her faithful old evening dress with her, but Anna had taken one look and insisted she wore one of hers.

Jennie was suddenly aware that Anna had lain down her menu, and was talking to her. '. . . the motor car, darling. We can go out up into the hills when you want a change from the beach.'

If ever she did, Jennie thought. It was wonderful lying there in beach pyjamas, or in Anna's case a daring two-piece swimming costume, feeling the sun soaking into her. For years Aunt Win had made her 'cover up' if ever she went into the sun, and yet here she was just soaking it up like a sponge – even if it did make her rather red afterwards.

'Look, there's an old chum of ours.' Anna indicated a table some way away where a beautifully gowned woman was dining with a man. Gowned was hardly the word, since the cream-coloured dress was very low cut. On her head was a sparkling tiara, and her face seemed slightly familiar.

'Schiaparelli,' Anna commented looking at the gown.

'Who is she?' Jennie frowned. 'Are you sure I know her?'

'You know *of* her. She's ex-Queen or as she would have it *Queen* Marta of Montevanya. Max's wife.'

'Of course.' Jennie remembered the pictures of the coronation, with the stern-looking Max, and a photograph of Marta in London with Queen Zita. 'So is Max here?' she enquired eagerly. Queen Marta's companion was a stranger to her. A pompous looking one too.

'Dear Jennie. As if any woman of fashion, let alone an

123

ex-queen, could be seen dining with her husband. Especially Marta.'

'Do you know her well?' Jennie was curious, remembering how good Max had been to her over the cottage.

'Unfortunately yes. I used to meet her at royal gatherings in Montevanya when I was young. She was some sort of relative on my grandfather's side of the family. I disliked her intensely.'

'But Max must love her?' she probed.

'Haven't you learned yet? Did love come into anything when my parents were so eagerly searching for a bridegroom for me?'

Jennie had a curious mixture of sadness for him if he did not love his wife and an odd hope that he did not love this ice-queen of his. 'No,' she answered, 'but it might have come about by chance.'

Anna shrugged. 'It makes no difference to Marta. She liked being a queen, she doesn't like being an ex-queen. Not many of them do, of course. She and Zita are therefore naturally great chums; they hold court in London, I gather, as though they still on the throne. They do hobnob with my mother, of course, but naturally not with Eileen – though she's too sensible to go near them. Nor is Georgius considered up to their standards, since he gives public performances for *money*.'

'How do they avoid Eileen since she and Georgius are so friendly with Max?'

'I gather Marta entertains. Max doesn't.'

'Poor Max.' Jennie fell silent. 'What a terrible life for him. First to fight for your country, then struggle to keep it independent, only to have Viktor marching back to make himself dictator.' She peered at his wife again. 'Who's she dining with?' she asked curiously.

'That, my dear, is one of the Hohenzollerns, ex-Kaiser Wilhelm's dynasty. I'm not sure which one. There are plenty of them.'

'Is she fascinated by German politics like Viktor, or is she dining with him because she's some sort of relative of Zita's?'

'Neither, would be my guess.'

'Then is he,' Jennie's head whirled, 'just her escort, or—'

'Her lover? Oh undoubtedly, I would think. I have it on the best authority that he rents the villa next door to hers.'

*   *   *

Jennie was home again. It all looked so peaceful. Cannes had been like Montevanya, a brief paradise. They went to Goreham Court first since the twins would be there. Lynette came racing out to greet her, and Jamie was only a step behind. Tom was behind them, but while Anna theatrically threw herself into his arms, Jennie saw his expression over Anna's shoulder.

'What's wrong?' she asked sharply, looking quickly at the children. They seemed fit enough.

'We had a good time in Cornwall,' Tom assured her, and the twins nodded vigorously. So she would have to ask Tom about this later.

When at last an opportunity arose, she was appalled at what he had to tell her.

'My fault, Jen. Jamie wanted to see where his father had been born, and I couldn't see any harm in it, so we went to Helston. I didn't know, you see,' he said apologetically.

She froze. The last communication she had had from Richard's father had been in answer to her letter telling him of Richard's death. The short answer had contained threats to the children, and insults about her. She had thrown it away, since there was nothing to be done. The man was mad.

'They knew the address,' Tom explained. Her heart sank, for she hadn't realized how deep their grief for their father was. Perhaps they even hoped they might find Richard in Cornwall. 'I think they had a plan to meet their grandpa all the time. Anyway, once he knew who they were, he dragged them inside and slammed the door in my face, shouting out that he wasn't letting them go.'

Dear God, the man really was mad, Jennie thought, her stomach churning. Suppose she had lost them? Suppose, like Anna, her babies had been snatched away from her?

'There was a bit of a to do,' Tom continued. 'I had to get the police and a magistrate involved and they managed to get them away from the old devil. I don't think they'd have believed my word, except that the children were terrified and he was frothing at the mouth when they broke in. They could see something was seriously wrong, and so we all went to the police station. He ranted and raved away, including accusing me of being your lover as well as your brother, which confused the issue.'

Jennie shuddered. 'Is it all settled now?'

'Yes. He's been bound over, and we got the hell out of Cornwall, I can tell you. Good job we went to Tintagel first.'

'Darlings,' Jennie sat with Lynette and Jamie that night, still shaky at realising how easily she might have lost them, 'in all the best fairy stories, there's always a wicked witch or a monster that has to be conquered. And you've done it now. Isn't that marvellous? That means you live happily ever afterwards.'

'But I don't like him,' Lynette wailed. 'How can he be Daddy's father?'

'I don't know,' Jennie said truthfully, 'but he's your grandfather, and he wants you too.' Did he? Or did he just want revenge for Richard's having escaped his power?

'He won't get us, will he?'

'Never.' She'd put it in her will that Dad or Aunt Win or Eileen should be the twins' guardian if she died unexpectedly. But that, she decided, she had no intention of doing. Life, Cannes had shown her, was an interesting experience, and besides, she still had her promise to Richard to fulfil. She was still aboard that magic train, heading for the next station, and her children were coming with her.

Nine

1930

Christmas was going to be even bleaker this year, and Jennie realized she was dreading it. It was her second without Richard, but the poignancy was just as keen as last year. And now fate had thrown another spanner in the works. Why did the poor old Flyer have to give up its steaming powers just at the beginning of the season on which they depended for sales? Add to that the effects of the slump which were really biting hard, and business was slack. The sales of the Winnie the Pooh books would be strong, but the occupants of Hundred Acre Wood couldn't miraculously produce a profit for the Flyer by themselves. Albert of course remained forever hopeful, or rather he *appeared* to be so. She suspected he had given up on the boiler long before she and Freddie had admitted the terrible truth. The Flyer would steam no more. The grandeur of steering its throbbing power through the lanes was over.

'Fortunately,' Albert had declared yesterday, 'I have been keeping my head to the ground, in a manner of speaking.' He frowned, as he considered his wording. He hated not to be exact.

The idea of Albert producing a new boiler from under his bowler hat amused her. As so often however, she had been proved wrong. Albert apparently lived next door to a lady (who, it transpired, was a widow – competition for Aunt Win?) whose nephew's friend had run a London bus company, which like so many nowadays had sprung up in the buoyant competition for trade. It had run 'chasers', buses that followed established companies' routes hoping to overtake their rivals' vehicles and take their trade. Unfortunately this one had failed to chase sufficiently well and his stock was therefore being sold extremely cheaply, and one particular bus even more cheaply. It had, Albert understood, been specially built with the Blackwall tunnel route under the Thames in mind. It was a double decker, at which Jennie's hopes had promptly subsided, since she and Richard had agreed that a single deck suited their purpose best. They rose a little, however, after Albert explained the bus was only three years old; also it was entirely enclosed, not only the top deck, which was unusual enough, but the rear platform and stairs as well. Moreover the sides of the top deck were curved inwards to accommodate the tunnel's roofing. Albert had looked at her expectantly when he mentioned this, and she did not disappoint him.

'So it would suit narrow lanes with overhanging branches,' she said with growing interest.

'Yes, Mrs P.' (Jennie wondered whether he would continue to call her Mrs P if he did marry Aunt Win, or whether Aunt Win would become Mrs H?) 'And,' he continued, 'should you be concerned about low bridges, I have – I trust you will not be offended – discovered that there are only three on our existing routes, but this with a certain amount of circumventing, should not prove a problem.'

'But what use could we put the top deck to, Albert?' This had always been Jennie's worry. If customers went up to the top deck they might not bother to go inside as well; those who went inside would not then go upstairs, even if it were made into a sitting area. Nor could they leave it empty, for that smacked of defeat.

Albert looked reproachful. 'I am sure you will think of some arrangement to suit.'

Would she? Her mind immediately went blank. Albert coughed. 'For instance,' he continued, 'a children's reading circle.'

'But—' Jennie pulled herself up short. But was not a word of which Richard approved, unless a considered argument followed. So what was her objection to a reading circle? Only that the Flyer was a travelling bus, but was not licensed to carry passengers between stops. Therefore it collected only a small number of buyers (or readers) at any one time. Suppose, she began to think positively, they stopped in the village, advertized the circle as an attraction one afternoon a week, and timed it for immediately after school.

'That,' she announced to Albert, 'is the most wonderful idea. Just think what fun Richard could have had reading his illustrated stories. And,' she hastily added, before he could intervene, 'think what *we* could do with it. Mary could come with her books . . .'

'Miss Harkness could also come . . .'

'Aunt Win?' She would enjoy reading to children, Jennie thought. Then, as she saw Albert's eyes still on her, she realized there was another Miss Harkness: 'Eileen too of course. With her travel books, and . . .' Albert was still watching her. 'And . . .' Where did that take her? To Georgius, to Christmas, to . . .

'*Conjuring tricks*!' she cried triumphantly. 'Wouldn't it wonderful if Prince Georgius would put on a conjuring show on the top deck?' He and Eileen were to stay at Applemere for Christmas with Michael and Anthony. 'Oh Albert,' Jennie realized she was leaping around in excitement, 'everyone would come, all sorts of people. How much is this bus, and how quickly can we get it?'

Its purchase seemed a conjuring trick in itself. Very reluctantly, Freddie agreed to investigate this bus which was languishing in a garage in Charlton, near Woolwich. If, *if*, he told her meaningfully, it was in reasonable condition and price, he would take her to inspect it, and *if* she purchased it drive it and her to the Dower House, and make some arrangement for the disposal of the old Flyer.

'One condition,' Freddie had added. 'Make sure *they're* not at home.'

She understood immediately, and gave her solemn promise. Anna had mentioned that she and Tom would be in London for the last week of November. Work, Anna declared airily. Her new novel was finished, and she needed to work closely with the publisher, if publication was to be by the middle of the year as usual. She would give no hint as to what her next shocker might be, and Jennie did not ask. Time enough to face any problems when they came.

The conjuring trick began well, for the price was much less than she had expected. They must be eager to get it off their hands, she thought. It was £200, which she hadn't got, but how could she object? She'd have to talk to the bank manager in very glowing terms. She fell in love with the bus immediately. It looked so compact, so *elegant*. If it was raining, people didn't have to get wet going from one deck to another. Even Jennie could see the bus needed painting, however. The top deck seated ten each side in two facing rows, which was ideal for her purpose.

The Flyer would soon be flying again, she rejoiced. All she had to do was paint her, get the motor overhauled, rip out the seating below, put in the shelves from the old Flyer, all in a matter of days, if she was to profit from the season. She gulped at the prospect.

'White,' said Jamie. 'Yellow,' said Lynette. 'Red,' decreed Jennie.

So she relented, ordering some white and yellow paint too. Not ordinary paint of course, but strong foul-smelling stuff, to cover up the original lettering as well as the present shabby brown overall colour.

The twins spent the weekend painting the front and back signs to insert where the bus direction indicators would have been. 'Shall we paint Applemere Two on it?' Lynette asked.

Jennie thought for a moment. 'No. It's still the first Applemere Flyer, still Daddy's original idea. It's just run by another bus.'

The twins rushed to and fro with piles of stock, removed from the old bus carefully keeping it in subject order. Posters announced the new arrival with a special new attraction: Mary Patcher reading her well-known children's stories.

As for Georgius's conjuring tricks, Jennie grew increasingly excited. Eileen had consulted Georgius, who had wanted to set forth for Applemere and the Flyer immediately. A compromise was reached that they would come to Applemere House two weeks earlier than planned, and Jennie didn't know whether she or the twins were the more thrilled.

On the Wednesday morning the twins went to school with great reluctance. 'We've done the work, why can't we be here?' they complained.

'Because you can't,' Jennie retorted amiably. 'Much more fun to come home and find it all ready.' They weren't convinced, and set off to walk to school in mutinous mood.

Freddie arrived half an hour later. When she saw the Flyer coming along the drive, she swelled with pride, wishing Albert could have been here too. Trust Albert, however. He wasn't going to miss a day such as this. As the bus approached she spotted him ensconced on the top deck, no doubt with his briefcase at the ready. He must have telephoned Freddie and made some arrangement behind her back in order not to be left out. As she ran up to the bus, he descended in stately fashion down the steps.

'What do you think of it, Albert?'

'A most suitable vehicle,' he declared. 'Or it will be, once it is ready.'

Underneath his overcoat he wore not the frock coat but an old suit he obviously wore for gardening. He had come prepared to work. And work they all did.

By the end of the morning, Jennie's eyes were stinging with the smell of the paint. It wouldn't be finished today, but a good start could be made while Albert and Freddie were busy with the shelving.

Work was going well – *too* well. There had to be a snag, and after lunch in the Dower House it arrived. Jennie left the men at the table to return to her painting, only to see a familiar car parked outside and, to her horror, Anna and Tom emerging from it several days earlier than planned.

'What's this old wreck doing here?' Tom enquired cheerfully.

'It's the new Flyer. The old one's given up. Anna, why not get settled back at the Court and I'll come up later?' Jennie appealed to deaf ears.

'I'll give you a hand with the paint,' Tom said approvingly.

'No. You must tired. I've done enough for today,' she gabbled. Suppose Freddie came out. She had promised him Anna and Tom would not be here. 'Why don't you go home?'

'Because I can't wait a minute longer to tell you,' Anna laughed. 'Guess why we're back early, Jennie.'

'I can't,' Jennie said wretchedly. Why did this have to happen? She began to steer Anna back to the car, but she wouldn't be steered.

'I'm pregnant,' she bawled, waving her arms ecstatically to the heavens. 'I'm having a baby. I really am! Isn't that wonderful?'

'Glad to hear it.' Freddie's voice of doom came from behind them. Jennie saw him standing in the doorway, and knew she had to get Anna out of here quickly, if she was to avoid

131

trouble. She opened the car door pleading with her to get inside.

Anna refused. She was staring at Freddie like a pugnacious puppy.

'Tom?' Jennie appealed sharply. Surely he would want to get Anna home quickly? But he didn't move either.

'No, Jennie,' he said quietly. 'This had to happen some time. Why not now?'

'Why not indeed?' Freddie began to stroll towards them. 'Congratulations, Anna. My first child. What shall we call it?'

Tom's face darkened. 'What the hell do you mean, *yours*?'

'Anna,' Jennie appealed again, and for once Anna listened, trying to pull Tom away.

'Steady, Tom,' she said. 'Freddie's out to cause trouble. You know it's your baby, so why get upset? Let's go.'

'*My* child,' Freddie said impassively. 'I've no doubt your stud here sired it, but you're still married to me, darling. Remember your old husband? Legally the child might be mine.'

Was he right? Jennie had a horrible feeling that he might be – and if so, what on earth was going to happen?

What happened was that Anna's conciliatory mood promptly vanished. 'Dear me,' she mocked. 'Does that mean you promise to maintain Tom's child and care for it, change its nappies, and pay for it to live?'

The mood was getting ugly, but Jennie was powerless. This was between the two brothers.

'Why not?' Freddie shot back, his eyes still on Tom. 'The courts don't think much of mothers who walk out of the family home.'

Anna was white with shock. 'I left you long before I conceived. At the very least I'll divorce you.'

'On what grounds?' Freddie asked, 'I could divorce *you*, but I'm not going to climb into bed with a hotel chambermaid just to provide you with evidence to divorce me. Why should I?'

'Go ahead. Divorce me,' Anna spat at him.

'So you can marry my brother. Not sure that's legal, is it? Anyway, your family would like that even less. Better a bastard grandchild than married to yet another peasant.'

That did it. Appalled, Jennie saw Tom's face change. At first he was inarticulate with rage, then spluttered:

'How many kids have you given her? You're bloody impotent and you talk about being a father. I'll have had three kids by Anna. What have you done for her? Nothing.'

'What the hell do you mean, *three*?' It was Freddie's turn to be completely thrown. Obviously reading the horror in Anna's face as confirmation, he turned to Jennie in bewilderment.

'Tom's joking,' she stammered. She could have kicked herself for her stupidity. There was no going back now.

'I'm not joking, Jennie, and you know it.' Tom was triumphant, in control.

So Freddie hadn't known the whole truth about Anna and Tom's affair before the war. Jennie had always assumed Anna had told him, but with Anna it was never safe to assume anything. Freddie looked like the baby brother she'd always protected. All the stuffing had been knocked out of him, just as when Tom had deliberately broken his toys. Tom was the elder brother he could never conquer, and it was still so.

'Anna?' Freddie turned to her with a face of despair.

Even Anna looked appalled at the situation. 'I was young, Freddie. I had the twins in Switzerland as war broke out. They were adopted and vanished.'

'And you never thought to mention it to me? Even though you'd slept with my own brother?'

Anna said nothing. Nor did Tom, though he was bristling with combined self-righteousness and fury. Jennie had to do something, however inadequate. A nice cup of tea, she thought hysterically. She heard herself saying, 'Let's all talk about this inside, shall we?' At least that might take the heat out of the situation.

'Keep out of this, Jen,' Freddie replied impassively, and then turned on Tom.

'I knew you'd had her way back before the war, but children too! God, what a fool I've been.'

'You still are, Freddie. *You are*,' Tom yelled, but he was calming down, Jennie saw. It must have been a shock to him too that Freddie hadn't known.

'This wasn't Anna's fault,' Freddie came back at him bitterly. 'She was a kid when you first got at her.'

Words stopped as Freddie threw himself at Tom with a punch to his face that sent him staggering back. As Anna

133

shrieked, Jennie tried to intervene but was pushed aside. As Tom rallied, the fight began in earnest. This wasn't just a disagreement, Jennie realized, appalled; this was sheer hate emerging. Albert at last managed to separate them by throwing a bucket of water over them both, and then marching Freddie back into the Dower House.

'Don't, Anna, don't,' Jennie found herself saying uselessly, as Anna burst into tears. Real tears for once. 'Why on earth didn't you tell Freddie about the babies?'

'It was a new start,' Anna sobbed. 'I thought the past was over. By the end of the war Tom had married, and there was nothing for me.' Tom came over to her, put his arm round her, and pushed her gently into the car.

Jennie went back into the Dower House to face the situation there. She found Albert tending Freddie's wounds, and mopping him up. 'Fine brothers we are to you, Jennie.' Freddie looked at her shamefacedly.

'The best,' she said stoutly. 'But it wasn't all Tom's fault, Freddie.'

Freddie made no comment.

Anna's baby was due in late May, she told Jennie a few days later. 'I couldn't tell you before, just in case it all went wrong. But now we're sure. Perhaps he or she will be born on the same day as Lynette and Jamie,' she said happily. She seemed to have recovered from the fracas remarkably easily, but then one never knew with Anna. 'We could have jolly birthday parties together.'

Jennie plucked up the courage to ask: 'Do you think Freddie might relent about divorcing you?'

'I doubt it. I asked him a year ago, and he refused. Tom's talking to Mary about it. We can't wait forever to be married. Besides, what's the point of marrying anyway? We're happy as we are. Or we were until all this happened.' She glanced at Jennie. 'I did love Freddie, you know. I tried to make him happy, but when Tom came back into my life, I realized I didn't. Beside Tom, he's so, well, steady.'

And that's what at one time she'd wanted, Jennie thought. Or had she? Was it possible that Anna had deliberately chosen to marry Freddie in order to be closer to Tom? She pushed this disloyal thought to the back of her mind. 'What about the baby?' she asked. 'It will be hard to grow up with unmarried parents.'

Anna laughed. 'Will it? They're both called Trent, aren't they?'

Tom had come to the Dower House alone to apologize to Jennie. Not to Freddie of course. 'That's between him and me,' he said. 'And don't worry, we won't embarrass you with a scene at the Station House at Christmas. That's Freddie's time. We're going to St Moritz anyway. I'll show Anna's circle a thing or two even if the Fokinghams stick their posh noses up. One day they might even speak to me.'

Jennie let this pass, although it puzzled her. 'I thought you didn't like grand places. That's why you didn't go to Cannes with Anna, isn't it?'

He looked surprised. 'Anna said it was a working holiday and she wanted to go alone, or with you because she thought you needed a holiday. She asked me if I'd take the twins somewhere, so that you would be free to come.'

Jennie was even more puzzled. Firstly Anna didn't usually think in terms of Jennie's welfare and secondly, what was this work? Although Anna had set off for one or two days alone in Cannes for research, so far there had been no mention of a novel set there.

Freddie simply seemed to be ignoring the whole episode, whenever she met him. She had quickly got in touch with him again and with the perfect reason for doing so. He could join their reading circles: he was good at reading aloud, as the twins could testify, and if he read Edith Nesbit's *The Railway Children*, the audience would meet a real live engine driver, who was a war hero into the bargain. He'd agreed, and was popular with the children, and Jennie's heart went out to him. Would he ever have children of his own?

The new petrol bus was working well though it took some getting used to after its steam predecessor. The painting had been somewhat haphazard, compared with the professional job Tom's men had done on the last Flyer. Jennie had lovingly painted 'Pencarek Books' herself. Tom had actually lent a hand too, though naturally she didn't tell Freddie that.

Two weeks before Christmas Eileen and Georgius arrived at Applemere House. The day after their arrival, the Applemere Flyer drew up outside with a triumphant toot, and Jennie and

Albert were escorted inside for mince pies and coffee.

'*Joa napotata*, Meeses Jennie.' Georgius bowed over her hand, preventing her from curtseying.

'We've decided on no curtseying from now on,' Eileen declared. 'Especially from me. Queen Zita thinks I should curtsey to Georgius every time I see him.'

'Me, I never curtsey,' Georgius rumbled. He was older now, grey-haired, grey-bearded and just right for a wizard, Jennie thought. She'd recently bought a few copies of an American book published before the war called *The Wizard of Oz*, and decided that Georgius would fit the bill nicely for the title role.

Applemere House had a much softer feel to it now, even though it was much tidier than when the Fokinghams were here. Then it had been a gracious blend of formal and informal, comfortable sofas and cushions, pictures of the Fokingham ancestors, photographs and magazines. Now the Fokingham paintings had vanished, and only one or two Deleanu ones remained. Michael had his own paintings displayed, and Jennie was surprised to find mainly English works, especially from the Newlyn School, which was almost pre-Raphaelite in its narrative appeal, and not a field she would have associated with Michael.

For his conjuring performances on the Flyer Georgius reluctantly allowed himself to be billed as Prince Georgius Deleanu, which overwhelmed the villagers until they began laughing at his tricks. Often these didn't quite work, and his bewildered 'Now, what I do wrong this time, plis?' as he looked anxiously at his audience, had them laughing even more.

To Jennie's delight, his appearances sold many books, because in addition to the extra trade in their usual stock, the audience often trooped downstairs to buy a small book of conjuring tricks to be performed at home which Georgius had hastily prepared and had printed in London.

All in all, Jennie thought happily, the future of the Flyer looked far more promising especially as Albert seemed to relish his position as part-time stooge to Georgius.

On Boxing Day, the combined Station House party, including Freddie, went to Applemere House where Michael and Anthony entertained them. To see Dad's arrival was a delight. It was his first formal visit there and he almost fought Stevens for possession of his beloved hat. Albert came too. The widow hadn't won yet, Jennie thought happily, even though no proposal seem to be forthcoming for Aunt Win. Only later did she hear that the next door widow, the by now famous Mrs Arbuthnot, was spending Christmas with her daughter over Gillingham way.

There was one extra Christmas pleasure at Applemere on Boxing Day. During a walk through the garden, Michael had a word with her. 'Are you still happy at the Dower House?'

'Of course.' Jennie was surprised.

'Applemere Cottage is free again. My aunt never moved in, or even showed much interest in it. I think,' he added apologetically, 'she just wanted to stake a claim to it.'

'No peasants in Applemere?'

'Something like that,' Michael agreed, and they laughed. 'I wondered if you'd like to move back? Tony and I would welcome it.'

She was both surprised and flattered, since Michael was clearly sincere. Her immediate reaction was to agree, but then she realized there was a snag. There always was, and it was usually the same one.

'I'd love to,' she said regretfully. 'But until Anna's baby is born, how can I? She needs me there.'

Oh to be back in Applemere, where Richard and she had been so happy. Would it be possible to be happy there again? Why not? Once Anna had the baby, Jennie would not be needed, and she could quietly return here with the twins. It was something to look forward to.

'Would the offer still be open next summer?' she asked hopefully. 'We must move back in time for the autumn school term?'

Michael grinned. 'Yes. We won't let it to anyone else.'

'And,' she hesitated, then plunged, 'the Flyer?'

'The barn would be yours.'

'Oh Michael, thank you. I'm so grateful.' She was glad of the offer, even if nothing came of it. On an impulse she kissed him, and to her pleasure he seemed pleased. Perhaps all the Fokinghams were human once one battled past their exterior front to the world. Or perhaps, it occurred to her, it was simply that Michael was happier now. Was that true of Anna too?

137

Jennie might be her friend, but it was a question she could never answer.

1931

'Wouldn't it be nice if you lived here all the time?' Jennie said wistfully to Eileen. She and Georgius had stayed on into January but were threatening to leave by the end of the month.

'Tempting,' Eileen teased. 'When I've hung my boots up for good we might consider it.' Those boots were extremely muddy today as she and Eileen were tramping around the Applemere gardens, in the hope of persuading Michael and Anthony that some serious work needed to be done if the pond (lake, as Michael used to call it) were not to disappear into quagmire and the woodlands into saplings and brambles. The present gardeners preferred to concentrate their efforts on the formal garden, which provided less of a challenge and more immediate rewards.

Looking at her beloved aunt's lively face and the greying hair that would never conform to any particular hairstyle, Jennie was resigned to the fact that the boots would continue to be worn for some time yet.

'You can travel abroad from here as easily as from London with Folkestone at the end of our line,' she pointed out.

'That's truc, but the gossip is of a different calibre in Fairsted to that of London. One hears things in London hotels that fail to be discussed in the Plough.'

'But they might be just as relevant.'

'True. In the last war all the best spies landed on the south coast. Nevertheless,' Eileen smiled at Jennie,' I shall bear your words of wisdom in mind. Georgius would be happy anywhere once he gets the idea of hiring the Crystal Palace or Albert Hall for a magic show out of his mind. By the way, Max is coming down next weekend. Do come over, he'd like to see you.'

Jennie felt flattered. It wasn't every day that she was invited to meet a king, even an ex-one. 'Is his wife coming?'

Eileen raised an eyebrow. 'No. And I am quite sure Anna filled your ears with all the gossip while you were in Cannes. Max seems to be putting a brave face on the situation, but there's a lot of shifting sand at present, both in the personal lives of ex-royalty and on the political front.'

'Is there any hope of Viktor being ousted?'

'Let's say that now that King Carol is safely back on the throne of Roumania and they are even ready to tolerate even that dreadful Lupescu woman at his side, the situation is looking better for monarchies again. Viktor must be highly annoyed that he settled for being dictator not king. And darling Queen Zita is of the same opinion. Some people like being royal, others are merely content with power.'

Because of the heavy snowfall at the weekend Jennie and the twins stayed overnight at the Station House, in order that she could walk to Applemere if need be. Need was, and so she left the twins building a snowman, and was about to begin her tramp over the snowy fields when the Applemere trap turned up to save her the bother. So she arrived in style, despite being wrapped up in every coat she had against the cold, not to mention displaying elegant wellington boots.

Max however looked disappointed that she had not come in the Flyer, and on an impulse she suggested he come back with her to see it.

He instantly agreed, but asked if they might walk instead. Would she mind? Not at all, she said, somewhat surprised.

'I enjoy walking in the snow here in England,' he told her. 'In London it's more difficult than here.'

'The quickest and most pleasant way is over the fields,' she told him, and then had a sudden doubt. Did ex-kings walk across fields? No matter, Max would. She was sure of that.

His curly dark hair had streaks of grey now, the eyes no longer laughed at her, and his face was sadder in repose than once it had been. Nevertheless she felt at ease with him after coffee as they set off.

'I don't know how to speak to a king,' she confessed frankly.

'It is very simple, Jennie. If one likes the king, then it is easy. If one does not, it is more difficult.'

'Then I find it easy,' she said smiling at him, trudging by his side. 'Why do you like snow in England? I can see why you would in Montevanya.' Too late she realized Montevanya might be a sore subject but he didn't seem to mind.

He took so long to reply she thought she must have offended him, but at last he spoke. 'I think because it covers most of what

139

man has done to our beautiful world, so that we can see what God gave us more clearly. We see the clear skies, the bare branches against them, the fields, the still waters and the mountains. From the Várcasá in winter we could see the snow—'

A sudden flurry of it dropping from a tree smothered him and she laughed. 'Snow has no respect for monarchs.'

'It is democratic. Snow feels as wet to me as to you.'

'Are you happy in London, Max?' she asked suddenly, surprising herself. She hadn't meant to mention anything that might impinge on his personal life.

'I like London. I know that is not an answer, but it has to pass as one. And you, Jennie, are you still sad because of your husband? Eileen told me of your great loss.'

'Of course, I am, but I have his two children and I have the Applemere Flyer.'

'Tell me about them all if you please.'

She glanced at him, wondering if he were merely being polite, or whether he was truly interested. He nodded, clearly amused as he noticed her doubt. So she told him all about Lynette and Jamie, and then since he seemed disinclined to talk of his own son, went on to explain what books meant to her, what Richard had wanted to achieve with the Applemere Flyer, and how she was trying to do the same with the new Flyer. Encouraged by his obvious interest she told him about the reading groups and Georgius's shows, and how, just as Richard had wanted, all customers, no matter their background, were brought together by the Flyer.

'I am glad I shall see it.'

She wondered whether she should take him into the Station House first, but the dilemma was solved for her. When she pointed out the Flyer standing in the station yard, he climbed eagerly aboard. She had left a small paraffin heater inside the bus, as protection against the cold, and it struck warm as they went inside. It was just as well, as once Max had inspected the upstairs deck and she had described Georgius' magic shows, he studied every book from *Winnie the Pooh* to the latest war memoirs.

'I have read many. They have changed in style, have they not?' he observed. 'When the war ended everyone was eager to write of their exploits, through relief at their survival. Now we get the considered truth, the bitterness and anger.'

'*All Quiet on the Western Front* and *Goodbye to All That*,' she said.

'And here you have *Sagittarius Rising*. Ah, that is good. The glory of the skies ruined by warfare. Mr Lewis is a fine writer.'

'Not all ruined,' she pointed out. 'If it wasn't for the aeroplanes developed in the war, we wouldn't have such good ones today. Amy Johnson would never have flown to Australia.'

'Perhaps.' He smiled at her. 'You are a great peacemaker, Jennie. Like Winnie the Pooh. Children all over the world love him and not just children, for we are all children when the dark comes.'

When Max came to the pile of Anna's books, he laughed. 'These I have read. Secretly of course. I fear my family would not approve.'

'Do you?'

'Probably. Nevertheless, Anna, like her mother, sees only one side of an argument. Why does no one ever try to see both sides? Do you do so, Jennie?'

'I try to,' she answered truthfully.

'Even when love is involved, either between men and women or within families?'

'Yes, it is possible to love and still see clearly.' She wondered if he were thinking of his wife and his own children. 'Does your son read *Winnie the Pooh*?' she asked daringly. 'Or is he too old for it now?'

'He did last year. Now he likes toy soldiers.' He hesitated. 'I fear he enjoys seeing the red-coated bearskin-helmeted soldiers of London too much.'

'All boys do,' she replied, and he looked at her gratefully.

'My wife tries to bring him up a future monarch. I do not think this is wise.' Then as if regretting his confidence, he added, 'Now tell me of your plans for the future.'

She told him of her hope that Eileen and Georgius would come to live in Kent, and she could put on more conjuring shows. Max laughed. 'You remember that day we went to the Tellestin House, Jennie?' That was the day they had gone out to see Georgius and Eileen's home in the Montevanyan countryside.

'I do. You were very kind to me.'

'No. I was not. And I was less than kind when we returned. I did not understand the situation then, but now I do. Has Anna changed? You are still her friend, I hear.'

'No change,' Jennie laughed. 'She is to have another baby in May, and perhaps she will change then, for she wants nothing more than a family.'

'And what will she teach that family? Kindness or bitterness?'

She could not answer that question, and indeed she had been wondering that herself. She was saved by Aunt Win's waving from the doorway. She took Max in to meet Lynette and Jamie, and Dad and Aunt Win, and he seemed to enjoy himself. Aunt Win quickly heated up some of her special carrot soup, which he ate with great relish.

To her surprise, when he came to leave, he asked her to walk back with him to lunch at Applemere House after which she could be brought home in the trap. He looked pleased when she accepted, and they set out again across the fields. This time the snow was driving in their faces, but not hard, and she hardly noticed it.

Max was right. This was the most beautiful season, she thought, looking at the pinky-grey sky, the branches of the barren trees and a solitary crow hopping dark against the white snow.

'Is life simple here in Fairsted, because of such beauty all around us?' he asked her.

'No, but we can *see* how lovely and peaceful it is, and that helps.'

He nodded. 'You can also see Applemere from here. That too is beautiful, is it not? A house that is sad because it has no family in it.'

'It knows how to wait,' Jennie said idly.

'And its gardens also. Do you like gardens, Jennie?'

A pang of love for her garden at Applemere Cottage came over her so strongly she almost cried out. And soon, soon, she would be there again.

'Yes,' she breathed. 'Oh, I do. Very much.'

He took her hand as she was about to climb into the trap after lunch. 'We shall meet again, Jennie. I said to you once that we would not. But now I know I shall come back to Applemere.'

Ten

If only she were at Applemere already . . . Jennie tried very hard to dismiss 'if onlys' from her life. After all, the Dower House garden was almost as nice as that of Applemere cottage, even if didn't feel like home. There had been too much unhappiness here, and too much struggle. Perhaps it was naïve of her to imagine that this would be instantly remedied when they returned to Applemere, but it was at least a hope, and one that was now only a few months away. Fortunately Anna had had few problems with her pregnancy, and the baby would be born shortly. Anna had refused to go to a London hospital for the baby's birth, or even to the Kent and Canterbury. Instead she was intent on going to the Valley Cottage Hospital in Marsham. Her reason? That it would shock everyone.

'Fancy having the notorious Mrs Trent in the next bed,' she said. 'Perhaps they'll think I'll cast the evil eye on their brats.'

Jennie found herself counting the days to the birth, for that would mark the beginning of her last few weeks here, as the baby would occupy Anna's time and thoughts. There was still no word of her new novel. True to form, Anna kept quiet about it, and all the publishers' travellers could tell Jennie was that publication was expected in July and its title was *The Island*. Jennie was becoming increasingly uneasy, since it didn't sound like a novel in either of Anna's former styles.

Jennie was hoping to return to Applemere in August, perhaps even in time for her birthday on the first. Meanwhile she had the twins' eleventh birthday to think of, and secondary schools for them.

Lynette and Jamie complemented each other in their interests; Lynette was still intent on books and drama and Jamie had requested a grown-up toolkit for his birthday. Jennie sometimes wondered if their diversity of interests would separate them in future, but she hoped not. Twins usually remained together even if they had to attend different schools.

What food to prepare for the birthday? The days of jellies and trifles were passing. There would have to be a proper cake, perhaps even salmon sandwiches. There'd have to be prizes for the treasure hunt, which meant a visit to the village shop – or should she donate present books as presents? Why not, after all? It all helped future trade.

She was still meditating on this problem while she planted a few late seeds in the garden. She wouldn't be here to see the crop, of course, but Anna and Tom might enjoy it; they had no vegetable garden of their own. A few weeks ago, she had had the bright idea of clearing a patch in the Applemere Cottage garden, so that she could grow some vegetables there for the autumn. Michael had no objections, and it gave her scope for using her spare energy. The more of that she used the better, for though the twins and family filled nearly all her heart, there was still a space left there which grew larger and keener by night, when she slept alone in the double bed.

She heard a motor vehicle draw up without surprise. It must be the delivery of manure she had ordered. She scrambled to her feet, and dusted the earth off her skirt, ready to go into the house for her purse. She never did so, for Tom appeared through the side gate.

One look at his face, and she knew something was badly amiss.

'Is it Anna?' she cried. 'Has she started?' No, it must be worse, she realized. Tom seemed smaller, shrunken into himself and his face was almost grey.

'Last night,' he tried to begin. Then just: 'The baby, Jen. You've got to come.'

'Anna's in the house?' Jennie was terrified. There must have been an emergency. Was the midwife, or even the doctor needed?

'Hospital.' Tom could hardly get the word out.

'Anna's in labour?'

He managed to shake his head. 'The baby – oh Jen, it died. They said—' He broke off as she immediately cradled him in her arms. 'It was dead. I guessed something was wrong these last few days, but she wouldn't admit it. Oh Jen. *Jen.*'

Her arms were tightly around him. He wasn't even crying,

the shock must be still too great. 'You've got to come, sis,' he repeated.

Of course she must go. She thought her heart would break for poor Anna, but then with sickening clarity she realized it might be worse news. 'Anna's physically all right?' She was almost too terrified to ask.

He couldn't answer, and Jennie was knotted with fear. 'She's not dead, is she?'

'They don't think she'll live,' he managed. 'I couldn't stop to telephone you. Jen, you've got to come *now*,' he said again.

She was already tearing off her gardening jacket and shoes as she ran into the house. She scribbled a note for the twins to go up to the Big House when they returned from school, in case . . . she forced herself to think this through . . . she was not back. The pain seemed to surge up into her throat as she jumped into Tom's car, and they hardly exchanged a word on the way to the hospital. What was there to say that could not be outdated by what they might find as they arrived at the hospital? If Anna died – no, she could not face that yet. It was bad enough that the child had died. How on earth would Anna cope with that loss, even if she did pull through? She would need help to go on living, and Jennie must give it to her. Anna had always been there, she was part of her life. Exasperating and mesmerizing though she was, life without her was unimaginable. Cold fear grasped her, as Jennie willed all her strength into Anna to live.

Tom was white and silent as they hurried into the small hospital to Anna's room. She had one to herself, and Jennie saw Tom glance at the nurse who nodded brightly. Too brightly, but at least it meant Anna was still living. Jennie almost cried in sheer relief for that must mean that there was hope.

She followed in Tom's wake into the room dreading what she might see. It was worse than she had feared: an old woman's face, sallow and sunken against the pillow, eyes closed and her tiny body huddled under the bedclothes. Jennie realized her hopes were in vain: Anna was dying. Even if physically she might be pulled through, Anna would need her mental strength to fight on, and there was none left.

Tom sat down, his large frame a stark contrast with the frail figure in the bed, and gently took her hand. Anna opened her eyes and he spoke softly to her. She was trying to frame replies and Jennie stood back, for this was between the two of them. Then Anna looked directly at Jennie. A hint of a twisted smile crossed her lips.

'Don't tell my parents,' she whispered. 'Promise.'

Jennie glanced at Tom, who nodded. 'No darling,' she answered, 'but there'll be nothing to tell. You'll get well.' The words rang as falsely in her own ears as they must to Anna. She would not get well, and they all knew it.

They remained at her side, awaiting her moments of lucidness, when she forbade them to tell anybody, not Freddie, not her parents, no one. Then at midday she relented. 'Michael,' she murmured, and Tom promptly left to telephone him. Michael was still in London, though being a Friday he would have been leaving the Foreign Office for Applemere later that afternoon for the weekend. He came immediately and was with them at four o'clock, and Jennie went out into the gardens while Tom and Michael took turns to sit by Anna's bedside. She couldn't leave with Anna so ill, and as the day was drawing to a close she telephoned to Goreham Court to ask Mrs Grant to keep the twins there overnight.

When she returned to the room, Tom was outside, white with shock. Anna was losing her fight, if fight there had been, and the doctor was on his way. Michael then emerged when the doctor arrived, looking so shaken that Jennie put her arms round him. The door opened once more when the doctor left, but what was the use of hoping now? He murmured words of sympathy and Tom hurried in, taking Jennie with him.

Anna looked at them with dull eyes. 'Tom,' she whispered. 'I need to talk to Jennie alone.'

He blenched, but obeyed her instructions. Jennie caught his sleeve as he left. 'I won't be long,' she assured him. Then she sat down at Anna's side putting her face close to hers so that Anna didn't need to strain to make herself heard. 'Don't leave us,' she pleaded. 'We need you.'

'You always were a romantic,' Anna managed to gasp. 'It's happening, that's all. Another bit of life. Now, Jennie, I have a plan—'

'Another one?' Jennie asked affectionately, half sobbing.

'It's there. Don't tell Tom, he's such a hothead.' The words

146

dragged out in short breaths now. 'There's something you must do for me.'

'Anything.' Jennie held Anna's hand.

'Promise me. Promise.'

'I will.'

'Find my babies, Jennie.'

Anna died ten minutes later, with Tom holding her hand, and Jennie and Michael at the end of her bed. Later Jennie drove Tom back to Goreham Court, and Michael came with them. He said he would ask Anthony to drive over the next day to take him to Applemere, and Jennie sensed that he needed to be with them. The old animosity between himself and Tom had either vanished or was temporarily in abeyance for they sat most of the night talking about Anna. She had never realized quite how much Tom had loved her, but it clearly emerged now. He made just one painful reference to the dead baby.

'I haven't even got the kid to bring up.'

Michael did not comment, but she guessed what he was thinking, if only because he asked if he could telephone his parents. There would be no heir to the Fokingham estate now after Michael himself, legitimate or illegitimate. It would not be an easy call to make and he was clearly anxious to get it over. When he had hung up, Jennie would have to telephone Freddie, and after that Dad and Aunt Win. Have to, have to . . . the words etched themselves onto her mind until the whole nightmare assumed an unreality that gave her the strength to cope. For the moment at least.

She must think about her promise to Anna. She had said Jennie should not tell Tom, and Jennie could understand why. Tom would get *too* involved, unable to judge what might be best for the children if and when Jennie found them, even though they would be over sixteen now and children no longer. Her promise would lie heavy on her, but she had made it, and that was that. Yet the task seemed hopeless. If Anna herself couldn't find her twin babies, how on earth could she hope to after all these years? Anna must have been confident, however; she hadn't said *look* for my babies, she had said *find* them.

Supporting Tom and Freddie helped anaesthetize Jennie's own pain. Only Tom, Jennie, Michael and Freddie were to be at the funeral. Definitely no parents, and her funeral was also to be that of her baby. She had insisted that her son be called Thomas.

Michael, to Jennie's great relief, volunteered to break this news to his parents. He hadn't told Jennie and Tom what they had said on the telephone that night, but the fact that on the Saturday he went back to London to see them suggested the news had caused both grief and furore. Jennie thought back to her friendship with Lady Fokingham, and her heart ached for her. Whatever her attitude to her daughter's antics, Jennie had never doubted her love for her. Why couldn't Anna have seen that too? she anguished. Michael returned the next day to Goreham Court to tell them that his parents had accepted the decision over the funeral, and were holding a service in London at the same time as that at Fairsted.

Which left Freddie. Whether Tom liked it or not, he was still Anna's husband, and he had loved her. Jennie had found him waiting at the Dower House when she went home the next morning, and promptly had despatched the twins on a mission to the village.

'Didn't she want to see me?' Freddie asked, bewildered rather than angry, when he recovered from the immediate shock. 'I can't believe it, Jen. I can't,' he burst out. 'I lived with her for nearly nine years, and she didn't even want to see me at the last. I've lost her, Jen. What's there to live for?'

'Anna hadn't the strength to think clearly, Freddie,' she replied gently.

'She had the strength to see you.'

Jennie was silenced. She couldn't explain that Anna had needed to discuss her last plan, particularly since it was such a sensitive one. It was between her and Tom, and Freddie was not involved, however much she felt his grief.

'What am I doing to do, Jennie? I'll have to see Tom, won't I?'

'Yes.'

'I said I'd never speak to the bastard again. It's him who did this, you know. He ruined all the hope there was for Anna and me.' He paused. 'Did she tell you I'd agreed about the divorce? I'd only have done it for the child, not for its bloody father.'

'Freddie,' she warned him, 'that's over, at least at present.'

'Don't worry. I'll be polite. Let's get it over with.'

148

They walked slowly up to Goreham Court, and found Tom in the morning room, slumped in a chair. Freddie was as good as his word, however, and pitched straight in.

'Let's get the funeral over, Tom. We'll sort the rest out afterwards.' Freddie must have realised this sounded inadequate. 'I'm sorry about the baby,' he added gruffly, 'and Anna. I know you loved her.' These too were inadequate words, but they served the immediate purpose, to Jennie's relief.

Tom stared at him, as though Freddie had no right to intrude even by mentioning her name, but he answered, 'You too, Freddie.'

Once the funeral had been discussed, Freddie and she left and returned to the Dower House. On the way Freddie paused to look behind him at Goreham Court, and it was only then that Jennie realized the terrible truth. Anna had left no will, and no known children, so Goreham Court, which she alone had bought, might pass to Freddie as well as her entire estate, once the probate court for intestacy had pronounced its decision.

So what about Tom, whom Anna had loved, and whose children she so passionately wanted? Oh, Anna, Jennie thought sadly, you had so many plans, couldn't you have planned for this?

The twins' birthday was two days after Anna's funeral, and everyone did their best to make it a happy day for them. But it was hard, and Jennie was glad when it was all over, and everyone had left. Even Aunt Win and Dad had taken the last bus home, and she and the twins were alone, and all her grief spilled over once they were in bed and there was no need to hold it back.

Once she was at Applemere Cottage her spirits would recover she told herself, and meanwhile she should plan what to do over her promise to Anna. She would have to see Lady Fokingham. Or would she? No, that wouldn't be sensible. Time enough to tell them once she had achieved her goal. She had to consider whether they might prefer the babies to remain 'lost'. They might even put obstacles in her way. After all, there had been recent legislation over illegitimate babies. Freddie must have been thinking of that when he agreed to the divorce on the new baby's account. Only he'd been mistaken about its helping the new baby, she realized. Both parents had to be free to marry when the child was born, in order for it to be later legitimized, and Anna had not been free. The divorce would not have gone through in time.

Where did that leave Tom? If the children were found, could he legitimize them if he could prove he was the father? She had no idea, but what she did conclude was that any mention of finding the twin babies might raise all sorts of spectres in the Fokinghams' minds, especially if they had realized Michael was unlikely to provide them with an heir after himself. He might want to bequeath his estate to the twins. Which made her all the more determined to do everything in her power to find them.

The Swiss nursing home was the starting point – save that that was where Anna had begun her fruitless hunt, and moreover Jennie didn't know where it was. The Swiss Embassy might have records, even Somerset House, since Anna was a British citizen. Or would the Fokinghams have obliterated all trace? Rome, why had Anna been in Rome? She had mentioned a Monsieur and Madame Roc – so were they French or Swiss French or just was that just a false name given by the home? Even if it was the real name, it might have been spelled Rock. Jennie hadn't seen it written down, so it could be British or American, or even German, Roch. That might explain the difficulty in tracing the couple once war had begun. Endless possibilities tugged at her tired mind; she was running round in a caucus race, like Alice in her Wonderland.

She visited Tom as much as she could in the following weeks, and sent the twins to visit him too, although she wasn't sure if this made it worse for him. He was remarkably quiet. She had grown up with Tom as the difficult brother, so greedy for everything, so boisterous. Freddie had been the easygoing one. Now the roles were almost reversed, Freddie was intransigent and non-committal. Tom had said there was truce between them until after the funeral at least, but that did not mean there was peace. In despair at Tom's lethargy, she asked him to come with her on the Flyer.

He shrugged. 'Too busy. Anyway, Mary does that.'

'We could pick different days. I could do with your help

on the paperwork.' That wasn't true, but it sounded good.

'I've plenty of that,' he said bitterly, and indeed he was sitting in Anna's writing room today, just staring at her desk.

'Sorry. Am I disturbing you?'

He grimaced. 'I'd been reading this.'

He tossed a letter over to her to read. It was from a London solicitor:

'Dear Sir, You are requested to arrange access to Goreham Court on Tuesday the third of July, for Sir Roger and Lady Fokingham to collect those of the late Mrs Frederick Trent's possessions as belong to the Fokingham family. You are entitled to have your solicitor present. We expect your confirmation by return of post.'

'How's that for a letter to the bereaved father of your clients' grandchildren?' Tom asked as she gasped.

Jennie tried hard to reconcile this ridiculous request with the Fokinghams she had known. At first she could not and then she remembered the way they had turned on her in Montevanya. There had only been one side of the story then – theirs. They had presumed her guilt without trial.

'But the probate court hasn't sat yet. They can't do that.'

'Of course not. Does that matter a damn to the Fokinghams? No. Anyway, why attack me? Brother Freddie is the probable legal owner of the whole bang shoot. I'm merely his caretaker. *His* solicitor has asked me to look after the place until the position is clear. And to continue looking after Anna's publishing affairs. Free of charge of course. The Administrator will be going through the results with a fine toothcomb. He's the chap the court will appoint to see everything's sorted out properly.'

'So you expect Freddie will get everything?'

'Yes, Jennie dear. If the child had lived it might have been different, but as it is Freddie will probably get the lot. At least he won't give the Fokinghams one penny. Nor, I imagine, take any notice of this letter.' He flipped a finger at the paper. 'Anna had no family relics, even though they seem to think she had the family crown jewels tucked away. Not very likely, is it? It was one of the last things she said to me. She made a joke out of it—' his voice cracked '—but she meant it. The Fokinghams wouldn't have a hope. According to Anna, it's like getting blood out of a stone, trying to get money out of

Freddie. Anyway, he'll see the Fokinghams off, if I know Freddie. Nothing moves until the case is heard legally, even if King bloody George himself comes down. I'm lucky Freddie hasn't sent in his legal mob to do an inventory already, in case I squirrel poor Anna's goodies away.'

Jennie was appalled. Surely Freddie wasn't so hard? 'What will you do, Tom, if Freddie inherits?'

'I don't know, sis. Freddie has indicated he might be gracious if he inherits. He's planning to sell Goreham Court lock stock and barrel, including the dower house and the farms, but he might keep the two cottages in the village, and let me have one rent free if I'm a good little boy. Funny old world, isn't it? Freddie who only wanted to drive trains, lands up not only a war hero but one of the landed gentry rolling in cash, and me who chased every shiny penny in sight am out on my ear, with precious little to look forward to. Lucky you're going back to Applemere, or he'd turf you out of your home too.'

Jennie felt wretched. 'Could you go back into the brewing business?'

'I've burned my boats there. Mary would see to that, and even if she wanted me back with her, I wouldn't go.'

'So what could you do?'

Tom considered. 'Be Dad's porter, I suppose.'

'Don't joke, Tom.'

'I'm not. It's some sort of job. I like working and seeing people. Now look at me, thanks to Anna's bloody family.'

'What did they have to do with it?' Jennie was puzzled.

'Everything, blast them. They're what drew Anna and me together in the first place. I've never told you about it. There seemed no point, but now Anna's dead—'

'Tell me now,' she said.

'I found her crying one day in Cornerstone Field. She must have been about fourteen. Asked her what was the matter. She told me she couldn't stand Applemere, and was scared of the straitjacket she'd be growing up into. Well, you knew about that part of it. I sympathized with her, instead of telling her everything would be all right. I hated them too. When I was about nine, his lordship and her ladyship came tootling along in their car one day, and knocked me off my bike. Instead of apologizing, noble Sir Roger gave me a penny and told me I was a brave little man. I wanted to take a swing at him then and there. And young Master Michael was sitting there too, giggling his head off.'

'But that's ages ago, and Michael has changed so much,' Jennie said.

'Fokinghams never change. Michael seems all right now, but deep down, he's not one of us. God, I loathed him when he had a go at Jack every time your back was turned. I guessed right away he was a pansy, and I told Jack he should watch out. Well he didn't, the fool, but that didn't give the Fokinghams the right to treat us like peasants.'

'I don't think they do,' Jennie said, trying hard to see both sides. 'They just live in a different world.'

'But they think theirs is best, the only one for civilized folk. We're the subterranean worms that serve them.'

'You say the Fokinghams drew you together, but that wouldn't have driven her into your arms.'

He glanced at her. 'Don't be mealy-mouthed, Jen. You mean bed. Yes, there was more. Anna kept seeking me out, one thing led to another, and one day—' his face changed as he thought of that private moment '—well, let's say she decided the time had come. I loved her, but Anna, she couldn't believe it. Everyone said they loved her, she told me, but it turned out they all had their own reasons, wanted something of her. So she assumed I did too, and decided to use me for her own ends. That's what she told me later. She didn't bargain on falling in love with me.

'Of course after the Fokinghams found out in Montevanya, they really dripped poison in her ears, and she found out later her mother had torn up the letters she sent to me. I didn't know about the children, and she didn't intend to tell me until later in case her parents guessed her plans. She was going to find them, and just bring them back to England so the Fokinghams would be forced to let us marry. The Fokinghams, always the Fokinghams.'

'They can't touch you now, Tom.'

'Can't they?' He tapped the letter. 'They'll carry on this sort of thing till the end of time. The only good thing is that it will be poor Freddie who cops this one.' He laughed. 'They can tell the Administrator of the estate I've pinched stuff if they like, but what good will it do them? They can't prove anything because I have nothing of Anna left. Not even their grandchild.'

As the summer dragged on Anna's death seemed to hang over everything and everyone like a heavy pall that could never be shaken off. Aunt Win suffered, Dad did, Tom and Freddie, and Jennie too, all waiting for the probate court to appoint an administrator, so that the world could move on again.

She was glad she had not gone to see Lady Fokingham about her quest, though it worried her that she had not visited her to talk about Anna. It would have been hypocritical, she decided, and had written instead. It was just as well, for when she spoke to Michael he told her that his parents had realized Tom might want to hunt for the children, and they had taken a decisive stance. Tom would have no legal hope of finding the children, since Anna was no longer alive.

So they had clearly decided that no heir beyond Michael was preferable to an heir by Tom. Jennie shivered. Anna's babies were their grandchildren, but they acted as though they were nothing at all to do with them.

'They also pointed out,' Michael said, 'that when I marry there would be even less reason to find those children for inheritance purposes and so Tom stands to gain little.' He laughed, but there was strain in his voice.

'Doesn't she realize yet, Michael, that it will never happen?' Jennie was appalled. So the Fokinghams were still living in a fool's paradise so far as Michael was concerned.

'No. Or if Father does, I think he would expect me to make the great sacrifice. Marry and make some woman unhappy, as well as myself, in order to provide another Fokingham. Or if I can't face the idea of a woman in my bed, marry her anyway and send her out to find another sire.'

'No. That's too much, Michael.' Jenny was indignant. 'It would be the same situation as with Tom.'

'It wouldn't,' he said bitterly. 'Whatever happens once the magic words have been spoken, written down, signed and sealed on a nice wedding certificate, is perfectly in order – from an inheritance viewpoint.'

'The Freddie situation reversed,' Jennie said wretchedly. 'Michael, I'm going to find those babies. Anna didn't want me to tell Tom though. Suppose I *did* find them, and they didn't want to meet him. It's possible. So will you help?'

'If I can. Though for your sake, Jennie, not for my parents.'

She had two hopes to move forward on. Michael had kept Anna's letters from the nursing home, and would look at them to see if the address was on them. The second hope, at least so far as her task was concerned, was *The Island*, which was published in July. It was neither a racy novel nor a clever satire on social life. Not entirely to her surprise, *The Island* was a triumphant and serious story of a young mother's hunt for her lost child after the war had ended. Anna had completed her own story, regardless of its effect on others, especially Mary who still might not know of Tom's twins' birth. The novel might carry on the story from *The Dishonourable Miss Sheringham* but the style was dull compared with that. The critics hated the book, but sales were good. Moreover, Jennie hoped it might prove a guide to Anna's search for her own children.

The move to Applemere and farewell to the Dower House took all her spare time in late July, and every night she longed for the day's arrival, to rid herself of nightmares and throw herself into work. When it finally condescended to arrive, she drove the Applemere Flyer over herself with the twins installed, and walked in the door of the cottage, half fearful that it might vanish before her eyes. The furniture was in place, thanks to Albert and Tom, there were flowers everywhere and Aunt Win was waiting for them with afternoon tea.

The twins raced through to the garden and came back shouting:

'Mummy, mummy, come outside.'

She ran into the garden to find it all cleared of brambles and even some of her old roses in bloom, which had survived their years of neglect. Her vegetable patch no longer looked a lonely oasis from weeds and rough grass.

'Michael and Anthony have been hard at work.' Aunt Win glowed.

The smell of scones baking in the range re-awakened memories. She had only to open the door and there she would find Richard, looking up at her with his smiling blue eyes. His presence was everywhere, but she didn't mind. She welcomed it. She was home. She was at Applemere again.

Eleven

Christmas at Applemere Cottage. Jennie could hardly believe how much difference her return here had made. She had the strength both to face her problems and to enjoy her memories of the past. With a light heart she remembered Richard and the twins making paper chains from some old railway timetables which Dad had given them. They were printed in several colours, admirably suited for garlands. When she produced these from their traditional yearly hiding place under the eaves of the cottage roof, the twins fell on them with whoops of joy, once permission had been granted to adorn the house for Christmas.

The celebration was signalling new hopes for 1932. In the year ahead there would be hope for the Applemere Flyer and perhaps even the slump might slacken this year, though so far there was no sign of it. Surely the new National Government drawn from different political parties to meet the emergency should be able to achieve *something*. Certainly books in every field were pouring off the presses, which was good, although some said that that was an indication of a yet worsening economy, during which people needed escape in the form of Hollywood musicals and undemanding novels. Mrs Christie's *The Sittaford Mystery* had been eagerly lapped up this year and for next year the publishers' traveller was promising a return of Hercule Poirot in *Peril at End House*.

Jennie had harvested her small crop in the cottage garden and promised it more for next year, planting seeds and cuttings. Now it looked bleak and bereft but under its soil life would soon be stirring. The twins had been separated for the first time, with Jamie at a boys' secondary school in Canterbury and Lynette at a girls' school in Folkestone. So far it had made little difference to their absorption in each other. School was merely a distraction from the kingdom of their own life from which even Jennie was excluded. She wondered if Anna's twins had the same affinity? She belatedly realized that she had been guilty of what she and Richard had tried to avoid for Lynette and Jamie, thinking of them as an entity. Appalled, she realized she didn't in fact know whether Anna's children were boys or girls, or one of each. Had Anna ever mentioned it? She didn't think so. She could not ask the only two persons who might know, Lady Fokingham or Tom.

'I have an announcement to make,' Albert informed them at Christmas luncheon. He sounded very solemn, but Jennie noticed the twinkle in his eye. 'Mrs Arbuthnot,' Albert began, 'who as you know lives next door to me, is moving to live nearer her daughter. She has,' polite cough, 'suggested that I move with her. In other words, we should be wed.'

A stifled cry came from Aunt Win, and two from Jennie – one for Aunt Win's sake, the other for her own, despite the twinkle. She couldn't run the Flyer without Albert, not only because she needed someone reliable on board, but because he was an invaluable source of information and, even more valuable, a staunch friend. Who else knew the intricacies of the discount system, who else knew every book from *Oliver Twist* to *Orlando*, from Josephus to Joad? Who else knew how to steer the Flyer through precisely the right spot to negotiate the bridge in Marsham Lane? Who else could, with his quiet 'ahem', draw her attention to a troubled engine as she drove along the lanes.

'However,' Albert added, 'I have informed Mrs Arbuthnot that I shall not be able to accept her kind offer of matrimony.'

A flood of relief left Jennie speechless, but Lynette piped up, 'I'm glad. Mummy needs you in the Flyer.'

Albert inclined his head in acknowledgement. 'I should of course have been most sad to leave the Applemere Flyer. However that was not my reason for preferring to remain here. My heart, I informed Mrs Arbuthnot – and I had never given her reason to believe otherwise – was another's, and even if that lady refused me, I could conceive of no other with whom I would wish to spend my life.'

Aunt Win glared at him, red in the face. 'And who, Albert, is she, might I ask?'

'You, Miss Harkness.'

157

'Albert?' She stared at him, then burst into tears, which puzzled the twins.

'Don't you want to marry Mr Hodge, Aunt Win?' Lynette asked.

'Of course I do,' she wailed.

Dad joined in with gusto. 'You'll have to kiss her, Albert.'

'I am in agreement with you, George.' Albert rose to his feet, took Aunt Win's hand, bowed over it, then kissed her to great applause.

Then: 'But I can't,' Aunt Win cried, to Jennie's horror. 'I can't live in Canterbury, Albert. What would George do without me?'

'I'll be leaving the Station House in just over a year, Win, you know that,' Dad said hastily. 'Don't you worry about me.'

'I'll look after him,' Jennie offered, frantically rearranging the cottage in her mind.

'Mrs P.,' Albert replied firmly, 'has enough to do running the Flyer. Now my idea is this, though you might not like it, George. I've grown fond of Fairsted, so how would it be if I sold my Canterbury home, bought one in Fairsted and we all live together, Win, George and me?'

In the excited talk that followed, Jennie could distinguish the word Flyer, Station House, attic rooms, but was chatting so hard herself she could not hear the gist of what anybody else was saying. Finally there was general agreement that Albert should move into the Station House after their marriage and that time could then be taken over the choosing of a new residence suitable for newly weds and their family: Dad.

The Christmas pudding had steamed on happily for another half an hour while this scheme and wedding dates were eagerly discussed. Everyone's opinion was sought, even Lynette and Jamie's, though Jennie took little part. She was too busy contemplating how marvellous life could be sometimes, and how unexpected. At its darkest hour it could turn round, and present news such as this.

Perhaps it would for Tom too, she hoped. If only he and Freddie could share in this sudden happiness. When the probate court decision had at last come through, everything had, as expected, gone to Freddie, but he had given Tom the choice of a rent-free cottage in Bossingham village, and a small fee in return for looking after Anna's royalties and publishing affairs.

Tom was in the process of moving from Goreham Court into Bossingham village, and had made that the reason for his not being present today. He'd find something to eat, he said, turning down every plea Jennie had made. He hated being beholden, as he saw it, to Freddie, and was determined to find another job – but nowadays when men were marching in protest for the lack of food in their bellies because of the unemployment there was little likelihood of that. She had tried to interest Mary in his plight, but she was intransigent. He had made his bed of thorns and now he could lie on it, was her view. After Tom left Mary, her father had ensured that no one in the brewing fraternity would offer him a job, even if there were any, especially him. His first employer, Mr Hargreaves of Fairsted Manor, was still seething at Tom's disloyalty in moving to Patchers brewery when he married Mary.

With Anna's death, all her earlier novels as well as the most recent had had a further boom, local speculation about the facts behind *The Island* was rife, and Jennie was glad that Tom was living in Bossingham, not Fairsted.

On New Year's Eve she lay awake thinking over the Christmas period and listening to the church bells ringing out to welcome the New Year. What would 1932 bring? Five terrible things had happened in the last few years, Richard's death, Anna's death, her baby's, Tom and Freddie's feud, and the final split with the Fokinghams. Did that mean, she wondered, she was entitled to ask her fairy godmother for five wonderful things to happen to make up for it? One already had, Albert and Aunt Win's forthcoming marriage. As she had left the Station House on Christmas Day, Aunt Win had whispered 'Omdurman' in her ear, and Jennie had laughed. In her childhood, the word had haunted her, a symbol of Aunt Win's grumpiness. Then she had discovered that Aunt Win's sweetheart had been killed at the Battle of Omdurman and all the grumpiness was explained – and vanished with Albert's arrival. No more disappointments now.

And there were still four more wonderful things to happen. Bliss.

The first came promptly. It brought Eileen and Georgius

back to Applemere House after having been in 'foreign parts', as Eileen put it, over Christmas. It turned out it was Montevanya, since Georgius wasn't exiled from it, as Max virtually was. Viktor must see Georgius as no threat, Jennie thought, since no country in its right mind would put him on the throne, even as a puppet. Indeed it could have helped Viktor since it was a sign to the public that all was friendly in the Deleanu family. On their way back, Eileen told her airily, they had called in to see one or two friends in Holland and Vienna. That must mean the political scene was hotting up again, Jennie realized. In Germany Hitler's Nazi party was rapidly gaining strength, over six million at the last vote, and Eileen told her that one of the Kaiser's sons, Prince August Wilhelm, was a member of the party. The outlook, she said, was not good.

Jennie welcomed Eileen and Georgius even more gladly than usual, for Georgius was all too eager to present more performances on the Flyer, which filled her gap left by Mary. He had some amazing new tricks, the magician's orange tree on which an orange appeared to gobble up a walnut, an egg and a borrowed handkerchief. Then a dish of spirits was set alight in front of the tree, bringing it to miraculous life, the tree blossomed and then the blossom became oranges. Real ones, which delighted the children. Naturally, with Georgius, one of the oranges proved to be a lemon. Jennie was grateful that her stock of books was on the lower deck of the Flyer otherwise they might have become fair game for other tricks of his that went 'just a little wrong'.

'I wish you were here all the time, Georgius,' she told him fervently.

'I also vish this,' Georgius rumbled happily, intent on building a pyramid of crystal glasses. Not hers, thankfully, even though hers were from Woolworths.

'Fortunately,' Eileen informed her, 'your wish is about to be granted, Jennie. We're moving to Kent.'

'To Applemere House?' Jennie could hardly contain her delight.

'No. To Goreham Court.' Eileen looked amused at Jennie's reaction of complete astonishment. 'I'm sorry, I thought Freddie would have told you.'

All this happening, and Jennie hadn't known. Sometimes

she felt she didn't know her own brothers. She didn't think Tom could have known about the sale either, for he might have mixed reactions to part of Anna's family moving in. Nevertheless it was his family too, since Eileen would be there. A just turn of fate, Jennie decided. What would Fairsted make of this, she wondered, as yet another unwed couple moved into Goreham Court? Gossip in peace, she supposed. Bossingham would bear the 'shame' of this news, as well as the glory.

'There's more to tell you,' Eileen added.

'It can't be better than your own news.'

'It's certainly different. Marie and Roger are selling Applemere House.'

Jennie's first reaction was that this was sad news, especially for Michael, for it must mean he would have to move. And then came the growing realization: what might it mean for her? The cottage would be sold too.

'Don't worry.' Eileen read her expression correctly. 'The cottage is safe.'

'And Michael?' Jennie realized how much she would miss him; it was almost as though his presence were a compensation for Anna's loss, and at least she could talk about Anna with Michael as she couldn't with Tom, who had simply closed off the subject in his mind.

'Don't worry about that either. I suspect Roger has taken a dive on the stock exchange during the slump otherwise he'd have handed it over to Michael as his heir. Anyway, Michael and Anthony are to continue living there at least for the present. After all, one of them might want to get married,' Eileen said mischievously.

At least her fairy godmother hadn't let her down too badly, Jennie thought. 'It's a shame though, in a way. It's been a Fokingham home for centuries and now it's leaving the family.'

'Not entirely. It's merely taking a sharp bend.'

'What do you mean?' Jennie frowned.

'Max has bought it.'

Jennie was first astounded, and then pleased at such a simple and obvious solution. Second thoughts brought concern, however. With Max would come Queen Marta, with all the ramifications that might mean for Fairsted. Worse was the possibility that Queen Zita might arrive in all her 'glory' too, unless she returned to her darling son Viktor. Nothing like hoping. Nevertheless, to have an ex-king living in the village might bring all sorts of problems. Kings were notorious targets for assassination, even ex ones, usually in case they decided to become active ones again, like King Carol. She comforted herself that Viktor must feel secure enough in Montevanya, without resorting to fratricide. After all, Max had abdicated of his own free will.

'Doesn't that please you?' Eileen lifted an eyebrow.

'I'm not sure,' Jennie replied frankly. 'Applemere's character will change if the whole Montevanyan family moves here. Queen Marta doesn't look the type of person to appreciate living in Applemere.' Jennie saw another major problem rapidly approaching. She had been assuming she was established in Applemere Cottage for ever, but one look at her and Queen Zita would whisk her out of it quicker than a wasp sting. With Richard's death Jennie's hope of buying a home had receded indefinitely, so if she had to leave Applemere Cottage, where would she go then? Life, she thought crossly, always had a trick up its sleeve and unlike Georgius's these tricks *never* failed to hit the mark.

'I'm happy to inform you that Max and Marta are divorcing,' Eileen told her cheerfully. 'I can't answer for Queen Zita, of course, but at least Max alone owns the house.'

Slightly better news. In fact, much better. 'Thank heavens for that. What grounds is Max divorcing her on?'

'You know Max. He's doing the decent thing – if one can call it that, under our stupid laws. He's letting her divorce him on grounds of adultery.'

'He has a mistress?' Why did this take her aback? She supposed she hadn't expected it of him somehow, despite his rakish past.

'He may have, but he wouldn't drag her in. It's the usual arrangement, I expect. Hotel chambermaid at Brighton, carefully caught in bed with him. Sitting up decorously, of course, but it's enough for the court. He says he has nothing to lose so why not?'

Poor Max. But how much happier he might be in the long run, Jennie hoped. Especially if he eventually came to live at Applemere. He would be her landlord, and a good neighbour, provided she didn't have to get the red carpet out for him each time he arrived. On the other hand, perhaps she could get paid by Southern Railway to rush up to the Halt with the carpet whenever royalty was expected to set its dainty foot to the ground at the Halt. Such daft thoughts kept her amused for some time.

So that, she realized, after Eileen had left, might take care of two more wonderful happenings. And it was only January the fifth. There was nearly a whole year to produce the last two. So let one be my finding out where Anna's babies are, she asked the stars that night. At the moment that looked as likely as asking Peter Pan to pop in from Neverland. The hunt was only inching forward and that over ground that she knew Anna must already have covered.

Jennie had read *The Island* many times now, seeking in it clues as to where she might turn. First she had thought there must be some included, secondly that there weren't any. When Anna was writing it, she would have had no idea that she would not live to see it published, which would result in her passing the hunt on to someone else. That argued that there would be no clues or at best only unconscious ones in the novel. Ellen Pargeter, a young nurse, falls in love with a French soldier during the war. He is killed, and she bears his son. His parents claim the baby, and promptly disappear. Ellen devotes her life to hunting for her son, and the novel ends triumphantly with her finding him years later. Had Anna, Jennie wondered, suddenly received a clue as to where she might search next, and where indeed had she searched? Or had Anna written the novel to console herself that anything was possible, knowing that her own trail of evidence had come to an end.

Jennie realized she could not even guess the answer until she had gone further along her own trail. Born in Switzerland the children would have to be registered at the local Swiss City Hall, and if the Fokinghams had so chosen, at the local British consulate in Geneva. So far so good. There would have been no compulsion for the children to be registered as British however, and given the Fokinghams' antipathy to their birth, they might well not have been. If they were, however, there was a chance that their birth certificate might have reached Somerset House since some, though far from all, consulate records had.

Full of hope that her quest was beginning she had visited Somerset House, only to discover that though there were some records for that year from Switzerland, no birth with the name Fokingham was registered. She returned home thwarted, deciding that as soon as Christmas was over she would go to Switzerland herself to make enquiries. If she could find the birth certificates, she reasoned, some record of the adoption might also exist somewhere, even if they didn't have formal adoptions in 1914. Going to Switzerland would mean she was walking in Anna's footsteps of course, but unless she followed the same false trails, she would not be able to take the search forward.

It was then that Michael had proved so helpful. From Anna's letters he had discovered that the nursing home was in the Montreux area. Montreux was on Lake Geneva some distance across the lake from Geneva itself. He wasn't hopeful that a visit would achieve anything, however.

'Think about it, Jennie,' he had said. 'If the consul didn't forward the certificates to Britain, why should he reveal any information to you? You have no direct status, and nor, knowing my parents, do I think they'd let the babies be registered in the Fokingham name.'

That had triggered a new train of thought for Jennie. She had already put a request through the Swiss Embassy to check their records, but after an agonizingly long time the answer had reached her that there were no births registered for twins in the Montreux area for early September 1914 under the name of Fokingham, or with British parentage. With Michael's comment in her mind, she returned to Somerset House and triumphantly discovered that twins, a boy Guy and a girl Bridget, were born on September the seventh 1914 to one Anna Avril. The certificates were left blank for the father, as was usual for illegitimate births, and Anna was the daughter of one Marie Avril, housewife, and Roger Avril, clerk. The Fokinghams, she realized to her amusement would not break the *British* link by not registering the births at all (only the Swiss law, which being foreign was not so important). They would, however, make it impossible, or so they would have hoped, for the children to be traced. Perhaps they knew Anna better than Jennie had appreciated. Avril, Jennie knew from Anna herself, was Anna's fourth baptismal name, and stemmed from an old surname in the Fokingham family. This was the first step achieved, Jennie gloated. Now the hunt was on.

And where did it take her?

Answer, Switzerland.

Jennie half wished she had taken up Eileen's offer to come with her, now she was on the train. She had refused the offer partly because she felt Eileen should be with Georgius as he struggled to adapt to country living (not that Georgius seemed to have much struggle), and partly because it was her problem, and she felt she should do it alone.

Mid January wasn't an ideal time to travel, but the sooner she went, the more time she'd have to follow up any clues before she gave her mind to Aunt Win's wedding in April.

'No point waiting, Win,' Albert had pointed out. 'We're not getting any younger.'

Aunt Win had seen his point immediately.

Jennie had gratefully accepted Eileen's offer to pay for her trip, even though she wasn't coming herself. There was no way the meagre profits of the Applemere Flyer would extend to Continental rail travel and hotels.

The winter sun was sparkling on Lake Geneva as the train steamed past snow-covered mountains into Montreux, or more correctly Montreux-Vernex since Montreux was composed of several villages spreading along the lakeside and up onto the white mountainsides. She decided it would be best to stay by the lake, rather than in the mountain village nearest the nursing home, and was pleased to discover the Hotel Pension Suisse had a garden running down to the lake. She would have an afternoon off exploring the Castle of Chillon, made famous by Lord Byron's poem about the prisoner in the crypt. She enjoyed the anonymity of being on her own, both here and in an elegant salon, whose fare was a far cry from sandwiches on the Applemere Flyer.

Next morning, refreshed, she took the cable car railway up to the village of Glion, and then a horse and trap 'taxi' to the home. The icy air was so pure up here, so fresh, it was easy to imagine Anna was with her all the way, urging her on. She could almost hear her laugh when she reached the home itself. She could imagine her here, so apparently free, so mercilessly chained into the prison, just like the prisoner in Chillon. The head of the home was a middle-aged man, whom she got to

165

see by sheer persistence, and she blessed her wartime knowledge of French. She took an instant dislike to his bland officialdom, and was hardly surprised at his reply, after she stated her mission.

'*Je regrette, madame,*' he began as her heart sank, 'you are mistaken. This is not a maternity home, nor has it ever been. This is a home for tubercular patients. I will check our records, however.' He spoke into his telephone and various books were produced remarkably quickly by a dour white-coated minion. 'Ah yes,' he examined them, 'it was true there was an Anna Fokingham amongst our tubercular patients. But only that. No mention of a child. Nor would there be.'

'I have seen the birth certificates,' Jennie informed him firmly. 'She had twins in the Montreux area, and she wrote letters home from this home.' She flourished the certificates before him, and after taking them reluctantly, he examined them carefully. Then, exuding triumph, he handed them back.

'These are for a Madame Anna Avril. You said the name was Fokingham. There is no Anna Avril in these records.' He decided to be magnanimous and show her the admissions ledger, as she did her best to explain in rusty French.

'I realize there is a matter of confidentiality, but that must be usual in cases of illegitimate births.'

'It is not a question of confidentiality,' he interrupted smoothly. 'You have been misinformed. Whoever this Madame Avril was, she was not a patient here. It is, and never was, permitted for babies to be born here.'

He brushed aside her further arguments, and it was obvious she would get nowhere. She thanked him stiffly, and left, doing her best to pretend to be satisfied. The trap was still waiting for her, but when she descended at the cable car station she decided to take lunch at one of the hotels in Glion village, before returning to Montreux. Local information might be invaluable, and no one would volunteer anything in the home itself. Here she fared much better, and was directed to an address in Montreux where a former nurse at the home lived.

Madame Théviers lived in the Avenue de Belmont, in an apartment of some style, which was a relief since it suggested she was not dependent on a meagre pension paid by her previous employers. She was a large lady all in black who

166

obviously enjoyed the products of the many patisseries in the town. At first she was wary, but as Jennie spoke frankly of her reasons for wanting to discover the truth, she became more human.

'*La pauvre*,' she exclaimed indignantly, as Jennie recounted the tale of Anna's betrayal by the Rocs, and then went on to tell Madame Théviers of the reception she had received at her home.

Madame cackled aloud. '*Mais oui*, it is and always was a home for tubercular patients, an *hôpital sanitaire*. And of course no births took place at the hospital. They make their money because they never speak of such births. We all knew that to one building, supposed to be for infectious patients, ladies were taken when they were *enceintes*. It was hidden in the woods. Their diseases were too advanced, we were told, for them to be mixing with other patients and the building had its own staff, very highly paid staff. There might have been babies, who knows, for patients arrived heavily wrapped in coats and left much thinner. There were stories and many laughs. Most of these patients were English, we were told.'

'What happened to the babies?' Jennie asked eagerly.

'There were many rumours over the years. Monsieur Robbins was very friendly with Monsieur Menton, the owner. We laughed that the law must not be broken, but it could be bent a little, if the clients were sufficiently distinguished.'

'Who is Monsieur Robbins? The consul from Geneva?'

'*Non*. He was his agent in Montreux. There are and were many English in Montreux, they have their own doctor, their own chemist—'

'Their own adoption methods?'

'Ah.' Madame cackled. 'Perhaps. I would not know. There is an orphanage near Montreux, run by the Soeurs de la Rose, a religious organization, you understand. Soeur Marie-Thérèse, the head of the orphanage, came sometimes to the home, as did Monsieur Robbins.'

'And this orphanage is still here?' Jennie held her breath. It all sounded too neat, the consul's agent, the home, the orphanage. But why not? Who would know or object to such discreet arrangements? Wouldn't it be logical for an orphanage to run an adoption service too? There was nothing illegal

167

about arranging such matters then. Only now was it more formal.

The orphanage was another taxi ride (by motor car this time, and thank you, Eileen) and though Jennie had been building up pictures in her mind of an austere Dickensian establishment, it proved to be a friendly, girls only orphanage, dressed in neat pink uniforms with ankle socks and print dresses. The sister in charge could not have been more amiable, and even proved to have been here in 1914, though not herself the famous Soeur Marie-Thérèse. Jennie's hopes soared, only to find that the smile, though probably genuine, hid as usual a wall of iron.

'*Oui, madame*, I remember Miss Avril,' she confirmed, 'because she visited us after the war was over, as well as when she was ill here before the war. She was English, the daughter of a doctor and his wife in the north of England, her mother told me.' The concluding smile suggested that it was as far as she was prepared to go.

'Do you arrange adoptions? Would you still have records here?'

The smile remained firmly in place. 'We do, but they are confidential you understand, for the children's sake.'

Jennie felt she was on slightly firmer ground now. 'Miss Avril herself told me that a Monsieur and Madame Roc adopted her twins, and this information could only have come originally from you, whether directly or through the nursing home. And as,' Jennie gained confidence, 'it was not a formal adoption, the confidentiality must be a matter of choice rather than law in 1914. Miss Avril paid your fee, she also later met the Rocs and paid them to return the babies. But they disappeared with her money, and she was betrayed.'

Perhaps she was saying away too much. Jennie had a moment's alarm, but comforted herself that no harm could come of that now. Still not a flicker of response from that placid face, even though it remained friendly as the sister said: 'I do not understand how that could have happened.'

'I have the name,' Jennie swept on, 'so would it not be possible for you to check your records and tell at least me how it was spelled?' That would give her something to go on.

She thought she was going to be refused, as still there was no response.

168

And then: 'I can see, Madame, you are not one to abandon your search easily.'

'I cannot,' Jennie said quietly. 'I made a promise to Miss Avril as she lay dying.'

Amazingly this changed everything. Jennie could have kicked herself for not playing this one earlier. A deathbed request was to be taken seriously. 'It is true we have the adoption certificate, recorded in our books.' Soeur Marie-Thérèse thought for a moment and then rang a bell. I will allow you to inspect the books yourself.'

At last! Jennie trotted behind the young nun as she took her to a small room adjacent to the main office, and soon Jennie was looking at the entry in the book, and then the certificate itself. Twins, a boy Guy and a girl Brigitte, born to Anna Avril, adopted by Mr and Madame P. Roc of ten Rue Bonival, Geneva. So it was Roc, not Rock or Roch.

Jennie was so relieved to have seen the spelling at last together with concrete proof of the adoption that she went back to the hotel almost dancing, despite the deep snow. Only later did the terrible thought come to her that there was something odd about the address. She sprang out of bed to consult her guidebooks, and her heart sank. Number ten Rue Bonival was the address of the British consul in Geneva, whose name was not Roc. It was possible, she supposed miserably, that the Rocs were on the staff there, but in her heart she knew it was unlikely. If it were so simple, Anna would have found them. Nevertheless, Anna's hunt had continued. How though, and *where*?

At Applemere Cottage discussions began on where to hold the wedding breakfast for Aunt Win and Albert Hodge. Goreham House was offered – no. Aunt Win decreed, it must be in Fairsted, and naturally Albert seconded this. Applemere House, suggested Michael. This too was politely declined. Not like home, Aunt Win decided. The Station House was her choice but this was promptly vetoed by everyone on the grounds that Aunt Win would either end up doing all the work or make the helpers' job impossible while she superintended them. So Applemere Cottage was agreed.

The day was fast approaching, and despite offers of help from Eileen and Lynette, Jennie decided to hire the help of

Alice Cowper, who needed the money since her husband had left her two years earlier. She was a good cook, as well as being an old sweetheart of Freddie's. Alice might cheer him up and – no, Jennie was not going to matchmake, even if this particular match did seem a good idea. Freddie and Tom had both agreed to be present, which was a relief, and Alfie and Arabella too. Mary had declined with apologies, which Jennie thought were genuine as she was fond of Aunt Win. Everyone was, and there was growing excitement in the village.

Jennie woke up at dawn on the wedding day and rushed to the window to see that sun was clearly visible. Three cheers. It was. This might be another precious wonderful happening and her fairy godmother could take the rest of the year off, if all her hopes came true. Eileen had insisted on supplying champagne with which to toast the couple, beer was provided and sandwiches, trifles and tea, all Aunt Win's favourites. The fishman had even made a special trip from Folkestone to deliver fresh shrimps. The garden was looking happy too, in its springtime colours and flowers. It might even be warm enough for guests to spread from the cottage into the garden. It would be a tight fit inside.

Aunt Win made a stately blushing bride in a white linen suit and hat, with apple blossom in it, and as for Albert – well, the frock coat had been replaced with a tailcoat, with new striped trousers and a dashing grey topper accompanying them. Albert turned out to have an extremely beautiful young relative, Dinah, the eighteen-year-old blonde blue-eyed granddaughter of his sister, and she made a striking bridesmaid together with thirteen-year-old Arabella and Lynette, all in pale blue.

The service seemed over in no time at all, and Mendelssohn's wedding march was then superseded by the church bells. The whole of Fairsted seemed to have turned out to cheer the happy pair along the lane to Applemere Cottage. Alice had remained behind at the cottage to have everything ready, and Jennie immediately went to her aid, while the unaccustomed sound of champagne corks filled the air. She was so busy with the food that it was not for some time she discovered there an unexpected guest. Max had been staying at Goreham Court, and had arrived with Eileen and Georgius. He looked far less strained, she thought, and thank goodness, he'd got rid of the beard.

She instantly began to curtsey, but he laid a hand on her wrist to prevent her. 'Not here, Jennie, please. Remember, I am Max.'

'You're visiting at the right time,' she said. 'Kent is loveliest with bluebells and apple blossom.'

'Alas, I am only here to discuss –' he shrugged '– dull things'.

'As dull as Viktor?' she couldn't resist asking.

He laughed. 'He and even duller. Mr Hitler for example.'

'No politics today,' Jennie said firmly.

'I agree. Are those the bluebells?' He gazed at the small patch under the tree in her garden. 'I have heard of them.'

'Yes, but there are many more in the grounds of Applemere House. You own a great many.'

'I have never seen them there.'

'I could show them to you now,' she said impulsively. 'You shouldn't miss them while you are here.' For a moment she wondered if she had been too forward, but Max looked pleased, which reassured her. With a word to Michael to explain, she led him through the Applemere gardens, past the pond she loved so much, where the last of the wild daffodils were still blooming together with the bluebells.

Max stared at them for some while before commenting, 'Perhaps I shall be another Wordsworth when I live here, only instead of marvelling at dancing daffodils, I shall write of the bluebells.'

'Don't you have bluebells in Montevanya?' she asked, but when he did not answer she felt humbled. 'I'm sorry,' she said, 'It must hurt very much to have no land of your own any more.'

'My own? No one owns land. It belongs to itself, its mountains, its fields and its streams, no matter what busy wars we human engage in over it. And yes, Jennie, it does hurt. I envy you, for you still wear your crown.'

'What crown is that?' she asked doubtfully.

'You are a bookseller.'

'I'm only a bookseller's widow.'

'You are the queen of what you do. Whereas I am merely an ex-king. May I crown you, Queen Jennie?' He picked several of the daffodils and came near to her.

171

'You may, humble servant,' She entered into his mood, removed her hat and bent her head towards him, so that he could twist the flowers into her hair. 'Now that I am truly queen,' she informed him,' I shall dedicate myself to my duty.'

She had meant the Flyer, but he mistook her. 'You wish to find Anna's children, so Eileen told me. You can trust me, Jennie,' he added, obviously sensing her immediate alarm. 'No word to anyone, and that particularly includes my Aunt Marie and Sir Roger. How are you getting on with this the task? If I can help, I will.'

She explained how slow the process was, and the limited progress she had made since Switzerland.

She had read *The Island* again and this time noticed that one apparently minor character, a solicitor called Bernard Robillaud, turned out to be a key player. Could this solicitor could be equated to Mr Robbins, the consul's agent in Montreux before the war? Robbins to Robillaud was not too great a hop. If she was right – and it was a big if – where was he now, eighteen years later? She had been sure he was no longer in Montreux. An enquiry to the Geneva consulate produced nothing, but Madame Théviers had proved a more productive source, though it had taken time, while Jennie waited impatiently. Then at last the letter had come two days ago. Mr Robbins had retired not to England but close to Antibes on the French Riviera. Initially Jennie had rejoiced. Antibes was near Cannes. Could that be the reason for Anna's visit to Cannes with her two years ago?

'I have discovered,' she told Max, 'that the agent of the British Consul who was so involved in the affair, a Mr Robbins, now lives in the south of France, near Antibes, and I think that might have been what took Anna to Cannes when we went there in 1930. I had been wondering whether it was worth going to see him again, even though Anna would have explored any avenue he suggested.'

She stared at the seat she and Anna had been sitting on when she first met Max. She'd only been fourteen then, and he a young man of nineteen. How long ago that seemed. 'Perhaps,' she continued her line of thought, 'Anna believed he'd lied over the information he'd given her at first, because she returned there two years ago.'

'It is possible.' He frowned.

She made up her mind. 'I shall go then.'

'Take care if so, Jennie. There might be more opposition than you imagine.'

'From Marie and Sir Roger?'

'More formidable. My mother.'

This was unexpected. 'Why?' she asked blankly.

'She believes strongly in the purity of the family name, Jennie. She believes the Deleanus have a divine right to rule Montevanya, and that Anna's children besmirch that ideal. She would stop at little, perhaps nothing, to prevent illegitimate children appearing in the public eye.'

'But she is an *ex* queen now.'

'And therefore all the more formidable. She believes the Deleanus must return to the throne of Montevanya, greeted like returning gods. If you go on seeking these children, you will be watched, and if you draw too close, prevented.'

'I'm not going to give up,' she said calmly.

'No.' He looked at her. 'I don't believe you will. Then please do me a favour. When you plan to go, telephone me at this number, not at my Kensington home, and tell me.'

She looked at him and laughed. 'You're serious, aren't you, Max?'

'I am. Especially where you're concerned, Jennie.' He leaned forward and for one wild moment she thought he was going to kiss her, as once he had done years ago. But if she was right, he thought better of it, and merely touched her arm, indicating they should return to the party.

Twelve

Jennie held her breath, as the operator telephoned through to Max's home. True, it was a Mayfair number, whereas his earlier home had been in Kensington, but suppose darling Queen Zita answered the telephone? She might still be living with Max. Then Jennie realized how ridiculous this was. Zita would never so demean herself as to pick up a telephone receiver. Jennie then pondered whom to ask for if a butler answered? For ex-King Maximilian? No, nor for Mr Deleanu. And certainly not for Max. She would play safe, she decided. Even if Max were informal, it was highly unlikely that his butler would be, and so she compromised with Prince Maximilian.

She was rewarded by a friendly enough voice assuring her she'd be put through quick as a flash, and quick as a flash she was.

'I thought I'd tell you—' she began, only to be cut off with:

'Jennie, I'll be coming to Applemere tomorrow so perhaps you could bring that *symphoricarpos* there about six o'clock when the Flyer is back home?'

Several sets of bells began to ring in Jennie's head, and highly amused, she solemnly agreed she could indeed deliver the said plant at that hour. It would be a pink one, she assured him. She hung up the telephone receiver, wondering whether there really were spies everywhere in the Deleanu households, not to mention the telephone exchange, or whether Max was being extra careful. She decided that it was probably the latter, though Max had never struck her as being over-cautious. At least he had reacted promptly to her call, and she felt a sudden rush of pleasure at the thought of seeing him. She had a lot to tell him, and it didn't include discussions on botany, although she supposed she had better produce something in the shrub line in case Zita or Viktor had hired a man with a black hat pulled over his eyes to hide behind the bushes in the lane watching every move in and out of Applemere.

Over two months had passed since Aunt Win's wedding, when she was unable to leave Fairsted because of her commitments, but now she was impatient to continue her quest. It was more than a year since Anna's death and Jennie was all too well aware she was still covering ground that Anna herself must have trodden. If only she had left some letters or diaries that might give her a clue, but there had been none. She had obviously been meticulous in keeping both Tom and Freddie out of this part of her life.

Clutching a hastily dug up flowering currant bush, Jennie felt rather like Alice in Wonderland with the flamingo tucked underneath her arm which kept poking its head round to look at her. When she arrived at Applemere House, it promptly poked out a branch right underneath her chin. She had decided that potential spies were unlikely to be experts in garden bushes and that any bush would fit the bill for Max's purpose. At least she hoped so. In fact it was Anthony, not Max, who opened the door.

'Tradesmen's entrance for you,' he mocked, seeing the bush.

'And I expected a red carpet,' she retorted, stepping into the hall.

'Alas, Max doesn't believe in them. You'll find him redesigning the garden, incidentally.'

'Oh. That must be worrying for you.' She sympathized, knowing how much he and Michael loved the gardens as they were.

'No, darling Jennie, it is not. Max has a delightful way of redesigning without one noticing, and if one does he points out that it was all one's own idea anyway. Furthermore one can't actually pinpoint the changes since everything contrives to look exactly the same. The very essence of royalty, wouldn't you say?'

'Politics are above my humble head, my lord,' she sidestepped, and he laughed.

With a quickening sense of pleasure she went through into the gardens to find Max and eventually tracked him down sitting on an old tree trunk by the pond. Even Michael had ceased calling it the lake now. It had lost all pretensions to being a centrepiece for a planned vista from the house, and had relapsed into a sprawling nature home for wild life and flowers. Max was deep in thought and did not notice her arrival.

'Max?' she said shyly and he leapt up apologetically.

'So you have my *symphoricarpos*?' he said.

'A near equivalent,' she told him gravely, placing it at his side.

'I am sorry,' he said awkwardly, 'about the need for such games.'

'Is there really such a need?' She still did not believe it.

'Very much. That is why I wished to talk to you privately.'

'About possible danger to me?'

'Yes, and also to me, since I hope you will permit me to come with you to France.'

She stared at him in astonishment, trying to divide her pleasure at his suggestion from logic. Would his presence help or hinder? She gave up the attempt. She'd love to have his company.

'I would not,' he continued seriously, 'accompany you as ex-King Max of Montevanya, nor indeed as Mr Deleanu. That would only defeat the object, which is to protect you.'

Jennie took a deep breath. 'Is there room on that tree trunk for two? I need to think this over.'

'There is always room for two.'

This wasn't strictly accurate. Two, she discovered, could indeed sit on it, but only if they were very close together. Did she mind? No. They had been close enough before in the barn during the Serbian Retreat, and feeling the warmth of his body next to her seemed entirely natural.

'I can understand,' Jennie said, 'that Viktor – if he is ruthless enough – would wish that you could conveniently disappear for ever, but surely your mother would not want that? Your enemy is only Viktor.'

'Perhaps. There is also the possibility that if my mother, in what she sees as her divine destiny,' he answered bitterly, 'were to see my disappearance as being in the greater good of Montevanya, a tragic accident might well befall me.'

Jennie tried hard to imagine a world in which mothers could countenance the murder of her own children. Even if Queen Zita had tacitly agreed to the assassination of her husband, her own children must be a different matter. And yet Greek legends had held such stories.

176

'It's surely unlikely,' she replied, 'and as regards me, wouldn't your mother's aim be to prevent Anna's children being found? She would have no reason to *kill* me. It seems rather extreme.' She tried to say this lightly, almost as a joke, but Max did not reply immediately.

Eventually he took her hand in his. 'Jennie, we saw war together in Serbia, did we not? We saw what it can do, the way it steamrollers over families, over moral taboos, over everything that lies in its onward path.'

She remembered the piles of corpses lying by the sides of the roads and mountain paths, not soldiers alone, but old men, women and children. She thought of the tomb of the unknown warrior at Westminister and the Whitehall Cenotaph. The innocent victims might be remembered afterwards but no one had time to think of them while war was still raging.

'You mean there is no room for the individual in war. But this,' Jennie said as she tried to think straight, 'is not wartime, and the individual does matter.'

'Not to those who believe that their cause is greater than the individual.'

'Like Herr Hitler.'

'Yes. The Nazi party is stronger by the day. It's possible, so Eileen and Michael believe, that he might even stand for Chancellor, which means a Nazi-dominated country. And the Nazis believe in the cause, rather than the individual, just as much as the communism does.'

Jennie was surprised at this. 'But communism believes in equality.'

'And those in power feel they must ensure that the cause of equality is not threatened by individuals. Eileen tells me that in the Soviet Russia under Stalin there are rumours of countless people disappearing without trace. That is what happens when dictators take power to pursue a cause.'

'Would Viktor do that—' she caught sight of his face '— *is* he doing that in Montevanya?' she asked in horror.

He nodded. 'Not yet in a big way, as there is no strong opposition to him yet. But the odd disappearance then grows into the many, fantasy grips the dictatorship, and the many become multitudes eliminated on the merest suspicion of dissent. In Montevanya the breeze might blow into a wind.'

'And,' Jennie hesitated, 'your mother is part of this?'

'Neither she nor Viktor would hesitate to cause a death, if they felt that their destiny, whether throne or dictatorship, is threatened by anyone. It could be you, me or Anna's twins or countless others.'

'I don't see how Anna's twins could threaten them. Both you and Viktor have sons.'

'If I were killed, Stefan would undoubtedly die with me. If there is sufficient opposition to Viktor however, it is possible that his eldest son might indeed be offered the throne. Nevertheless Anna's children, being five years older, might provide a rallying point for strong opposition to Viktor or his family, especially if I and my son were dead.' Max turned to her, and gave his crooked smile. 'Now tell me I too am gripped by fantasy.'

'I do,' Jennie said decidedly.

'When one considers that thrones have been offered to British newspaper owners, Lord Rothermere that of Hungary, for example, and that of Albania to Lord Inchcape, perhaps my fantasy would not seem so outrageous to Viktor.'

Jennie stared at the Applemere pool before them, and the wild roses and willow trees sprawling at its side. Here in this magic garden such a world as Max described seemed far away. This was a Peter Pan Neverland in which one could dwell for ever. Once one grew up, however, Neverlands were only an occasional blessing, and entry had to be earned.

'I shall still go to France,' she said quietly.

She felt his hand tremble around hers. 'I understand,' he replied. 'I expected nothing else of you. So this is what I want you to do.'

He must have sensed her instant recoil at his taking over her plans, because he continued gently, 'Believe me, Jennie. This is necessary.'

'I would like know the times of the trains to Nice,' Jennie said to the concierge in the foyer of the Grand Hotel on the Cap d'Antibes, in as loud a voice as she could manage for the sake of prying ears. She needed her movements to be known.

She had enjoyed her two days here in suitably grand style. She had at first refused Max's demand that she buy some stylish clothes at his expense, but Michael had told her not to be so foolish. If Max said that it was necessary it was.

178

Once here, she was glad, as this was no place for old linen dresses that had come out of winter storage for the past four years, with hemlines being stitched up and down in a vain attempt to keep up with fashion. She had watched the tennis, she had relaxed with cocktails on the beach, she had visited the town and the botanic gardens. She had seen no killers lurking behind trees. Max seemed to think she would be in no danger at first because Viktor and Queen Zita might be interested to know where Mr Robbins now lived, but Jennie was of the opinion that they could as well find that out without stalking her. Indeed they might already know where the twins were. That was an uncomfortable thought.

The hotel ran its own car service to Antibes railway station and since Max was sure that her movements would be noted, it was part of his plan that she should take one. This hotel was host to the rich and the famous, and Jennie felt one of them herself by now, and was almost sorry to be leaving. *And she must be seen to do so.*

She chattered gaily to the concierge while the car was summoned, wondering which of the other guests milling around might be a hired spy. On the basis of Mrs Christie's method of choosing the most unlikely candidate for murder, it might be the English dowager with the lorgnette, or the *baggagiste* carrying her suitcase and one small bag to the car. Would he suddenly produce a handkerchief full of chloroform or plunge a dagger in her back? Neither, it seemed. She arrived at Antibes station, and duly purchased a ticket not to Nice but to Cannes.

Minutes after boarding the train, a nondescript French girl handed in her ticket and strolled out into the Juan Les Pins sunshine, leaving her suitcase steaming merrily on towards Cannes. So far the plan had gone smoothly. Leaving the suitcase in the compartment, she had visited the lavatory with her bag, just before the train reached this intermediate stop, then quickly removed her light outer coat to reveal a badly fitting linen dress, exchanged smart shoes for sandals, and exquisite hat for a sunbonnet and thus clad she had descended at Juan Les Pins railway station. Her heart had been pounding, half convinced that the placid-looking nun or the austere gentleman with top hat and monocle reading *Le Monde* was about to turn into a killer. If so, she had foiled them, as there was no sign of pursuit.

She jumped aboard the electric tram to return to Antibes, breathing more easily now that that she had a short time before any pursuers could catch up with her. She was still sure, however, that the opposition would know exactly where Mr Robbins lived and could be waiting on the doorstep for her. Nevertheless, Max was determined not to take chances, and so, once in the Place de la Victoire in Antibes she waited impatiently for the next tram that would take her into the foothills of the Alpes Maritime. And there at the village of Biot, six kilometres away, she would meet Max.

Suppose he wasn't there? They had agreed that if the worst happened and he failed to make the rendezvous, she should make her way back to England immediately however great the temptation to keep the appointment with Mr Robbins. The suspense began to prickle at the back of her neck as the tram rattled its towards Biot, where Mr Robbins lived. It stopped on the outskirts of the village by a small river, and she descended, to find no sign of Max.

Suppressing panic she began to stroll towards the village, rather than remain conspicuous by loitering where she was. In a few moments a group of French workmen in berets and blue *blousons* overtook her, laughing and joking. She felt a hand taking her underneath her arm, and turned indignantly to find herself looking into Max's laughing face.

'I make a good workman, yes?' he said.

Jennie felt limp with relief. 'Excellent. What are working at, Monsieur Max?'

'I am a very temporary student at the school for horticulture and agriculture here. Jennie, were you followed?'

'No, I noticed no one. Anyway, they're probably waiting here for me.'

'But they do not know when you will come, that is the point. So you must see Mr Robbins as quickly as possible.'

'I can't go like this.' Jennie looked down at her shapeless out of fashion dress. 'Remember I left my suitcase in the train.'

'You look beautiful, but fortunately,' he smiled at her, 'I had thought about that. Voilà, you shall see what I have done. You must change immediately.'

'My appointment is for tomorrow.'

'Yes, so first we go to our cottage, and then you go *today* instead.'

Jennie saw the sense of this, save for one respect. What cottage? She couldn't remember this in their plans. A small country auberge had been mentioned, and she reminded him of this.

'A small auberge is just where they would expect us to stay,' Max pointed out. 'And that is where we might take dinner after you have seen Mr Robbins.'

'And lunch?' she asked hopefully. It was already two o'clock and French breakfasts were hardly substantial.

Max laughed. 'How practical. I shall buy a baguette and cheese in the village while you change.'

The cottage was tucked away on the edge of the village, with a view down to Antibes and the sea, and sure enough, inside she found another set of clothes awaiting her in a suitcase. They were hardly Coco Chanel or Schiaparelli standard, but exactly what Jennie might have chosen for herself, a pale blue dress and jacket. She wondered whether Max had provided underwear too. After all, he hadn't specified how much she should bring. Sure enough, she found this too neatly packed. Embarrassment at his obviously knowing or guessing her correct size gave way to amusement. Perhaps he was in the habit of personally equipping harems?

'How do you like being dressed by me?' Max asked with straight face, running his eye up and down her when he returned from the village.

He wasn't going to win this round. 'Excellent. You have a new career as a floor salesman in lingerie ahead of you.'

'I shall look forward to it, if all customers are like you.'

'Are you coming with me to see Mr Robbins?' she asked hastily.

'No. You look like an English lady tourist and therefore completely able to look after yourself. I will keep you in sight all the time however, to ensure no one is following you with a stiletto.'

It was light conversation, but suddenly she shivered, and quickly turned to the baguette and cheese to take her mind away from bogeys under the bed. Her grandmother had scared her once by telling her that if good children didn't go to bed old Boney would be coming to get them. Who was this sinister figure who came round collecting the bones of young children, she had thought fearfully. Confusing him with bogeys under the bed, she checked every bed in the house scrupulously for many months before reluctantly climbing into her own until Aunt Win got to the bottom of this mystery and assured her that old Boney was just Napoleon and that Her Majesty's redcoats had made short shrift of him years ago. But the sensation of that early fear lingered and it came back to her now, despite Max's presence. The sunshine could hide as many dangers as the night, and if Zita's thugs were following her . . .

Max pulled a silly face at her, obviously sensing her sudden seriousness at his remark. 'I will lie across the threshold to defend you tonight, never fear.'

Which reminded her of something else. 'Just as well, she laughed, 'I see there is only one bedroom here.'

'Can it be that once again you are mistakenly crediting me with lustful thoughts towards you?'

'It wasn't so mistaken last time,' she pointed out defensively. As a young man at the Várcasá in Montevanya he had very definitely had lustful intentions.

'Ah. But we kings learn quickly that business comes first. How can I both protect you and seduce you at the same time? You may choose one only.'

'Protection,' she said promptly, wondering if this were game or otherwise.

'I too choose that, for many reasons.' He paused. 'You are not just any woman Jennie.'

'I was once.'

He came towards her and kissed her cheek. 'But not now. Or ever again.'

Mr Robbins lived in the picturesque Place des Arcades in the middle of Biot village, and now she was on public view again Jennie was glad she was playing no grand lady now, only herself. What would Richard have made of this charade, she wondered, with a quick stab of agony. Gently she put his memory aside for later. She must concentrate on Mr Robbins.

He proved to be a short grey-haired frosty-looking man, the kind who would make an excellent bank clerk, but hardly a manager, she decided instantly.

'I'm so sorry,' she apologized. 'I know my appointment was for tomorrow but I made a mistake in the day. Is there any chance you might be free today?'

182

'If you wish, Mrs Pencarek,' came the bank clerk's reply. 'As I doubt whether I can be of help to you, it would be unfair to suggest you return at the correct time merely to convey this news.'

She followed him into a sombre, rather drab room, which showed every sign of there being no Mrs Robbins about. This was a bachelor's room with frills and furbelows missing. There were a few photographs, which suggested that there had once been a Mrs Robbins and indeed a family. The backgammon board and chess set, lying on a small table, had the air of being well used, which suggested he was well established in Biot with a coterie of his own kind.

Jennie repeated her story, which was more or less the truth, though given in more detail than in her letter to him.

'Yes,' he agreed non-committally. He probably did register the twins' birth in Montreux and indeed he thought he recalled the name Avril, and certainly, now she came to mention it, Fokingham. On the matter of the adoption certificate and the name Roc, however, he became distinctly chilly.

'How could I be concerned with this adoption certificate? I fail to see how I can help you.'

'Because I understand you were friendly with Sister Marie-Thérèse of the Soeurs de la Rose orphanage, as well as with the owner of the nursing home, Monsieur Menton.'

'I was. The British community in Montreux is not so very large. But does that affect anything I have said?'

Jennie was sincerely grateful that her bank didn't have a cashier like Mr Robbins. 'I am following in my friend's footsteps,' she explained. 'She made enquiries both at the time and after the war, and I am sure she must have come to see you. She seems to have reached a stage beyond me, which suggests that there is further information for me to discover.'

'Such further information obviously led her nowhere, or you would not have been asked to investigate.'

Not a bank clerk, she decided. A barrister in a court of law. 'She died before she could complete her search.'

'I am sorry to hear that. A sad life.'

Was that a fair final verdict on Anna, Jennie wondered. This man could not know the truth. To him the word sad was a cliché to cover an awkward moment. Anna had not had a sad life. A tragic one perhaps, but she had done so much that

183

was positive in writing her novels, in loving, and in her war work. She had lit up some people's lives for ever, even though others had been blighted. Sad was a negative word. The Greek idea of tragedy was that one's own failings caused one's downfall, and that certainly applied to Anna.

'I wish I could help you,' Mr Robbins continued.

'Can you recollect *anything* about Anna Avril other than the name?' Jennie took advantage of his pious wish. 'She must surely have come to see you at least once while she was trying to track her babies down.'

He frowned in concentration. 'It's beginning to come to me. She came to my office in Montreux – yes, not long after the birth of her children. She did not stay long for I could tell her nothing, though I did—' he paused to think again '—have the impression Avril was not her real name. Perhaps that is why it has lingered with me. Of course it often happened that false names were given.'

'I am sure it did,' Jennie agreed, hoping that this didn't sound sarcastic.

'The thought occurs to me,' he added carefully, 'as doubtless to you also, Mrs Pencarek, that if Avril was not her real name, perhaps the name of the adoptive parents was false too. Such a pity Soeur Marie-Thérèse is no longer with us to help.'

Got you, Jennie thought triumphantly, as she replied sweetly, 'Indeed. Especially since the Rocs' address was given as the British Consulate in Geneva.'

She had floored him now and his expression rapidly changed. He seemed highly annoyed. 'There were many British tourists displaced by the war, stranded temporarily in Switzerland,' he snapped. 'The British Consulate was no doubt a temporary address.'

'Did I say they were British?' Jennie replied evenly, trying to suppress excitement. Why did he assume that?

Mr Robbins looked mildly surprised. 'I assumed they were with a name such as Rock.'

It was Jennie's turn to feel taken aback. It was true that she had thought of that possibility herself, but to hear it from the bank clerk suggested he could have had no involvement in the adoption. 'It was Roc, spelled in the French way, on the certificate.'

There was a certain smugness now about Mr Robbins. 'I

have been told that on such certificates that the nationality of the person writing out the certificate, particularly if not a legal document, as this could not have been, influences the spelling of the name. I suggest since the British Consulate address was given, the name should have been spelled Rock.'

'I hadn't thought of that.' Jennie's heart sank. The fact that Bridget was spelled in the French way was depressing confirmation that he was right.

Mr Robbins pressed his advantage. 'If the name Rock was false, you might well find that the real name was something akin to it, say Stone, or Mount. My experience leads me to suggest this.'

Jennie's heart sank even further at the thought of the endless permutations this would present. Where to start? 'I hadn't thought about a British connection.'

'Then I suggest that you do so, Mrs Pencarek.'

As she left the house, she saw Max sitting in a café. Strange what a difference clothes made. Who would recognize the ex-king in this casually dressed French worker? Without a sign of recognition he paid the waiter and began to amble after her. Once out of the village square, however, he caught her up quickly.

'We must leave sooner than I thought,' he told her. 'Two suspiciously well-dressed gentlemen are in the auberge. They arrived in a car with French number plates but it was a British Rover, and so I think we should take what luggage we can and leave. News of newcomers whether in cottages or hotels travels quickly in a village like this.'

'By tram?' The thought that what had seemed a game now appeared reality had shaken her. No longer was she taking part in a Dornford Yates novel, and even if these nameless pursuers remained in the shadows, she would never be sure they would remain so.

'No. We should walk through the fields to Antibes. Can you manage that?'

Four miles in flimsy shoes? Jennie gulped. 'If there's dinner at the end of it,' she said bravely.

'Two dinners if you wish, *ma mie.*'

It was a long walk, and an even longer wait for dinner, as Max decided that once in Antibes they should immediately take the train elsewhere. He chose La Napoule, a small port and resort not far from Cannes. Cannes station might be watched, but La Napoule was too small, and from there they could continue tomorrow towards St Tropez and then onwards back to England. The nameless shadows were taking their toll with a vengeance. When they reached England again would she believe in them as she did this evening or see them as fantasies? She would have to believe in them, she realized despondently. She would have to battle on with the problem of Rocs, Rocks and Steins, even though the task seemed hopeless.

Once in La Napoule, Max risked establishing them in a small family hotel, not the grand one for visitors. And after that came, at long last, dinner at the de la Plage restaurant. She had to restrain herself not to fall instantly on the basket of bread on the table but wait for their fish to arrive. At last however she was able to tell Max about her visit to Mr Robbins, and he listened attentively. 'So where do I begin?' she concluded. 'I'm moving in circles. Assuming that Mr Robbins is right and the Rocs were British—'

'Should we assume that?'

'He was trying to help, Max.'

'Why should he?'

'Common humanity.'

'Does that exist in this affair?'

'It's your family involved, Max.'

'And like all families it has strengths and weaknesses. Mr Robbins is not of my family, but he could well have been paid to see my family's point of view.'

She frowned. 'If so, then he must have been involved in the whole plan, right from the beginning, not just the birth certificates. So why should he be so reasonably helpful to me?'

'So that he could suggest the name Roc was a forgery. Perhaps it is the true name.'

'Anna would have found them. No, I'm sure it a false name. Anyway, Mr Robbins gave me a hint as to what the name might be.'

'That was very generous of him. Why?'

'Because—' She stopped, a sudden uneasiness coming to the surface. 'I don't know,' she admitted. 'Max, am I going mad? Didn't he miss out something?'

'Tell me what it was.'

She thought back carefully. 'He said he remembered Anna Avril coming to see him at the beginning of the war, and specifically mentioned Montreux, not Biot. But Anna must have gone again to see him at least once after that, and I told him so. Why didn't he refer to it?'

'The obvious answer is that he wasn't trying to help her at all, or you.'

'Why not? I have to see him again.' She found herself rising from the table as if to set off immediately, but Max put out a restraining hand.

'It would be a pity to leave so soon just as our *St Pierre au chablis* arrives. And Mr Robbins would be waiting for your return, together no doubt with other friends of ours.'

'Then what should I do next?' she demanded in frustration.

'*We* think,' Max replied. 'And my first thought is that Mr Robbins was very anxious to persuade you that the Rocs were British, which means that probably the reverse is true. They are French, Belgian, Swiss, even German. But not British.'

'That narrows the field at lot,' Jennie said ironically. 'And, Max,' a terrible thought occurred to her, 'we've forgotten Italy!' How could she have done so? Memories welled up of Anna on Rome station platform in 1915. That was where the Rocs said they lived, and which turned out to be false. Quickly she explained to Max. 'How on earth did Anna get that information?' she finished. 'All I have so far is a British consulate address in Geneva.'

'Whatever information she had, it led her nowhere,' he reminded her. 'But it will do so for us, Jennie.' He clasped her hand in his, and the restaurateur smiled benignly.

'He thinks we're just two middle-aged lovers,' Jennie laughed. Why she laughed, she did not know, for delightfully it felt just like that

'Is middle age too late for love, do you think?' he asked blandly.

Jennie wanted to take her eyes away from his. But she couldn't, for that would give him his answer: no age is too old for love. 'Of course not,' she replied briskly. 'But one takes it more carefully.'

He kissed her hand lightly. 'You are wrong, Jennie. Oh so wrong. And you will see that you are.'

Jennie felt a tide of fear sweep over her, as though the path before her had opened up and plummeted her into unknown depths. She had taken it for granted that with Richard her capacity for such love again had died, and yet here was her body saying that it hadn't. That as spring came, so might love. It would not be the same but it could be as strong.

'When will you come to Applemere?' she asked hastily, for the sake of saying something, anything, to fill the sudden silence between them. 'I mean, to live there, or won't you do that?'

'I shall, and I think very soon now.' He carefully restored her hand to her.

'And your mother?' Might as well know the worst.

'She too. It is better to have a problem beside you than festering far away.'

'Oh.' She digested this thought, not at all sure she agreed with it.

'She will not harm you, Jennie. And she will not harm us. Do you understand?'

She shied away from understanding. It was too soon, perhaps for both of them. 'You mean the hunt for Anna's children.'

He smiled. 'Of course I meant that.' A pause, then: 'What has been puzzling me, Jennie, is what I shall do at Applemere. Now I think the answer might come once I am there.'

'Can you define what you mean by do?' Jennie asked. Memory took her back to Richard and his reactions to the loss of his leg, his terrible refusal to marry her because he could not see the way forward. Did Max feel like that, now that he had lost his throne?

'I will try, Jennie, I stayed here in La Napoule once with Marta. There is a harbour here where we moored our yacht.'

'Oh.' Jennie felt deflated. So that's why Max had chosen to come here. To relive a happy time with Marta.

'There is an ancient castle here which was fast falling into ruin when it was bought just after the war by a reclusive rich American called Henry Clews, a sculptor. He and his wife Marie see very few people, but agreed to see me since I am interested in gardens. Marta was bored, I regret to say. The Clews spend all their time fashioning their castle into medieval splendour once more, and in creating superb gardens. They have a great sense of humour so some of the carvings and

188

sculptures are funny despite the grimness of others. That is in the medieval tradition too. Jennie, you are wondering what this has to do with me and Applemere.'

'You want to do the same? To create new gardens?' This sounded a terrible idea. They were perfect as they were.

'Not the same,' he reassured her. 'It seemed to me that Henry and Marie are creating a wonderful object, but it is for themselves only; it says nothing to the world at large. For me to do the same at Applemere would achieve nothing to satisfy me. So many royal exiles remain like the Clews, cultivating their own patch, which only replicates for most of them the world they have just left. Like my mother, they become more royal than when the throne was theirs, while they wait hopefully to be restored to their true position, as they see it. That is not for me. I have to find some drawbridge to take me over the moat that kingship set up for me, and out into the world. One must create, yes, but also reach out to touch people's hearts and lives. You do that with the Applemere Flyer, and I must find my own way.'

'From Applemere though. How can that help?'

'It must show me the way. And until I find it, Jennie, I have nothing to offer anyone, no heart and no kingdom. A displaced king must find his own way first.'

Thirteen

Nearly everyone was here to celebrate her birthday. Albert and Aunt Win were sitting under the pear tree. Georgius was demonstrating conjuring tricks to Lynette and Jamie, with Eileen and Dad egging him on. Lynette in particular was engrossed in Georgius's weird and wonderful dramatic displays, so much so that Jennie wondered uneasily whether her daughter might be heading for a future on the stage – and if so, what Richard might have thought of that. Times had certainly moved on since prewar days. Jennie at Lynette's age could no more have thought of drama school than flying an aeroplane. Parish bounds no longer marked the limits of one's existence, even though this cottage remained the centre of her own world.

Michael and Anthony were talking to Tom to her great pleasure. Freddie was deep in conversation with Dinah, that pretty great-niece of Albert's. She could hear his laugh as Dinah asked shyly:

'Engine drivers are like explorers really, aren't they? Don't you sometimes want to keep right on driving and driving as far as China or even Australia to see what it's like?'

'There's enough in Kent for me,' Freddie replied gently, his eyes fixed on her.

'That's natural,' Dinah said quickly. 'You were in the war, weren't you? Uncle Albert told me so.'

From the look on Freddie's face, Jennie's hopes for his rekindling his interest in his one-time sweetheart Alice Cowper seemed to have come to nothing. Freddie, she admitted, was quite capable of looking after his own heart.

She wished Tom could do the same. He was still estranged from Mary, although at least his children were here, Alfred and Arabella. As for work, he had settled down to doing odd jobs combined with his role in Anna's affairs. Something, he had said carelessly, would turn up, but the lost look in his eyes denied this optimism. She wouldn't worry about that today, Jennie decided. Her actual birthday had been last Monday, but she had chosen today, Sunday, to celebrate it, and the sun had shone on her. Her family was here. There were flowers, there were sandwiches, there was a green woodpecker in the tree at the far end of the garden, and a robin was hopping about expectantly.

Rather like her, she thought ruefully. The *nearly* everyone meant one omission. She had hoped that Max would be here, but there had been no sign of him. Michael had not mentioned him, and nor had Eileen. Jennie had not seen him since they returned from France, at the end of June. Furthermore, watching Tom with Arabella and Alfred rubbed it in that she had got no further in her hunt for Anna's twins. It was made all the worse by her suspicion that she was being deliberately misled, but she could see no way forward.

This was a double celebration, for Win and Albert had at last bought a cottage in the village into which they planned to move shortly. Dad would be retiring in January next year and coming to join them. Marriage suited Aunt Win. There was a definite gleam in her eye, and her gaunt face had filled out, allowing her inner softness to shine through.

'How's the Applemere Flyer?' Eileen enquired, sitting down on the grass next to Jennie. Much better than a chair, Jennie and the twins always agreed. On the grass one could see fairy rings, grasshoppers and all sorts of tiny flowers which were invisible from higher up. In chairs one was bothered by wasps, which might not spot you lower down.

'Doing well, surprisingly. Plenty of entertainment books sold, no sales on the *Revelations of a Soviet Diplomat* front.'

Eileen laughed. Georgius had waxed so enthusiastic about this book that Jennie had been persuaded into buying several copies – just as Richard might have done, and with the same result. None of them sold. Even Albert had looked askance at the purchase, and there they still remained. 'Door stoppers,' she admitted ruefully to him yesterday. *The Private Life of Greta Garbo* had been far more to Kentish rural tastes. Her films were a magnet and even Jennie had looked in the mirror to see if her own features might adapt to soulful musing. They wouldn't.

'I bought the new Christie at Hatchards,' Eileen said idly.

'Tut, tut. What about supporting local talent?'

'I'll do better,' Eileen promised. *'Peril at End House* is her best yet, don't you think?'

'It reminds me of Applemere House.'

'Why? Applemere isn't a siege perilous, is it?'

Eileen spoke so oddly that Jennie glanced at her. 'Not with Michael and Anthony there.'

'Max is the owner though.'

Jennie hesitated. 'I was hoping he'd be here today.'

'Did he know about it?'

'Yes. Michael said he'd told him.' What had she been hoping for, she wondered? That Max would come rushing down from London just because it was her birthday party? Hardly.

'Are you in love with him, Jennie?'

Was it so obvious? 'I don't know,' she answered.

'Don't you?' Eileen asked drily.

'No.' Jennie glared at her. 'Perhaps yes.'

Eileen sighed. 'So the old harpy was right.'

'What's Queen Zita got to do with it?' It was obvious whom Eileen meant, and Jennie was in belligerent mood. This was nothing to do with anyone save her and Max.

'Quite a lot, I'm afraid. I don't know all the ins and outs, but I do know there was a right royal set-to between ex-Queen Zita and ex-King Max on the lines of—'

'Don't tell me,' Jennie interrupted. 'That peasant woman, in other words me, is not one of us. Have nothing to do with her.'

'Worse, if you do decide you love Max. It was on the lines of "No child of mine marries beneath him".'

'Marries?' Jennie felt a shock run through her. How stupid. She hadn't even got that far, yet it seemed a perfectly natural progression. Or had she in her heart of hearts seen herself as Max's wife? So far her permitted day-dreaming had always ended in his arms. Eileen's words crystallized her thoughts, and she began to laugh.

'I don't see anything much to laugh at,' Eileen said frankly.

'I do. If the harpy seems me as a serious threat, it must mean that Max—' Jennie stopped, unwilling to put into words her growing hope.

'I agree. It means Max obviously feels strongly about you.

But don't rejoice too soon. Zita holds cards you don't know about. I wouldn't mind betting she played one or two aces during that battle. And there'll be more up her sleeve.'

'What are they?' Jennie asked with foreboding.

'Money is one. Max owns Applemere but nothing else. The income he was awarded at his abdication was stopped by Viktor, so Max is dependent on his mother for money. She can cut off the supply any time she likes.'

'That isn't a problem so far as I'm concerned.' Jennie frowned.

'Darling Jennie,' Eileen said fondly. 'Max might see it as such. The other ace is his son.'

'Stefan is with Marta.'

'Supported by Queen Zita.'

'She wouldn't deprive them of cash. Stefan is part of her dynasty.'

'Think of Tom,' Eileen reminded her gently. Jennie glanced over to see Tom still in animated conversation with Alfred and Arabella. He was actually laughing, the first time she could recall that in ages.

'Oh.'

'Quite. Oh it most definitely is. At the drop of a hat Zita could cut off all contact between Max and Stefan. Marta sleeps in her pocket. Correction, she spends her days in Zita's pocket. Her nights are a different matter.'

Jennie knew exactly how she'd feel if she was told she could no longer see Lynette and Jamie. Her stomach seemed to turn over inside her, and she realized just how much she had seen the future as a wonderful mixture of Applemere, her children, and Max. Now she could see how much she had been fooling herself, even though if Max had love or just desire for her, she supposed the role of king's mistress might still be open. She wouldn't be applying. Not with Zita in the background, a persistent bloodhound baying at her heels.

'How are you getting on in the hunt for Anna's twins?' Eileen tactfully changed subjects, though hardly to a more welcome one.

Jennie struggled to bring her mind back from Max. 'Which way do you turn when you're lost in the desert?' she tried to joke.

'The sun's a help. So is a map,' Eileen answered practically. 'The desert isn't just miles of empty sands. It's full of colour and landmarks once one knows where to look.'

'And if one doesn't? I'm still lost. Anna was my map, but I can't read her, so I'll have to stick to the sun.' And at the moment the sun didn't seem to be helping much.

'Didn't Anna give you *any* clue?'

'No. Only "Find my babies".'

'Nothing else at all?'

Jennie thought back more carefully. 'Nothing important. She just said "It's there. Don't tell Tom, he's such a hothead. There's something you must do for me."'

'What did she mean by "it's there"?'

'I suppose that the path and clues were there if we knew where to look.' This was leading nowhere, Jennie thought dejectedly.

'Not much of a map, I agree.' Eileen closed her eyes, and Jennie watched her angular face, thinking how much she loved her.

The eyes flew open. '*How* did she say it?' Eileen demanded.

'Say what?'

'It's there.'

'She gasped it out,' Jennie replied unwillingly, not wanting to relive that moment.

'No,' Eileen said impatiently. 'Where was the emphasis? Did she say "It's there," all on one level, or "*It's* there," or "It's *there*"?'

Jennie thought back once more to that terrible time, doubting if she could remember accurately now, but forcing herself to remember. 'She said "It's *there*". I'm fairly sure of that.'

'Which assumed you both knew what "it" was. Did she mean the hunt itself, the answer to the riddle, a clue? Any of them, I suppose.' Eileen answered her own question. 'But where is *there*? Any ideas?'

The nursing home? The orphanage? Montreux? What would have been uppermost in Anna's mind? Jennie concentrated. Something shared, Eileen had said. Unlikely to have been any of these therefore. But they had been in Cannes *together* . . .

'Biot?' she suggested doubtfully. 'Mr Robbins? But he was only personally concerned with the birth certificates, not the adoption.'

194

'You said he was chummy with the orphanage and with the nursing home owner.'

'Yes, but even so,' Jennie tried to think logically, 'as he was directly responsible only for the birth certificates, why should the clue – if that's what Anna was trying to give me – be focused on him and not the other two? Biot can't be what Anna meant.'

'Why not? They were all in it together. Anna said *there*. She didn't say *him*, so what did she mean, do you think? Biot generally, Robbins' home, his desk, his garden? It might be something she saw when she waited for him.'

'He wouldn't have left vital clues about Mr and Mrs Roc around.'

'Play up, play up, and play the game, girl,' Eileen quoted blithely. 'Suppose you were Anna. What would you have seen in that home? What *did* you see?'

Jennie closed her eyes and began to describe everything she could remember, from the stone tiles in the hallway to his desk in the study, the photographs, the backgammon board, the chess set. *Play up, play up and play the game.* Memories of interminable French estaminets, memories of men hunched over chessboards with their glasses of *marc* beside them, and foul-smelling cigarettes . . .

'Perhaps they all played chess together,' she produced triumphantly. 'Sister Marie-Thérèse, Monsieur Menton and Mr Robbins.'

Eileen saw it immediately. 'That's it, of course. Well done,' she cried. '*Roc*, Jennie. The English call the chesspiece a rook, but the French for it is *roc*. That's how the name got on the certificate.'

'So we should be looking for Mr and Mrs Rook?' Jennie's head was spinning.

'Too obvious,' Eileen said. 'Rook and Roc are too close if they really wanted to put a false name.' She thought for a moment, then: 'How about this? In chess the rook can also be called the castle.' She was glowing with excitement, but Jennie was not convinced.

'Robbins urged me to think that the adoptive parents were English, which Max and I take to mean they were in fact French or some other nationality.'

'He's a *chessplayer*, Jennie,' Eileen said impatiently. 'He

195

might have been counting on your disbelieving him. No, I think Castle is a distinct possibility.'

Jennie rocketed up to hope then down again to the depressing reality. 'There are as many Castle surnames as Stones, and Rocks. Anyway, why should our three chess-players all be in a joint plot to find a suitable name for the adoptive parents?'

'There could be one reason.'

Jennie stared at her, and then she saw exactly what Eileen implied. All three were involved because there was a fourth person masterminding the twins' fate. Lady Fokingham, no doubt with her husband firmly behind her. It hadn't been a question of just handing over the baby to strangers to be adopted. Lady Fokingham had been far more deeply involved. Even now Jennie didn't want to believe it. She had liked Lady Fokingham and still did, even though their ways had parted. Now she had to face the probability that the Fokinghams had known all the time where the children were.

With the children's return to school in September and the autumn books to order for the Applemere Flyer, Jennie had plenty to do to override her frustration. She hadn't yet heard whether Michael had tracked down any Castles in the Fokingham prewar circle, nor had she heard any more from Max – or indeed about him. Daily she feared hearing the news that Applemere was to be sold.

Unexpectedly in mid-September, Michael warned her: 'Keep your head down this weekend, Jennie. My revered Aunt Zita is coming to stay.'

'At Applemere?' Jennie frowned. 'Why not Goreham Court?' This seemed odd. Georgius was her son, after all.

'I can't help suspecting, Jennie, that you are her target.'

'She can't turn me out of this cottage, can she?'

'No, but my aunt specializes in the unexpected assault. I suggest you disappear for a few days.'

Jennie decided against this. Moving out of her home would be surrendering to the enemy without a fight.

She paid the price. Michael was despatched to fetch her for 'an audience', as he put it. 'You might as well come now and get it over,' he pointed out.

196

Jennie would have preferred the battle on her own home ground, not Queen Zita's, but as she didn't want her cottage contaminated with the queenly presence, or for the twins to be upset, she obediently went to Applemere House. Any hopes that Michael would be present at the 'audience' were promptly dashed, when she was ushered into the living room. This was usually a pleasant room, but this latter-day Miss Havisham was casting a dark shadow over it. Jennie decided to award her a curtsey. She was an ex-queen after all, and there was no point in deliberate rudeness. It won her no approval however.

'Sit down, Mrs Pencarek.' The Harpy sat gimlet-eyed in the regal armchair as if it were a throne. Her long skirts, worn in an age used to the freedom of shorter lengths, seemed to accord her the status of Queen Mary herself.

'Thank you.' Jennie sat in the spindly chair allotted to her. 'Is Lady Fokingham well?'

'She is.'

'Please give my best wishes to her.'

'I shall.' The Harpy's tone left Jennie in no doubt that she would not. Obviously best wishes were not conveyed between peasants and Deleanus. Jennie was amused to find nothing had changed. In fact, as Max had said, Queen Zita was more royal than ever now. No doubt armed henchmen stood outside the door, waiting to burst in if Jennie suddenly produced an axe.

'I requested your presence here, Mrs Pencarek, because I need to know what you consider your position to be with regard to my family.'

'I am Max's tenant.' Mistake to call him that? Yes, on consideration, Jennie realized, but it was too late now.

'You have been a help to the Princess Marie, Lady Fokingham, over the years, she tells me, despite your support of my late granddaughter.'

'I liked and respected them both.'

'Respect? That seems a strange word. My unfortunate niece was led astray by first one of your brothers, and then another.'

'Anna knew her own mind.'

The Harpy let this pass. 'You see yourself merely as my son's tenant here.'

'Yes.' Let her make the running.

'It would not be true then that you see yourself as future chatelaine of Applemere House?'

Jennie struggled to keep her temper at this body blow. 'Who suggested that I did?'

'My nephew Michael.'

Jennie refrained from showing the recoil she instantly felt. Michael would not have betrayed her so. Zita was trying to undermine her, taking her by surprise. 'How could I be chatelaine of Applemere? The idea is ridiculous.'

'I am glad you see it to be so. Your pursuit of my son made me fear otherwise.'

'Your son Viktor?' Jennie asked politely.

'Do not trifle with me, Mrs Pencarek. Maximilian.'

'Surely your son is able to shake off pursuers.' Her stomach was in turmoil but she was holding on. 'Indeed he has already done so, to my knowledge.' That should fix her, Jennie thought triumphantly.

'I presume you allude to your visit to the south of France with him, where my son foolishly chose to elude the bodyguards employed to look after his personal safety.' Zita paused, having delivered this masterpiece. 'However enticing you may be, Mrs Pencarek, I would point out that although my son has had mistresses and indeed still has, it would be unfortunate for him to continue such an arrangement with one of his tenants, particularly one so different in status to himself.'

Continue? How dare the woman. And what was all this about Max having a mistress? Another Harpy device, surely. 'He is a divorced man, your majesty. I am a widow. The church would see mine as the superior status, rather than your son's, I am sure you would agree.'

'Do not bandy words with me, Mrs Pencarek. I wished to see you in order to judge the type of person with whom my son was embroiled. Now I have, and if you continue your hounding of him, I shall act immediately.'

'Do I take it I shall require bodyguards myself?' Jennie replied icily. 'Are you threatening me?'

The eyes blinked. 'Naturally not. You are a passing irritant. However, there are other means to achieve your absence from his life. I have the welfare of my grandchild to think of, as well as that of my country. And that welfare will not be threatened by a travelling saleswoman, or by my son's foolish indiscretions or by upstarts claiming to be your nephew and niece.'

Jennie was confused for a moment. Then she realized. This *was* a threat. She was shaking as she walked out, escorted by two liveried footmen who were not to her knowledge employed at Applemere. Had she been stupid to take on Queen Zita? No, better the devil you know, she decided. One thing was after all now obvious, and she should have realized it a long time ago. It had not been Lady Fokingham or even her husband who had masterminded the adoption of Anna's children.

It had been Queen Zita.

To her surprise, Jennie felt the Applemere Flyer braking. This was not one of the usual stops at Stelling Minnis. Perhaps Albert wanted to eat his sandwiches. No, she could there was a customer waiting to get on. She could see the dark hat and jacket and put aside her paperwork to greet him. The man climbed aboard, doffing his hat to her, and to her amazement she discovered it was Max.

'Are you allowed a short break, Mrs Pencarek?'

Emotions tumbled over each other. Shock, puzzlement, relief, pleasure – and that was the greatest.

'Of course,' she heard herself saying.

'I'm sure you won't mind, Mr Hodge,' Max said gravely, 'if I take Mrs Pencarek for a short walk on this delightful afternoon.'

Albert, it appeared, was only too delighted, and not a muscle on his face moved as Jennie gathered up her coat and followed Max.

'What are you doing here?' she asked, as they walked along the grassy path over the common. Stelling Minnis was miles from Applemere, so this could be no chance meeting. A thousand explanations whizzed through her mind, some flattering, others far from that, and logic sorted out the only one that fitted.

'I made enquiries about your route, and drove here to wait until I saw the bus. Not quite Sherlock Holmes' standard, but I was quite pleased with myself.'

She struggled to keep the conversation light. 'Are you trying to escape from your bodyguards again?' The leaves were falling now, their soft golds and browns covering the ground around them and underfoot. It was the dying of the year, which seemed a fitting time for what she assumed would be a goodbye talk.

He understood immediately. 'I heard from Michael that my mother had talked with you.'

'If talk is the right word,' she answered, aware of a bitterness she hadn't intended in her tone. This wasn't the Max of France. Here at her side this was the careworn ex-king, with all the troubles of the world on his shoulders, and she shouldn't be adding to it. She must make the parting easy.

'I regret that my mother sees it as her right to talk to anybody as she chooses, as she is head of the family.'

'Surely Viktor is head,' Jennie replied evenly. 'And even if that were not the case it makes no difference to whether she is entitled to speak as she did or not.'

'She believes it does. I do not. Many would still agree with her however, and it is hard for me to cut myself off completely from that way of life. Do you understand, Jennie?' he pleaded.

'I understand what I have always understood,' she answered sadly. 'That you are of a royal family and I am not. And that your world is not one I could ever live in.'

He flinched. 'That is why I want to live at Applemere Jennie, and be as far from my family's former royal world as I can.'

'But you have come here—' she had to interrupt this *now*, it was too painful '—to tell me there is no future for us at Applemere save as landlord and tenant. And perhaps friends?' Did she want that? No. It was too late for mere friendship.

'No. I have come because I love you, Jennie.'

'Oh Max.' She looked at him dumbfounded, and he seemed just as uncertain for it was a moment before he took her into his arms and she was crushed against him. Then he lifted her face to him and kissed her as he had twice before. But not like this, not like this. She forgot everything save her need to be with him, and the knowledge that his love was what she wanted from life, and hers what she could still offer to it. He unbuttoned her coat, his arms reaching inside to hold her the closer. So close, she could hear his heart beat, And then he released her. 'If this were summer, Jennie, if we were younger, if this were more private, I'd show you how much I love you. Even though—'

She went very cold.

200

'I can't offer you Applemere,' he continued. 'Applemere was my way forward. Together we could reach out to touch the world, but now it wouldn't be possible. You see that, don't you?'

'Yes.' The Harpy had blackmailed Max over his son Stefan. How could she not understand?

'Jennie, there is nothing I can do. I didn't know how hard it would be for either of us.'

He kissed her again, and they walked back to the Flyer in silence. She climbed aboard and watched him walk away out of her life. Of course his son came first. Without that they could have built an Applemere together anywhere. Tears were falling down her face as she asked Albert to drive on.

He coughed. 'I've often found,' he ventured, 'that life has an odd way of twisting round in circles. If it's right, it will find a way, though it might not be the way you expect.'

'Not this time, Albert.' The dream was over.

Fourteen

1933

Jennie fumed when she read the entry in her pre-war *Baedeker's Guide*. To keep her mind off Max, she had mused over the name of Castle for months, and with the coming of the New Year her brain had at last agreed to click into action. Zita, it had told her, equalled Montevanya. What a fool she had been not to see Zita's hand behind this plot earlier. She felt she had wasted all this time when if only she had applied her brain at the outset it might have been avoided. There would have been no need for trips to Switzerland or France. Instead she had been led by the nose, dancing like a puppet to Queen Zita's strings. There was the answer before her in black and white. *Montevanya, British Vice-Consul-General Philip Castleton.* Mr P. Roc, himself. In all probability the adoption had been planned even before Jennie had left Montevanya on her ill-fated visit in 1914.

Her next step was now obvious. She must check the current guidebooks, since he was highly unlikely still to be in Montevanya. On her next Canterbury day to meet publishers' salesmen, she therefore hurried to the library to see what she could find. Not entirely to her surprise it brought her to a dead end. The Embassy in Montevanya was no longer listed; in other words, His Majesty's Government no longer approved of the regime, which must be awkward for Sir Roger Fokingham, Jennie thought with glee. There were still a legation and consulate maintained there, but Philip Castleton was no longer listed. So where was he? Another posting? Retired? That was possible, she supposed, even though to be retired now the Castletons would have made rather elderly parents for the twins.

Jennie welcomed this leap forward. At least the hunt would

take her away from brooding over Max. During the silent months of winter Applemere House seemed to be waiting for something to happen, almost as heavy-hearted as her, she thought fancifully. Then she laughed at herself. How ridiculous. And yet perhaps there was a little truth to it. Here in the cottage she lived snugly with the twins; its four walls kept out winter's hardship – well, apart from the leak in the attic roof and the damp patch in the front wall. Applemere however did indeed seem to be slumbering and not peacefully. When she went to tell Michael the latest developments this impression was confirmed. The living-room, once so full of life, now seemed dark and listless, and Michael seemed almost lost in it.

'The last time I was in this room,' she observed ruefully to him, 'it was to face your mother.'

'At least you've avoided that pleasure.' He paused. 'Is it Anna again? Is that what's brought you here?'

'Yes.' She pulled a face. 'I've been an idiot. I've found the Castles, but too late. In fact, they're Castle*tons*. He was British vice consul in Montevanya in 1914.'

Michael was horrified. 'If you think you've been an idiot, I feel a much bigger one. I probably met him at the Várcasá.'

'If you had, Anna would have recognized him, because she met the Rocs. Perhaps the castle didn't stoop to entertaining mere consular staff.'

'Possibly. I take it the gent isn't still in his post?'

'No.' Jennie hated asking for Michael's help yet again, but she had no choice, if she was to push her task onwards. 'Could you—?'

'Oblige? Of course. They are my nephew and niece too, remember. The only family I'll ever have,' he added.

For a moment she saw his usual façade slip.

'Does Anthony not have brothers or sisters?'

'Hundreds of them, but it's not the same, is it?' The mask came briskly back. 'I'll look Castleton up in the records. Though bear in mind my illustrious father might have had a finger in the pie. Files have been known to vanish.'

With Sir Roger's position at court and links with the Government, this it was all too possible, Jennie supposed. She decided to be optimistic, however. 'Let's hope not. After all, your father must have known Anna's investigations hadn't yet got so far as finding the Castletons. Queen Zita must have kept him well in touch.' She shuddered at the thought that Anna's every step must have been dogged by the Queen's mobsters. Except as regards Tom, she thought. Even Zita hadn't been a match for Anna there.

'I'll get on to it right away,' Michael assured her. 'Consular names are on public record after all, so even my sainted aunt and father can't have dabbled too much.'

Jennie privately thought she wouldn't put anything past Queen Zita, or the Fokinghams. It must be hard for Michael, since although he wasn't close to his parents he was still on good terms with them. He was a good diplomat in his private as well as his public life, she decided. A new nightmare occurred to her.

'Suppose the Castletons changed their name after the adoption?'

'They couldn't do that and still remain in the service,' Michael assured her. 'I'll ferret around. 'I won't be here next weekend, so I'll telephone you.'

Jennie seized her chance. 'Is Max coming then?' she asked innocently.

Michael laughed. 'No, darling Jennie. Max is away travelling somewhere. Nursing a broken heart perhaps.' He cocked an eye at her and she flushed.

'No more than I am,' she muttered.

'Ah. I'll say no more. I've nothing to say in fact save that he might be travelling with Eileen. Private visits, of course. Nothing official.'

This sounded ominous. Jennie had believed Eileen had at last given up her 'travelling' work, and the fact that Georgius had made the last visit to the Flyer alone was simply due to her being too busy to come with him. '*German* private visits?' she hazarded a guess.

She knew Eileen was concerned about the German situation. On the face of it everything looked calm on the international front. In December Germany had even returned to the Geneva Disarmament Conference and together with Britain, France and Italy had formally renounced force in favour of diplomacy to resolve international differences. Internally, however, Germany was in turmoil with no one leader able to pull all parties together. Unfortunately Herr Adolf

Hitler's powers of oratory had united the National Socialist German Workers' Party so successfully that he could well achieve his aim of using those same powers as Chancellor, if the present chaos persisted. Beside him, Eileen's opinion was that the Kaiser would seem a model of good conduct. In fact Hitler was making moves to suggest he wanted the Kaiser's family back in power.

So were Eileen and Max in Germany? To Jennie the fact that they were together suggested Montevanya. Were there moves afoot to oust Viktor? Or was it Viktor himself they had gone to see? Whichever it was, she wished heartily that both of them were here, safe in Kent.

She longed to ask Michael if he thought Max would sell Applemere but restrained herself. Michael looked at her mockingly, as though he knew exactly what was in her mind, and she wasn't going to give him the pleasure of confirming it.

'Paris,' he told with her with relish on the telephone a few days later. 'Couldn't be easier. That's where Mr Philip Castleton is now. Not the Consul-General nor the Vice-Consul, so his career hasn't exactly blossomed, but there he is at the consulate, and I've got his private address. He lives in Vincennes, on the outskirts of Paris.'

It seemed all too easy. As she hung up the receiver, Jennie felt as though she'd just launched herself down a helter-skelter. There would be no stopping her now till she reached the end of her journey. She'd go to France, she decided, as soon as she'd spoken to Albert, and Eileen too, if she was back. She would be needed to help Albert on the Flyer. The sooner Jennie left, however, the less likely Queen Zita would be to hear her plans, and that was one reason she wasn't going to announce her visit to Philip Castleton in advance. She would have to take the chance that he might be out, working in Timbuctoo, on holiday in Biarritz, or working over the weekend.

She would have to talk to him first, obviously. If the twins were at home it would be unthinkable to announce who she was. She supposed she could not assume the Castletons were villains themselves, despite their double-crossing of Anna. They might have been desperate to have Anna's children, and who knew what lies they might have been fed at the time by Her Majesty's henchmen, or even the Queen herself?

There was only one hitch to Jennie's plans: Eileen.

'I'm coming with you,' she informed her, when Jennie popped into Goreham Court to ask her about the Flyer.

'I'm better alone,' Jennie rejoined. She was set on her task now, and there was no danger facing her in France, except perhaps to her feelings.

'No, you're not.'

'If you're worried about the wolves following Little Red Riding Hood through the Vincennes woods, you needn't. The witch won't know my plans.'

'Don't joke about it, Jennie. You were lucky last time because Max was with you. This time it's different. You're obviously getting near the truth.'

'The only people who know I'm going are Michael, me and now you.'

'Zita found out last time.'

'Because I'd written to Mr Robbins. I'm not making that mistake again.'

'Hmm.' Eileen grinned at her. I'm still coming. Posh hotel or bottom of the barrel? I'll pay.'

Jennie gave in. 'You'd see spies everywhere in a posh hotel. How about a nice respectable family guesthouse?'

She had one more mission before leaving on what Lynnette and Jamie in resignation called one of her Get-Away-From-Us holidays. They liked staying with Albert and Aunt Win, but Jennie longed for the time when she could be less mysterious about her travels.

This last mission was a delicate one. The village pub, The Plough, was up for sale, because Joe Brown was getting too old to run it any more. Aunt Win had suggested that might be just the job for Tom. He was too much alone out in Bossingham, and with his knowledge of the brewery trade he would be well suited for it, even though it was a different side to that he'd tackled before. It would take him out of himself, Aunt Win had declared.

Jennie had been very doubtful, but then saw how perfect it might be, provided Tom were prepared to change his way of life completely. Tom was sociable by nature, or had been before his affair with Anna, and it was high time he exercised these skills again. There was only one problem. He had no money, and the pub had to be bought.

'And I told young Master Freddie,' Aunt Win had said to Jennie with great satisfaction 'that after he'd bought the Plough for Tom he ought to be thinking about getting wed again.'

Jennie groaned. 'I'm sure he loved that.'

'He did,' Aunt Win said complacently. 'He said he would let me know when the wedding would be.'

Was he just pulling Aunt Win's leg, or had he been serious? Jennie longed to know. Meanwhile it was her job to sell the idea to Tom, but she failed dismally. Conscious of her coming visit to France, a subject she must avoid at all costs, she did not handle the meeting well. At first he seemed interested, then dismissed it for lack of money, then showed slight interest again when she said that was arranged – followed by a blazing row, when he found out what the arrangement was.

'Don't you think I hate it enough being his private charity?' he shouted. 'When this slump's over and there are decent jobs around again, I'll be all right and brother Freddie will have to whistle for his skivvy. He can look after Anna's business affairs himself, instead of flinging his weight around with me.'

'And suppose that never happens,' she had shouted back. 'What are you going to do? Waste the rest of your life?'

'I've got no life,' he yelled at her.

And whose fault is that, she wanted to say, but held back. He wasn't going to reply that it was his. She saw the desperation in his eyes. If only she could hold out some hope for finding his children, but it would be fair on nobody to do that.

After that row, she had been glad to leave for France, especially with Eileen. Now that it was a *fait accompli* she was grateful for her presence. 'No sign of Zita's hoods,' she said lightly on the boat across the Channel. 'Anyway, I've brought my cavalry with me. I hope you're suitably armed.'

'You're an innocent in this game,' Eileen replied equably, and proceeded to point out so many suspicious characters, explaining why each of them could be Zita's mobsters, that Jennie didn't know whether she was joking or serious. As no doubt Eileen had intended.

It wasn't until they were in the train heading for Paris however that Eileen talked of her travels in Europe – and then to Jennie's relief mentioned Max. That meant the subject could be discussed, and she wasn't going to raise it herself.

'What happened between you two?' Eileen asked. 'Max tells me he's having to sell Applemere.'

A chill came over Jennie. Even though she had expected it to happen, those words had a terrible air of finality about them. Perhaps she had been hoping even now for a reprieve. For her or the house, she wondered, but she knew the answer. It was her. Fond as she was of Applemere, it was Max who filled her thoughts day and night.

'To Michael?' she managed to ask.

'Perhaps, although I gather Anthony isn't too keen. He wants to live nearer London. Now don't edge away from the point, which is Max and you. Did you let Zita win?'

'I had no choice,' Jennie said wryly, 'How could I divide Max and his son, when I'm doing all I can to reunite Tom with his? Sauce for the goose, I think.'

'So that's the ace Zita played.'

'Yes. It was clear when Max visited me. We did—' Jennie swallowed for the memory was still raw '—talk, and I said I understood. He wanted to live at Applemere and with me, but with that threat hanging over him it was impossible.'

'Ah,' was all Eileen replied, for which Jennie was grateful. There was to be no reprieve, and she had to wrestle with that knowledge.

Despite the reason for the visit she enjoyed the evening in Paris, especially since Eileen had picked a small hotel on the Left Bank and seemed to know a remarkable number of small restaurants. The one she eventually chose was definitely not the sort of place to which Zita's troops would follow them, if only because it was too small for them to escape notice. Even though Jennie was sure they had no unwanted company on this trip, she realized tension was mounting inside her for the next day's meeting (or lack of it), but nevertheless she managed to consume a remarkable amount of good food.

They had agreed to take the train together to Vincennes the next morning, Saturday, and that Eileen would wait at the entrance to the park for her to join her. At the Gare de Bastille they were pushed near the front of the platform by the crowds and Jennie had her first pang of doubt that they weren't being followed. An accident here would be all too easy, and she found herself stepping hastily back from the platform edge and clutching Eileen's arm. When the train arrived however,

208

they were still safely together, and once seated there seemed no sign of gentlemen with designs on their lives. Only a forest of *Le Monde* newspapers rustled around her. This week had seen important political changes. Adolf Hitler had indeed become Chancellor of Germany, the only candidate who looked as though he could succeed where other more venerable politicians had failed in forming a government.

'Viktor must be jumping up and down with glee,' Eileen said wryly. 'Good news for dictators everywhere.'

'I thought you said Hitler was a monarchist.'

'I said he was claiming to be so. What actually happens remains to be seen. It could be just a ploy to get the Hohenzollerns' support.'

As they stepped down at Vincennes station, Jennie was relieved to smell fresh air again, after the stuffy smoky atmosphere and definitely garlicky smells of some of the breath around her. Not Eileen's of course. Here she felt more anonymous, amid suburban houses and the nearby park and château of Vincennes. The Castletons lived in the Avenue de Paris, a tree-lined road not far from the chateau, in a small villa set back from the road with high gates. Barren trees reared protectively above the fences, presenting a formidable appearance.

Now that she was here, Jennie felt very calm, however, no longer inclined to believe the old woman carrying the baguettes under her arm was really following her with the intention of clouting her with them. She parted from Eileen, breathed deeply, went in through the gates and rang the doorbell.

A black-clad maid answered it, and Jennie asked confidently for Monsieur Castleton, giving her real name. If he knew it, she reasoned, he would certainly want to see her, for he would guess that she wouldn't be put off by a mere refusal, as that might do his cause more harm than good. If he didn't know it, then he would at least be curious as to who she was, especially as she had announced her credentials as coming from Mr Robbins of Montreux.

'*Entrez, madame.*' The maid disappeared and Jennie held her breath, for at least this implied he was at home. Whatever happened it was going to be a difficult interview, but when the maid returned she was not surprised to be told to follow her. Step one achieved, she gloated. There was a silence about the house, however, which did not bode well for the twins

209

being here. Nor did the glimpses of the rooms they passed suggest a rumbustious family life, or indeed any signs of everyday life. She was taken to what was obviously Monsieur Castleton's study, not sure what she expected, save a chilly reception through which she would have to fight her way. Even that proved wrong however.

A fire was blazing in the hearth, and Philip Castleton sat not at the imposing desk but in an armchair by the fire, immediately rising as she entered. He was urbane, tall, grey-haired, classical-featured and perhaps in his early sixties. What was so unexpected was the smile, however. It looked genuinely friendly, Jennie thought, rather than a crocodile baring his teeth. That might imply he didn't know who she was. Once again she was to be surprised however.

'Do please sit down, Mrs Pencarek.'

Battle was joined, she thought warily, as she obeyed. 'It wasn't Mr Robbins who suggested I came here, Mr Castleton. I should make that clear. It was a name I thought you might recognize, however.'

'I do. I also recognize yours, Mrs Pencarek. You come from Applemere, do you not? And you have come to ask me about Anna Avril's children.'

'Anna Fokingham.' Jennie recovered quickly from this opening salvo. He wasn't hostile at least, that was clear – even if mystifying.

'I am involved only from the time of the children's adoption.'

'Save that you must still be in touch with the Fokingham family to know who I am.' She could be just as friendly, and just as sharp. No point holding back.

A laugh now. This man didn't seem tense, which was odd. He was completely sure of himself – or was that a professional trick? 'Of course I am. Now, tell me Mrs Pencarek, what exactly do you want of me?'

'News of the twins. Anything about them. Anna Fokingham was my dear friend, and their father is my brother, as you must know. When she died she asked me to find the babies she had lost all those years ago.' The words sounded to her like a stranger's, even though they fell from her own lips. Jennie could hardly believe that she was here at last. She had to choose the right words, or she would fail at the last hurdle.

'Then I am truly sorry for you, Mrs Pencarek.' Philip Castleton looked troubled. 'Nevertheless the babies were adopted to give them a new life and moral questions therefore arise about disrupting that life in any way.'

'If I was not aware of that,' Jennie said, 'I would have gone about this visit differently. The twins are eighteen now, however. In under three years they will be twenty-one and will be of age, and can decide for themselves whether they wish to meet their true family.' She saw the shake of his head, and her heart sank. 'Do they know they were adopted?' she asked.

'No.' He must have seen her stricken face, for he added gently. 'I'm sorry.'

'Are they here?' She was almost choking.

'I'm afraid not.'

'Will they be back shortly? Could I see them just for a moment, in your presence?' she pleaded.

'No.' He didn't speak harshly, indeed he still looked worried.

'I understand you must have made promises to the Fokingham family, and to Queen Zita, and that you have to consider them first but I wouldn't do anything to jeopardize their happiness. You—'

'I don't think you understand the situation,' he interrupted. 'They do not *live* here, otherwise I might have considered your request.'

Not live here? Jennie felt it like a physical blow.

'The situation is not as you seem to assume,' he continued. 'It was not my wife and I who brought up Guy and Bridget.'

'I don't understand.' A terrible feeling of complete helplessness swept through her, followed by indignation. 'The coincidence is too strong,' she cried. 'You were at the Montevanya consulate, you know the Fokinghams and Queen Zita, you knew Mr Robbins. You must—' She felt tears perilously close, but they were of anger and she fought them back. She had to keep a clear mind. 'The name Roc was on the certificate and that must have been you.'

'It was,' he agreed. 'However, adoptions were not so formal before the war, Mrs Pencarek, especially as war had recently broken out with all its chaotic effects. It was our daughter and son-in-law who took the babies, and that was the reason I had to betray Miss Fokingham by letting her believe she could get the babies back. We could not risk her finding out the

211

truth. Had it not been for the war, she would have received her money back too. My arrangement for that broke down.'

Every question answered. Jennie felt sick and dizzy, but had to press on. 'Why was it so important she didn't find out the truth?'

'Important to my family, Mrs Pencarek. You see, my daughter could have no children of her own. It was a terrible fate to face so young in her life, for she was only twenty-two. She and her husband have brought up the children as their own.'

'But where is she? Where do they live?' The appalling chasm opened up before her once again.

'I cannot tell you that,' he answered inevitably. 'It is not in Paris, however. Nor is her husband British. And their name, naturally, is not Castleton.'

Jennie hardly knew how she got out of the house and found Eileen again. Eileen took one look and marched her into the park towards the nearest café. They had to walk past the military buildings and the château, presenting an all grey February bleakness that offered no hope. The café at least was within the public park by the lakeside, with children and families all round, which restored some normality, especially as Eileen ordered strong coffee for them both.

'Tell me,' Eileen said firmly, when Jennie had drunk it.

She managed to blurt out the tale. 'The children could be anywhere in the world,' she finished, 'and I'll never know.'

She wouldn't. Queen Zita would see to that. There had been no need to send the mobsters after her this time, no need for Philip Castleton to hide away from her visit. Indeed Zita would be only too anxious for Jennie to reach the Castletons alive, in order that the full hopelessness of her task would become obvious to her. And it had.

On her return Jennie faced a fresh problem. Aunt Win hurried to the cottage full of concern. Tom had visited her to say that he'd heard from the Helston solicitor. Richard's father had died in an asylum. The funeral had already taken place, but a family presence was needed immediately. His home had been rented, and what little money there was had been donated to his church. There remained only personal possessions to be sorted out quickly.

Jamie and Lynette refused point-blank to come with her, for which Jennie was grateful. She had felt she had to ask them, since he was their grandfather, but their nightmares about their earlier visit still haunted them from time to time, and it was too much to expect. Once again Aunt Win took over their welfare, but to her pleasure, Dad, who had just retired, announced he'd be delighted to come with her. It was the first time he'd left Kent, and to him Cornwall seemed as far away as Timbuctoo.

It turned out that the chief attraction was the train journey to Cornwall on the Great Western Railway. He had decided that all his life he'd waved trains through his station but travelled on very few. Now he was going to make up for that. The Plymouth and Penzance Express was his first venture. He sat spellbound at the scenery, especially at the River Exe and the long Dawlish beach where the train ran right by the side of the sea past spectacular red cliffs. Just as Dad thought life couldn't get any better, the train pulled into Plymouth, where a ten-minute wait gave him an excuse to stroll around the station. He only just made it back just in time, thanks to his stationmaster's watch, which still accompanied him everywhere.

'Oh me, oh my,' he declared, as the train moved off towards Saltash.

'You sound just like Mole in *The Wind in the Willows*,' she told him, highly amused. Dad didn't hear her, he was too entranced by the sight of the Navy below him in the Sound, and by the Brunel bridge across the Tamar to Cornwall.

She had picked a hotel in Penzance rather than Helston, thinking Dad would be happier by the sea there than in the inland town, but he chose to come with her on the bus to Helston anyway.

'You need help, my girl,' he informed her. 'A gruesome business it is, clearing out memories.'

It was, even though there wasn't that much of it to do. It took time, however, as she had to bear in mind that in future years Lynette and Jamie might want any photographs or letters. She found so much of Richard here, including his sketchbooks of his childhood drawings, and was glad she had Dad with her. At least Richard's father had kept them, which showed some humanity, she supposed. There were old photographs too of Richard's ancestors, all bundled together in a brown paper bag, as though they had been pushed in there just to get them out of sight and out of mind.

When the task was finished after three days of work, she took Dad on a bus ride down through the Lizard peninsula. She remembered Richard telling her about the terrible journey his father had taken him on when he was only five to the inland village of St Keverne, in order that he should view the corpses of the victims of the wreck of the SS *Mohegan* in 1898. Richard had been forced to gaze at the rows of dead bodies and told to reflect on the wages of sin. What sin, he had thought, even as a child. These were innocent victims.

Jennie looked at the memorial cross that had been erected to the victims, and thought about the misery that his father had brought to his family. Just as Queen Zita did, his father had tried to control those around him, but Richard had defied his father. He had found his own life and used his strength to cheer and cure people.

She had vowed to do the same. She had tried with the Applemere Flyer, and thought she had succeeded as far as she could. With Max she might have done more. Now it was time for her to go on alone again. She had a sense of Richard being very close to her, strengthening her, telling her that Zita had no power over her now.

She still wondered how that power had come about. How had Queen Zita known so much about Jennie's movements? She couldn't doubt Eileen's loyalty, but what about Michael's? Had she taken his help too unquestioningly? Had he played a double game throughout, pretending to befriend first Anna and then herself, whereas all the time he was reporting both to his parents and his aunt? She couldn't believe it. After all, as he had said, they were his nephew and niece too. What other explanation could there be, however?

Zita had known she was going, and that was how Philip Castleton had had plenty of time to think out how to receive her. Could that warm sympathy have been feigned? The interview had certainly gone as he wanted. She had assumed the quest was at an end. Could she have been misled, just as she had by Robbins and the Montreux nursing home? If so, could the story of Castleton's daughter be a fiction?

'Funny old world, isn't it,' Dad observed, tucking into a

214

plateful of fried fish and chips in Penzance later that day. 'Who'd have thought it?'

'Thought what, Dad?' She had been lost in a dream. Across the bay they could see the fairytale St Michael's Mount, with its castle perched on top of the huge rock cut off from the shore by a narrow channel. She imagined Max and herself living there, she imagined them living in one of those fishermen's cottages. Anywhere with Max, where she could be alone with him and the twins. It wasn't possible, though. Life wasn't a fairy tale, and dreams were all they were.

'That places like this existed,' her father explained. 'All the time we're working away in Kent running trains and selling books and all the time this is here—' He waved a fork at the harbour outside the window, with its fishing boats and ferries, and the bay with St Michael's Mount in the distance. 'Pity we can't put a penny in the slot from Kent and see how things are done down here. Like what the butler saw, eh? Never mind the butler's ladies. He should have an eyeful of all this beauty.' The fork was waved again.

The only butler Jennie had ever known was old Stevens at Applemere House and he was hardly a jolly old soul, eyeing up buxom women. He was the stern face of Applemere. He'd been there forever. Of course he had. Jennie suddenly felt sick, and put down her knife and fork. He was so much part of Applemere, he faded into the background. He might be working for Michael, but his allegiance could always have been to the Fokingham family, which through Lady Fokingham included Queen Zita. So simple, so stupid of Jennie not to have realized. By dint of using his eyes and ears and with discreet questioning, Stevens could know pretty well everything that went on at Applemere House, and at the cottage too. Jennie's movements were hardly secret.

How easy it was to see things clearly from a distance.

'We should do this more often,' Dad said happily. 'There are other railways I'd like to see. One up north somewhere. Settle and Carlisle. Freddie would pay, wouldn't he?'

Jennie envied Dad his dream. His was realizable. Hers was not.

Fifteen

Every avenue Jennie explored turned out to be another cul-de-sac. Now March was here with its early signs of spring as if to remind her that years were passing without success – at least on Anna's behalf. Thank heavens for Lynette and Jamie, whose boisterous lives combined with the Applemere Flyer left her little time to reflect on her frustrations over the Castletons, or, worse, on the ache in her own heart. With spring looming she was even more painfully aware of it. Her slow awakening to her feelings for Max had made their sharp conclusion all the harder to bear.

On her return from Cornwall she had visited Michael, both about Stevens and because she was conscious that the issue of Anna's children affected him as much as her. Michael would be forty this year and she sensed that every member of his small family was becoming more important to him.

'I'll look into it, Jennie,' was his verdict after she had explained her conviction that Philip Castleton had been misleading her. 'I'm not hopeful but it's worth a try.'

As it turned out, there was no need for a very demanding try. He had made one telephone call to Paris and there proved to be no Philip Castleton working in the consulate or even in the embassy.

'That's not what the Foreign Office files say.' he told her gloomily. 'I can make further enquiries about him, but I suspect it will be in vain. My beloved aunt will have covered every tiny detail, Stevens or no Stevens.'

Michael acted promptly on her revealing her suspicions about the Applemere butler, and Mr Stevens abruptly vanished from the house, shortly to reappear in Fokingham House in Kensington, or so Michael ruefully told her later. Did that mean that the Fokinghams, and not Queen Zita, had been paying him to spy on Applemere? she asked. Michael laughed.

216

His mother would never in a million years suspect her sister-in-law of such underhand doings. Stevens, no doubt, still took, and earned, his double wages.

'How about the house I went to in Vincennes?' Jennie asked as a last try in tracking Philip Castleton.

'He might own the house there without working at the consulate.' Michael brightened up at this thought of a possible chink in Queen Zita's armour. 'I'll look into it.'

'How?' she enquired politely.

'My dear Watson, I have my methods,' was the only reply she received – deservedly so, perhaps.

His methods, it transpired, were Eileen's web of contacts, which had just reported back. 'We were taken for a ride,' Eileen admitted ruefully. 'The house was rented.'

Jennie's heart plummeted, even though she had expected no less. She should have followed her instincts about the Vincennes villa not feeling like a family home, and questioned Philip Castleton further, much further, while she had the chance. 'At least it explains why the old lady with the baguette didn't attack me.'

Eileen laughed. 'Don't let's blame ourselves too much. After all, she could have been Zita in disguise, determined to watch the flies enter her spider's web. The owner of the house is a Count Louvich, a name Georgius remembers from Montevanyan days. We were caught fair and square.' She glanced at Jennie. 'So where next?'

'There isn't a single "next" on the horizon,' she had to answer.

Except for the Applemere Flyer. There was always something new to absorb her there. Albert was still stalwartly supporting her, even though he would be sixty-two this year and was beginning to murmur about his rheumatics. There was brisker trade now, slump or no slump. Detective fiction was snapped up eagerly; *Lord Edgware Dies* was Agatha Christie's current contribution, and Dorothy Sayers was still a firm favourite with buyers. *Cold Comfort Farm* was still selling like hot cakes too, although Jennie wondered what Richard would have made of this hilarious parody of his beloved Mary Webb and other such writers. He'd probably have laughed, just like her, and a wave of misery came over her. No one, no one like Richard. Not even Max, for whom her love was completely different.

217

Everybody seemed to be reading nowadays, whether it was poetry, biography, war memoirs, fiction, or even political books. Jennie somehow acquired a working knowledge of all of them, quickly assessing which were good, which were poor. She listened to what the publishers' travellers said, and listened to what readers thought. They had readers' afternoons on the Flyer for this very purpose, and in addition she had her own instinct to go on after skimming through each book, even if she didn't have time to read them all thoroughly.

'Has anyone bought the Plough, yet?' she asked Albert.

'Not yet. Young Tom should hurry up or it'll slip through his fingers. He's daft not accepting Freddie's offer.'

'Is he doing any casual work apart from looking after Anna's royalties?' Aunt Win tended to know much more than she did about Tom's doings, so Jennie had fallen into the habit of treating Bell Cottage, where she, Dad and Albert now lived, as the fount of information.

'Not that I know of, Jennie. Mind you, he doesn't come into the Plough any more, so I might not know. Your aunt's said nothing, though.'

At least Albert called her Jennie now. There had been a turning point when Albert understood that calling her Mrs P. was no longer appropriate in view of their new relationship, and had therefore decided on her full name of Imogen. That hadn't lasted long, thank goodness.

'That Mr Stevens doesn't come in of a night, either,' Albert continued carefully, his eyes on the road.

'No, he doesn't. He made a swift departure to work in London.'

'I never took to him. Always asking questions, he was. Asked one too many, I've no doubt.'

Stevens' departure however did not help her over the question of Philip Castleton. Michael had not yet reported on the further enquiries he was making. She didn't expect much from him, and this proved just as well.

'There's no Castleton to be found any more,' he told her. 'I've crawled over every consulate file. He was in Montevanya until 1914, then in Rome and then in Paris, where apparently he still is. Only he's not.'

So that was why Anna went to Rome. Of course. True, she was looking for the name Roc, not Castleton, but something must have sent her there. Whatever it was, it had failed, however, whether the Castletons were there or not. It was probably another red herring, another false entry.

'I presume it *was* Castleton whom you saw in Vincennes?' Michael asked. 'Suppose he was my aunt's fancy man whose real name is Alfonse Smith?'

Jennie managed a laugh, but it was a hollow one. How *did* she know it was him? Her head spun as she tried to think it through. 'Why,' she reasoned at last, 'put a false Castleton there when the real one could tell the truth far more tellingly? She needed to convince me, and she did. A false one might slip up on detail.'

'True.' Michael sat down in relief. 'So tell me again what he said.'

'He said,' Jennie repeated, 'that it was his daughter and son-in-law who took the babies. They are not in Paris. Nor is her husband British. And their name naturally, he pointed out, is not Castleton.'

The oddness of this struck them both together. 'Why,' Jennie spelled it out, 'did he bother to specify that the husband was not British?'

'It could be,' Michael said cautiously, 'that it was the natural thing to say in the circumstances, in case you thought they'd be living near the Fokinghams.'

'But,' Jennie tried to keep the lid on her excitement, 'near *Zita* and the Fokinghams. Wherever they were during the war, Zita's been living *here* since Max's abdication. Do you think—' she eyed Michael, scarcely daring to hope that he'd agree with such a fantastic notion '—that's where they are now? Near here? If Castleton isn't in Paris he could be here, in London, and the story of his daughter a fiction. Zita warned him I was coming.'

'It's possible, all too possible.' Michael was trying to curb his enthusiasm. He failed though. 'How old did you say Castleton was?'

'Early sixties. Perhaps younger. Still of working age.'

'He could have left the service. No,' he thought again, 'not if my aunt is paying him. He would need to be in government service so that she could keep an eye on him. So . . .' Michael paused, frowning, 'perhaps he's still in it, but invisible to us.'

'Where do you make someone invisible? Where do you hide a leaf?' Jennie crowed triumphantly.

'On a tree.' Michael swallowed. 'I'll go through the Foreign Office like a dose of Epsom salts on Monday, Jennie, and I'll telephone you in the evening.'

'No,' Jennie cried in anguish. 'I can't wait. I'll take a day off. Monday's usually quiet anyway and Albert can manage alone, especially if Aunt Win goes with him.' She wasn't going to wait a moment longer than she had to.

Jennie sat in St James's Park despite the nip in the spring sunshine, trying to enjoy the sight of the ducks on the lake, the young children out with nurses and the busy kings of Whitehall striding along in private talks with each other. She waited an hour until at last she saw Michael crossing the road from Horse Guards Parade towards the park. He wasn't running, he didn't need to, for they were both sure they were on the right track now. Steam full ahead, she thought exultantly.

She watched him look round for her, spot her, and then come to sit on the bench beside her. 'Well?' she asked, as though there were all the time in the world.

'Philip Castleton does work for the Foreign Office, Jennie. I feel a fool, though it's not entirely my fault. He's in a sub-department run jointly by the Board of Trade and the Foreign Office, called the Overseas Trading Department, which deals with the commercial consuls abroad. It works out of a house in Old Queen Street, but of course they have automatic access to the Foreign Office. All he or my aunt had to arrange was to change one set of records.'

'Shall we go to Old Queen Street now?' Stupid question. Of course not. There would be no point in talking to Castleton again, and would only alert him.

'It's his home we need to find, Jennie.' Michael paused. 'And we have to agree on exactly what we want as a result of it. What are you looking for?'

'I want to know *where* the twins are, of course,' she answered promptly. 'And to see them, if not to meet them. I'd like to keep their faces in my memory, at least until they come of age. I'd take it from there, after that. Is that enough for you?'

'You told me they don't know they're adopted.'

Jennie nodded. 'That's what Castleton *said*. He might have been lying.'

'Unless we know that for sure, we have no choice but to assume he wasn't. So, yes, your wish is enough for me too. But what about Tom? He has to know at some point.'

'But which?'

'It's a risk,' Michael said. 'He might do anything.'

'The way he was treated, he might be entitled to.'

'That's not fair on the children.'

Jennie could see the muscle twitching again. There was little love lost between Michael and Tom, which wasn't going to help. 'What would Anna have wanted, Michael? To tell Tom when they are twenty-one? That's over two years away. If we continue this hunt and find out where they live, I have to tell him. So shall we stop now or go on?'

Michael sighed. 'I ought to say stop now, Jennie, but with this madman in power in Germany who knows what might happen? We don't want to risk losing them again. I suggest we find them, but make absolutely certain Zita doesn't know we've done so.'

Jennie had to restrain herself from instinctively looking over her shoulder. Zita's shadow was a long and dark one. 'And Tom?' she asked.

'You must decide that, Jennie. Just remember the risk if Zita or my parents discover he knows where they are. They'll make the children disappear quicker than Houdini.'

Jennie spent the rest of the day in the nearest reference library, checking telephone directories for the London and Home Counties. After her earlier exhilaration, this was a dispiriting job. If Philip Castleton lived here he was keeping his name out of the directory. When at last she found it, listed in Kelly's Directory, it was almost an anti-climax. She stared at the entry, close to tears in relief. Mr Philip Castleton, Dunosova House, Blackheath. His home was even named after the capital of Montevanya. She had trailed round Europe hunting for Anna's children, when all she had needed to do was to take the train from Fairsted station, change once or twice and alight at Blackheath. She had even walked over the heath once, when she and Richard had taken the twins to Greenwich Park to see the Royal Observatory and to jump up and down on the meridian line.

Poor Anna. After all her efforts, they had been within her reach the whole time. What wickedness for her family to stand aside, watching her hunt through their spies, laughing at her. On an impulse Jennie decided she could wait no longer and would make her way back to Fairsted through Blackheath, just to discover where exactly the house was. She would not, she would *not*, linger in the hope that Guy and Bridget would appear. After all, they could be wrong, she had to remind herself. Perhaps the story of the daughter was not a fiction, but a truth. But everything in her was shouting out that at last they would shortly be seeing Anna's son and daughter. The fourth glorious gift from her fairy godmother had arrived.

'What do you want?'

'Thank you, dear brother,' Jennie said tartly, 'for that welcome.' She *had* resisted the temptation to try to see the twins, in favour of telling Tom first and this was all the thanks she got when she called at his cottage in Bossingham. All she had done in Blackheath was find Dunosova House, which proved to be one of those bordering the heath itself, not far from the church.

'Sorry,' Tom muttered. 'You'd better come in.' He peered outside. 'Are you with the Flyer?'

'Yes, but it's lunchtime. Albert can manage.'

She looked round the cottage in despair. There was no sign that lunch or indeed any meal, or any kind of comfort, were priorities here. No wonder he had lost so much weight.

'Not quite the Station House, is it? Tom said defensively, as if daring her to agree.

She did. 'No.'

'Now you'll ask how I can live like this,' he jeered. 'Easy. What else is there to do?'

'The Plough,' she snapped, then mentally kicked herself. She had come here to be diplomatic, not to stir up trouble.

Tom went red in the face. 'So you're in on it too, are you?'

'On what?'

'Master Freddie's new plan to solve all my problems.'

Jennie must have looked as bewildered as she felt, for he condescended to explain. 'Freddie has bought the Plough. You must have known.'

She hadn't. It was good news, if only Tom would see it that way. 'That's marvellous, Tom.' She tried to sound warm and encouraging, but it was a forlorn hope confronted by Tom's sullen face.

'Not for me. He expects me to run it and I've told him he can think again. He'll be selling this cottage so I'll be out on the street, but I'm damned if I'll be beholden to brother Freddie and that's that.' He glared at her.

'What will Freddie do with the pub if you don't take it? He wouldn't want to run it himself.' She was exasperated. It was Freddie who had been the injured party in the break between them. Tom had run off with his wife, yet Tom seemed to think he was the victim.

'I couldn't care less. I won't be there. Anyway, what did you come about, if it wasn't the pub? A sisterly visit to make sure I'm feeding myself properly?'

She fired up angrily. 'Believe it or not, something more important.' She knew she shouldn't embark on this, while he was in this mood, but she couldn't stop herself. 'Tom, we love you and worry about you,' she pleaded.

'Bloody kind of you. So what's so important about that?'

She decided to plunge right in. 'Do you see Alfred and Arabella now?'

'Only when they fancy bringing a bowl of broth to their poverty-stricken father.'

She couldn't stand this any longer. 'You've two other children.'

There was a stillness in the room. 'What about them? They've gone for good.'

It was all going wrong, it was not as she had imagined this talk. Tom should be misty-eyed, caught unawares. Instead he looked like a bull ready to charge at the faintest wave of the flag she held. 'They're called Guy and Bridget, and I think I know where they are.'

She watched his expression change from sullen anger to explosion point. 'Where?' he bellowed at her.

'Before I tell you, I have to explain.'

'There's nothing to explain. Where are they? How long have you known? God, first you keep it from me for years that they were born at all, now you think you have the right to waltz around interfering *again*.'

223

She swallowed. 'I've known about a week. I've had to consider what to do.'

'You've no bloody right to consider anything. They're my children.'

'Not legally,' she flashed back. 'They weren't when they were born and they're not now.'

'Don't talk to me about legal rights. They're mine, and you know it.'

'Listen, will you, Tom?' She struggled to regain calmness. 'If you don't, I'm not going to tell you about them.' She felt as if they were children again, and he the big brother whom she adored but could never quite please enough. For a moment she thought Tom would fly at her, but he must have thought better of it. He sat down abruptly, and let her talk. She only held back the information on where they now lived. He listened, and, to do him credit, in silence.

'You've been tracking them down since Anna died,' he commented when she'd finished at last. He didn't seem angry now, only bewildered. 'And you never told me.'

'What could you have done?' She couldn't tell him Anna had forbidden her to involve him.

He managed a twisted grin. 'Screwed the bloody necks off those Fokinghams, that's what.'

'What good would that have done?'

He shrugged. 'You've all known about this? Eileen? Bloody Michael? Aunt Win? Dad – the lot. Who the hell do you all think I am? Some kind of kid who has to be left out of the party in case he gets too excited?'

'Yes,' she replied smartly. 'Look at you now.'

'Wouldn't you be furious? Where are they, Jen?'

'I can't tell you yet, Tom.' How could she? In this mood, he'd ruin the whole plan.

This time she thought he really would seize her. He wanted to shake the living daylights out of her, that was obvious.

'The children don't know they were adopted.' She did her best to keep calm. 'They won't be twenty-one for two and a half years, and even then it would be a shock for them to know. They've obviously been well cared for.'

'Those blasted Fokinghams,' he groaned.

'No. To be fair, I think it's those blasted Deleanus and Zita in particular.'

224

'Do you really expect me to do nothing?' He glared at her.

'Not till they're at least twenty-one, and then you should think about it carefully.'

'Where are they?' he said dangerously, eyes glittering.

'I can't tell you, Tom,' she said again wearily, getting to her feet. 'Not till you're ready to promise that you'll put them first, and not yourself.'

He ignored this. 'Have you seen them?' he demanded.

'No. Michael and I propose to try to see them from a distance, just so that I can know I've done my best for Anna.'

Tom lost all control. 'Get out, Jen, and don't bloody well come back,' he shouted. His eyes were bright as though he were crying, as he slammed the door behind her.

'Let me talk to him,' Eileen said firmly, when Jennie dolefully recounted what had happened.

'I don't think even you could do anything. He's got to come to his senses alone.'

'There's another factor you've discounted, Jennie. One that makes it imperative you keep track of those twins. Have you been following the recent events in Germany?'

Jennie shook her head. What time or energy had she for politics?

'Mr Hitler has now declared himself official dictator of Germany, not just Chancellor,' Eileen continued.

Was this important? Jennie couldn't see it affected anything. It was very little more than Michael had been pointing out. 'He's been acting like one already.'

'Now that's official, the Nazis are moving fast. They've already opened a camp for enemies of the Nazi party in Dachau. No opposition for them, you see. And, worse, there's a boycott of Jewish shops and businesses and of professional Jews.'

'There's always prejudice against them in many countries,' Jennie said, her mind full of other matters, 'even here.'

'This one's official government policy. *That*'s rather different from other countries, except perhaps Russia.'

'Does that really affect Tom's children? I know Michael thought it might change Zita's plans.'

'The stronger Hitler becomes the more secure Viktor will feel. He's an ardent supporter, remember. I've been keeping an eye on his chumminess with the Kaiser's son, and remember

225

Zita is the Kaiser's cousin. I wouldn't mind betting that she sees her crown floating straight towards her again.'

'But Victor is a dictator. How could he take the throne again?'

'He's ruling a small country that longs for the old days.'

What concerned Jennie more closely however was the thought of Queen Zita departing to join him. 'If Zita leaves Britain, you think the Castletons would go too?' Jennie frowned. Whatever Lady Fokingham wanted, Zita's voice would probably be obeyed, one way or another.

'It's possible, so I'm going to talk to Tom myself,' Eileen declared.

'Talking to a brick wall isn't easy.'

'Poor Jennie. Don't look so sad. Happiness has a way of popping up very unexpectedly.'

To Jennie's amazement it did. Two days later Aunt Win came bustling round to tell them that Freddie was getting married again, and of course the bride was Albert's great-niece Dinah. Jennie had met Dinah several times now, and was delighted. She obviously adored Freddie, wanted nothing more than to make a home for him, and yet she was an independently minded girl with a mischievous sense of humour. Life, Jennie thought thankfully, was going to treat Freddie much better from now on. Her fifth gift from her fairy godmother and the last one she could expect. They wanted the wedding to take place in Fairsted in June. Jennie found herself immediately embroiled in discussion of where the wedding breakfast might be held.

'What about the Plough?' Jennie asked, when all venues had been rejected.

Aunt Win's nose wrinkled up. 'Most unsuitable. Too small, both itself and the garden.'

'I meant, is Tom going to take it over after all?'

Aunt Win sighed. 'Oh that silly boy. No. Why can't he be sensible?'

The second piece of good news arrived twenty-four hours later, when Tom himself appeared in the cottage garden. He was scowling. 'I've done what you said, Jen. I've thought, and I agree. If you and bloody Michael haven't seen the twins yet, I'll come with you. I don't have any right to ask you after the way I've behaved, but I do. Can I come?'

226

In answer she flung her arms round him and hugged him.

'But before you get too excited,' he growled, 'I'm not giving in over the Plough.'

They chose a Sunday, counting on the probability that the Castletons would attend morning service at the church on the heath. Jennie decided they couldn't risk being seen in or near the church since she at least would be recognized, so they ensconced themselves by the lounge window in the hotel on the road from the church to Dunosova House.

'This could all be a wild goose chase,' Tom pointed out gloomily. 'You've no evidence that this is the Philip Castleton you're after, have you?'

'No,' Jennie answered, 'except the house's name.'

Tom ignored this. 'Or that the kids are even here?'

'No.'

'Or that it's not his daughter who's bringing them up in Sydney, Australia?'

'No.'

'And yet we're here,' Tom said, even more gloomily.

'We are,' Michael muttered though clenched teeth.

'It could be a big let-down.'

'So can Christmas,' Jennie said crossly, 'but it doesn't stop it happening every year. Tom, let's play the game we used to as children. Let's wish never to be "Disappointed at Omdurman". If we're disappointed at Blackheath, are we going to spend the rest of our lives being disappointed?'

Tom grinned. 'No, sister dear.' Nevertheless he could not sit still, he paced restlessly round the lounge watching people come in and out, and returned to the window every few seconds.

'Can't we stand outside the church?' he pleaded.

'You could, but we can't,' Jennie pointed out. 'Castleton would recognize me, and probably Michael.'

For a moment she thought Tom would go alone, but he didn't. Nor did he resume his perambulations. Instead, he stayed with them at the window, fidgeting with his glass.

'There,' Jennie cried at last. 'People are coming out of the church.' She watched, eyes fixed on the groups beginning to stroll towards them. Two false alarms and then there was no doubt.

'That's him,' she said quietly, almost crying with relief as she saw Philip Castleton.

'And them,' Tom whispered at her side. A young man and girl were with Philip Castleton. The girl wore an azure blue jumper suit and matching hat, looking so like Anna that Jennie felt a lump in her throat. Her twin, dressed in smart suit and hat, had more the look of Tom about him. Both were fair-haired, both were laughing at something Castleton said as they passed the hotel window. Guy and Bridget were lively, almost joyous, and they were *there*.

I've done it, Anna, Jennie thought. At last. And for the first time she had thought of them as Guy and Bridget, not the anonymous missing twins. This time she couldn't hold the tears back.

For a few seconds she felt like rushing out after them but she couldn't do it. Tom did though, while Jennie and Michael watched in agony lest he ran up to the group to catch his son or daughter by the arm. For one moment they feared the worst, but then he must have thought better of it. She watched Tom standing in the road staring after them as they passed onwards, oblivious. Then he quickly turned and hurried back into the hotel. He glared at them, as though to say he'd made his point.

'We'd better be going,' Michael said practically, obviously anxious to steer Tom out of temptation's way. 'We can lunch on the way home.'

Jennie thought for a moment Tom would insist on staying, but he didn't and as meekly as a lamb, with not even a protesting baa, he walked away with them to Michael's car. He didn't even demand to see where his twins lived.

As they parted at Fairsted, where Tom had left his ancient Ford, he said to her after Michael had driven off, 'I've been thinking, Jen. Perhaps I should take up the Plough job. You never know, I might make a go of it.' He glanced at her. 'Fancy a drink?'

The decision made, Jennie was relieved that Tom made instant arrangements to take over the Plough and was even, to Jennie's amazement, seriously talking to Aunt Win about serving food. This would be unheard of at the Plough, or indeed at any other pub she could think of. Jennie was so used to thinking of the Plough as a male preserve into which the occasional woman might be allowed under strict escort that the idea of food seemed laughable. Tom, however, maintained that during his time at Bossingham, he would have been only too glad of a sausage roll or sandwich in the pub, and he couldn't be the only one with no wife at home to cook for him.

Aunt Win had more things on her mind, chiefly Freddie's wedding. The wedding breakfast problem had been settled by Freddie and Dinah. Freddie had bought Fairsted Manor, which had come on the market after the death of Tom's former employer, Mr Hargreaves. Dinah seemed delighted – although in Jennie's view she'd have been delighted at anything that pleased Freddie. Albert was as proud as punch that she was to be lady of the manor.

So the manor would have a train driver as squire. Jennie was amused. Times were changing indeed. More lines were being electrified, and Freddie was a steam man through and through, like Dad. Perhaps he saw his engine-driving days coming to an end, though she couldn't imagine that. She sighed. With the Fairsted line single track now, even Dad was forecasting the worst. Perhaps Freddie would have a new career as lord of the manor. She couldn't imagine that either. But that was the fun of life, not knowing what might lie around the corner.

On the great June day, Dinah made a beautiful bride, and she would make a good wife for Freddie, Jennie thought thankfully. Poor Anna. No doubt she'd intended to be a good wife for Freddie too, to try to be 'normal', not the product of a Fokingham upbringing, but for her the quiet life had not been possible.

Freddie and Dinah left at five o'clock for a honeymoon in France, but the sun was still warm, and when Michael said to her, 'It's a shame for you to go straight home, Jennie. Come to Applemere House with us,' it was tempting. Her twins were busy clearing up in the manor, and the idea of those peaceful Applemere gardens in June seemed irresistible. She'd worked hard to prepare the wedding breakfast, so she didn't feel guilty about leaving.

Michael left her to go into the garden to find Anthony while he prepared drinks and she wandered out into the gardens. The scent of roses was strong in the evening sun, as she walked towards the pond which she knew was Anthony's favourite spot. She spotted his garden hat from afar and hurried to join him. Except that when she grew nearer, she sensed something odd.

It wasn't Anthony. It was Max, wearing that ridiculous panama hat which didn't suit him at all. Her heart seemed to somersault as she walked – floated? – towards him, forfeiting every happiness in the world for this moment. No ex-king this. It was Max. *Her* Max. The one she had lost, and her heart thudded painfully at that thought.

He rose to his feet from the tree trunk, removed the ridiculous hat and took her into his arms. She thought she should resist at first for it would only make the memory of what she had lost worse. Then she forgot everything save for the sound of his voice and the feel of his arms around her. No need for words, no need for anything, save the fact that he was with her, completing the day.

'Why are you here?' she eventually asked with a shaky laugh. Then she realized the only possible reason. 'You've come to tell me you're selling Applemere.'

'I am not selling it, Jennie.'

She didn't take in the words for a moment, especially since he went on to say: 'I've come to tell you we made a mistake, you and I, when we last met. Eileen has told me how you felt, but I did not understand, nor you me. I thought when we talked last – how could I have done so?'

His words weren't making sense, and he tried again. 'When we spoke last, we agreed we could not marry because I would have to sell Applemere.'

She looked at him dumbfounded. 'No! It was Stefan,' she stammered. 'I love Applemere, but you more, so much more. But your mother would have stopped you from seeing your son. I thought that's what you meant.'

'Oh Jennie.' He took her in his arms again. 'She might have tried, but with you at my side she would never have won. Never. It wasn't until Eileen came to tell me about your finding Anna's children that she realized we were at cross-purposes. I didn't dare to hope, but now I do. I haven't come about Applemere. I know I could never sell it. It is my future.'

The soft evening sun seemed warmer and brighter now.

'You want to live here?' Jennie was dizzy with the happiness. She was aboard Richard's magic train to a future she had only dreamed of.

'Of course. Could I have come here on a night such as this if I did not? I love it, Jennie. It is true my mother and Viktor have cut off my income, but Applemere is mine. My mother is returning to Montevanya. It is settled. Viktor has declared it a monarchy again, with Mr Hitler's backing.'

'And your son?' she asked with dismay. Would he be parted from Stefan after all?

'Even Marta sees the sense in keeping him away from Viktor. She has stood out against my mother, as have I. Marta is marrying again, and Stefan will live with her somewhere unknown to Viktor or my mother.' He paused, stroked her cheek, looking earnestly into her eyes with such love she thought she would faint with pleasure. 'So, Jennie. We have no money, you and I, but we do have Applemere.'

Even now she wasn't sure, and asked stupidly, 'I can still live in the cottage?'

He looked dismayed, then perhaps seeing the expression in her eyes, said softly, 'A king should have a queen. She should not live in a cottage but at his side in the palace even though the rain comes through the roof and beetle eats its wood. Would your children mind very much moving to Applemere House. Would they take me to their hearts?'

'If we go gently.' She was sure of it. Lynette and Jamie liked Max, and it should be an easy path.

'But we shall arrive, Jennie?'

'Of course.' Her reply was half sob, half laugh, or perhaps half disbelief, half joy. All she knew was that she was happy beyond her wildest hopes. Freddie's news hadn't been the last gift from her fairy godmother. This was it, and the best of all.

'What shall we do at Applemere,' she teased him, 'apart from love each other?'

'We shall reign there in poverty, you and I, but rich beyond belief. You can take the Applemere Flyer out if you still wish, and I could come with you. I can design my garden, and sell my plants perhaps. And we must create a new Applemere together.'

'How?' She knew what she would do, but what had Max in mind?

'Applemere should not be ours alone,' he replied. 'We

should share it with those who have the eyes to see it, be they laundrymaids, emperors, princes, Aunt Wins, Fokinghams, or farmboys. It would be the life I've always wanted, Jennie. The Várcasá, you remember, stood high above the town, and as a boy I would look down at the town and think what a short step it would be to walk down the hill and become part of the life at its foot. You remember we did that once together? It wasn't a possible future for me then, but it is now. Applemere doesn't exist alone, it has a village around it, which is part of it.'

She swallowed back her tears of happiness. 'But that's what I want too. What I always thought Applemere might be.'

'So when shall we begin?'

'When everything is right.'

'When will that be?'

'Soon, very soon, Max.'

He kissed her then, first gently, then more urgently, until she was lost in a sea of love and hope. 'You remember I told you once,' he whispered, 'that only one of our family ever married for love.'

'I remember.'

'Now there will be two.'